The

RIPPER

of Storyville

BOOKS BY EDWARD D. HOCH

The Shattered Raven
The Judges of Hades
The Transvection Machine
The Spy and the Thief
City of Brass
Dear Dead Days (editor)
The Fellowship of the Hand
The Frankenstein Factory
Best Detective Stories of the Year 1976-81 (editor)
The Thefts of Nick Velvet
The Monkey's Clue & The Stolen Sapphire (juvenile)
All But Impossible! (editor)
The Year's Best Mystery and Suspense Stories 1982-95 (editor)
The Quests of Simon Ark
Leopold's Way
Great British Detectives (coeditor)
Women Write Mysteries (coeditor)
Murder Most Sacred (coeditor)
The Spy Who Read Latin and Other Stories
The Night My Friend
The People of the Peacock
Diagnosis: Impossible, The Problems of Dr. Sam Hawthorne
Twelve American Detective Stories (editor)
The Ripper of Storyville and Other Ben Snow Tales

The RIPPER

of Storyville

and Other
Ben Snow Tales

Edward D. Hoch

with a Ben Snow chronology
by Marvin Lachman

Crippen & Landru Publishers
Norfolk, Virginia
1997

Cover painting by Barbara Mitchell; cover design by Deborah Miller

Crippen & Landru logo by Eric D. Greene

ISBN (limited edition): 1-885941-18-8

ISBN (trade edition): 1-885941-19-6

Printed in the United States of America on acid-free paper

FIRST EDITION

10 9 8 7 6 5 4 3 2 1

Crippen & Landru, Publishers
P. O. Box 9315
Norfolk, Virginia 23505-9315
USA

E-Mail: CrippenL@Norfolk.Infi.Net
Web: http://www.avalon.net/~scott/cl/

FOR JIRO AND KAZUE KIMURA

CONTENTS

INTRODUCTION

I

In a way this collection of my first fourteen stories about western detective Ben Snow is really two books in one, so it's only fitting that the introduction is in two parts. The character of Ben Snow owes its existence today to a pair of editors, Hans Stefan Santesson and Eleanor Sullivan, who could not have been more dissimilar. Both were close friends of mine and both harbored a special fondness for Ben Snow, an unlikely character to turn up in the pages of a mystery magazine.

Hans, a longtime mystery and science fiction editor, used a handful of my stories in *The Saint Mystery Magazine* and *Fantastic Universe* until both magazines suspended publication in 1960. After some months in limbo, the Saint's creator, Leslie Charteris, worked out a deal with a new publisher and *The Saint* resumed publication in both the United States and Great Britain. Hans suggested I try a new series for him, about a western detective character. Thus was Ben Snow born, with a name combining Bruno Fischer's detective Ben Helm with that of Mr. Snow from the hit musical *Carousel*. Ben's horse, Oats, was christened much later by *Ellery Queen's Mystery Magazine* editor Eleanor Sullivan, who knew of my admiration for the writings of Joyce Carol Oates.

Ben was a fast draw and a crack shot in those early stories, so good with a gun that he was often mistaken for Billy the Kid, who died a year before Ben Snow's first recorded adventure. I believe both of them were born in 1859, despite some confusion noted in Marvin Lachman's excellent essay and chronology at the end of this volume. The first two stories, "Frontier Street" and "The Valley of Arrows," were written and submitted almost simultaneously in late 1960. Hans Santesson bought them both, for the British and American editions, but chose for some reason to publish "The Valley of Arrows" first. Now these two stories have been restored to their rightful order. The only other changes are a few words, mainly about Native Americans, which seem contrary to the language in later stories.

Because the British edition of *The Saint* began publication six months ahead of the U.S. edition, most of the early Snow stories appeared first in England. They received favorable comment from the beginning, and one of the greatest thrills of my young career occurred at a Mystery Writers of America cocktail party when Cornell Woolrich insisted on meeting the author of "The Ripper of Storyville" so he could tell me personally how much he admired the story.

One of the problems in assembling this collection has been the quality of a few of these early Ben Snow stories. I believe "The Ripper of Storyville," "The Flying Man" and one or two others are worth preserving. Our first thought was to collect only these stories together with the later ones. However, it seemed that each of the seven had something of interest, some plot point or historical background important to the saga. After all, where else could you find Ben Snow solving a presidential assassination or journeying deep into Mexico?

So here they are, all seven of them. Read them with a bit of tolerance for a young writer.

II

There were no new Ben Snow stories published from January 1965 till May 1984. My other series characters were doing well and I had virtually forgotten about Ben until the spring of 1983 when mystery writer John Ball announced plans to revive *The Saint Mystery Magazine*. I was writing frequent stories of locked rooms and impossible crimes by that time, and the plot for a new Ben Snow story sprang immediately to mind. A steamboat would vanish on the Mississippi River, much as Conan Doyle and Ellery Queen had made trains disappear between stations.

When I saw John Ball at a party during Edgar Awards week in 1983, I told him the good news. I would revive the Ben Snow series for *The Saint*. He looked at me and said they wanted no historical mysteries, only those set in the present day. Ben Snow was dead again.

But the idea of the vanished steamboat was just too good to abandon. It had to be written and it had to be a Ben Snow story. I spoke to Eleanor Sullivan, who'd become editor-in-chief of *Ellery Queen's Mystery Magazine* following the death of Fred Dannay in 1982. She liked the idea, and Ben was back in business. He's been at *EQMM* ever since, thanks to Eleanor and her successor, Janet Hutchings, who has a special fondness for the historical mystery.

That is, really, what the Ben Snow stories are—not westerns but historical mysteries. In these stories the reader will find him solving mysteries in such distant places as the beach at Kitty Hawk, North Carolina and a wax museum in Sacramento, California. In addition to that vanished steamboat we have an old-fashioned locked room involving a phantom stallion and an early air conditioning machine. Perhaps best of all we have "The Trail of the Bells," Eleanor Sullivan's personal favorite among the Ben Snow tales she published. Enjoy them all.

Edward D. Hoch
Rochester, New York
June 1997

FRONTIER STREET

A tinkling piano—there was always a tinkling piano off somewhere in the corner—mingled with the clink of glasses and the murmur of voices as the man called Ben Snow pushed his way through the swinging doors of the Golden Swan . . .

"Is Len around?" he asked the tired bartender. "Tell him Ben Snow is here."

The man nodded and moved down the bar, still polishing the beer mug he held in one hand. Over the bar Ben saw the ten-foot-wide painting that gave the place its name—a painting of a single golden swan surrounded by unclad bathing girls in a variety of poses. Len, they said, had brought the thing West himself, on trains as far as they went and then the rest of the way by stage and wagon. It wasn't much as art, but cowhands and ranchers often came from miles around just to see it.

Now, with the tobacco smoke hanging in layers, there was nothing much else to look at in the Golden Swan. The piano player looked bored, pounding out some old song Ben hadn't heard since the days back in New Mexico. Business wasn't too good this night at the Golden Swan—only a few customers who looked standard, only a few drifters like you found in any bar west of Texas.

"Come in, Mr. Snow. I'm happy you could come!"

Ben focused his narrow eyes on the short, smiling man in the doorway at the rear. Len Antioch—the power on Frontier Street, the boss of the Golden Swan, with his brother a force to be reckoned with in Arizona. Short and smiling, but somehow very deadly.

Ben had never really spoken to the man during his two months on Frontier Street. That was why the summons this morning had been so strangely unexpected. Now he simply shrugged and followed the man into the rear office, not knowing just what to expect.

Inside, beyond the door marked *PRIVATE*, Ben Snow settled down into one of the few comfortable chairs in town, opposite the battered desk that served as Len Antioch's home base. "Well?" he asked quietly.

"Drink, Mr. Snow?"

"Too early in the day."

Len Antioch grunted. "Then I'll get right to the point. I know who you are, Snow. I've known for the past several weeks."

"Who I am?" Ben repeated, pretending to be puzzled.

"Let's not fool around," Len said, the smile fading quickly from his face. "I want a job done. The new deputy sheriff . . ."

"Killed? You want him killed?"

Len Antioch's smile returned. "I see we speak the same language, Billy."

"The name is Ben, remember? Ben Snow."

"Sure, Ben. A thousand dollars for the deputy's body before sundown."

"A thousand . . ."

"It's a lot of money, Ben. It would be a lot of money even back East, and out here it's a fortune."

"You could hire a gun for fifty dollars," Ben observed, unconsciously shifting the holster on his hip.

"Not one like you, though. Not one like you. I want the best and I pay for the best. A thousand bucks if the deputy is dead by sundown."

Ben Snow got slowly to his feet and walked over to the desk. Without seeming to change his expression he shot out a lightning fist and caught Len on the tip of his jaw. He staggered backward, crashing into the wall behind him. "What the hell!" His hand automatically shot toward the desk drawer, but Ben already had dropped the lightning right hand to his own gun.

"You've got me confused with someone else, Mr. Antioch. I'm not a hired killer. Remember that."

Then he turned and was gone, and Len stared after him with hatred in his eyes . . .

For Ben Snow it was a town like many others, and Frontier Street was a path that seemed to lead through the center of his life. The story was always the same, wherever he went. Always it started with the rumors, then the whispered tales, finally the open accusations. On Frontier Street it was no different. He remembered all the men he'd half-killed with his fists when they said those familiar words. And the few he'd brought down with his Colt when all else failed.

He went into the little lunchroom across the muddy street from the Golden Swan, sat down at a soiled wooden table and signaled Gus for the usual. Old Gus sometimes seemed like the only real friend he had in town. The only male one, at least.

"Hello, Ben. How's things today?" Gus had been a gold prospector some time, years before, until an Indian arrow lost him his left arm. Now he cooked food, such as it was, for the cowhands who wandered into town.

"Great, Gus. Busy?"

"Two people all morning. Nobody eats anymore."

Ben was just clearing his throat for an answer when the door swung open behind him. He never liked to sit with his back to the door and now he turned quickly to face the newcomer. It was the deputy, Reilly, the man Antioch wanted killed.

He was a handsome young man with features deeply tanned by years under the desert sun. A dark scar on one cheek was the only blemish, and even this could be overlooked in a town like Frontier. A much more important blemish on Reilly was one not quite visible. He was an honest man who took his job seriously.

"You're Ben Snow, aren't you?" he asked quietly.

"That's the name."

"You were just talkin' with Len Antioch."

Ben's muscles tensed. "You get around." He watched the light glisten off the deputy's badge, saw his hand dropping toward his gun.

"Draw, Snow! I know who you are," he shouted suddenly, crouching into a gunfighter's squat.

But he was too close, and Ben was too fast. Gus screamed a warning from behind the counter, and that was all the distraction he needed. His big fist smashed into the side of Reilly's head, sending the deputy sprawling. His boot came down on the man's gun hand and the fight was over as quickly as it started. He put his lips close to Reilly's ear as he yanked him back to his feet.

"Listen, dope—I didn't take Antioch's money. I'm not going to kill you or anyone else if I can help it. Now leave me the hell alone."

He pushed the deputy back into a chair and headed for the door, tossing Gus a quarter for the lunch he never got. There was no peace anywhere on Frontier Street today. Maybe in Cathy Norris's dress shop, he decided suddenly, crossing the street once more. It should be quiet there.

Cathy was older than Ben—almost thirty-five, he guessed—but she had a certain youth about her that went well with her middle-aged business sense. He liked Cathy, liked her better than any of the other women he'd met during these months in Frontier. She ran a dress shop just down the street from the Golden Swan, a shop that annually imported the latest New York and San Francisco fashions for quick sale to the forty or fifty females young enough and rich enough to still care about their clothes.

Cathy had come West with her mother and father ten years earlier, and like so many others they'd met the Utes in the Colorado Mountains. She'd wakened screaming one morning as the arrows rained down upon them, and when it was all over she found her father's body outside the wagon. The Indians had carried off her mother but somehow missed her. The experience would have broken most women in their mid-twenties, but Cathy had survived it with only a touch of hardness and cynicism to show for that day. She'd told Ben the story almost the first time they'd met, as if proud of the tragedy.

"Well," she greeted him with the usual smile, "what's the good news this morning, Ben? Come to buy a dress?"

"The news is all bad. I've been up an hour and I've already used my fists on two men."

"Not the sheriff, I hope," she said, going on about the business of arranging a great fluffy dress for display.

"Just as bad. His deputy, Reilly."

"No!"

"And Len Antioch, too."

"Are you crazy, Ben? If Reilly doesn't lock you up, Len will probably shoot you."

He dropped into a chair and rubbed his forehead with a leathery hand. "It's always the same, in every town."

"You know what they say about you?" she asked, her voice suddenly low.

"I know what they say. I've listened to the same whispers for nine years now."

The door of Cathy's shop swung open and Sheriff Vic Pedley strolled in, his iron-gray mustache glistening with tiny drops of sweat. "What's this all about, Snow?" he asked without preliminaries, in the familiar slow voice of an old lawman. "You slugged my deputy over at Gus's place."

"It was one of those things, Sheriff. He went for his gun without any cause."

"Says he had cause. Says you're workin' for Len Antioch and his brother now."

Ben looked the sheriff up and down, watching for any move that would signal a sudden drawing of his gun. But there was none—the lawman apparently wanted only to talk. "It's not true, Sheriff. I had conversation with Antioch, but that's all. I don't work for gamblers."

"Then suppose you tell me just who you really are. You rode into town two months back without a word, and you've just been around ever since. You don't work at any of the ranches, and you don't work for Antioch. What do you do?"

"I'm on my way to California," Ben answered. "Just stopping over in Frontier."

"On your way from where? New Mexico?"

Ben's body tensed. "I've been there. Years ago."

"Nine years ago?" Sheriff Pedley's hand was poised over his gun as he spoke.

"Let's all get some coffee," Cathy suggested, brushing quickly between them. "Let's go over to Gus's and have some coffee."

The tension eased for an instant and Ben relaxed. He didn't want trouble in front of the woman, and apparently neither did the sheriff. But before anyone could make a move for the door it opened once more, to admit a breathless Deputy Reilly.

"Quick," he gasped. "Someone's killed Len Antioch . . ."

S omeone had indeed killed Len Antioch, and already Frontier Street was alive with the news. Men on horseback rode shouting past, and from all directions came running people converging on the Golden Swan. It was as if the President had died.

"Everyone out," the sheriff was shouting to Reilly. "Clear everyone out of here. Give us room to breathe."

"That means you too," Reilly said, pushing Ben back through the office door. Beyond, in back of the big old desk, Ben caught a glimpse of a bloody head and a hand stretched out across the floor.

He walked back across the muddy street, against the rush of people, and collared Gus on the opposite side. "I need some coffee and food. How about it?"

"Sure, sure. Did you see him? Did you see Len's body? Who killed him?"

"They don't know yet. It looked to me like someone had beaten him over the head with a pistol butt."

Old Gus snorted, opening the door with his one good arm. "Probably that no-good brother of his done it. You know Harry?"

"Seen him around," Ben mumbled, deep in thought.

He drank his coffee in silence, and it was twenty minutes later when the sheriff joined him at the table. "Got a few questions to ask you, Snow."

"Go ahead."

Pedley's face was grim. "What did you and Len talk about this morning?"

"He offered me a thousand dollars to kill Reilly," Ben answered honestly.

"You accepted?"

"No, I hit him and knocked him down and left. I'm not a hired killer, whatever you and everyone else might think."

Pedley's eyes narrowed. "You say you knocked him down . . ."

"He was alive when I left him, if that's what you're wondering. I hit him with my fist, not with a gun butt."

The sheriff played with his mustache. "I'm going over to talk with Len's brother, Harry. Maybe you'd better come along."

"If you say so." He paid Gus for the food and followed the sheriff back across the street. The crowd was breaking up now, reforming itself into little groups of three or four to talk over the situation, to guess and speculate and wonder. And Ben noticed a good many of their eyes on him as he crossed the width of Frontier Street.

Deputy Reilly was in the little back office with Harry Antioch, but the body was gone now—bound no doubt for the undertaker at the end of the street and then on up to the graveyard on the hill. Reilly lounged in a corner chair, rolling a cigarette. Harry, looking gray and worried, sat behind his brother's desk.

"Well, Harry," the sheriff asked, "what's the story?"

Harry Antioch turned steely eyes on Ben. "This is the guy that killed my brother," he said quietly. "Everyone knows who he is."

"He denies it, Harry. And his story's pretty convincing. Claims Len tried to hire him to kill Reilly, my deputy."

Reilly got to his feet at the mention of his name. "I knew that's what it was. And I figure this guy would do it, too. I was givin' the Antioch brothers too much trouble lately. They had to get rid of me."

But now Harry was on his feet too. "Why in hell don't you guys all go back to punching cows? My brother and I weren't hurting anyone. We run honest games for the boys, with never no trouble. Everybody was happy till Reilly became a deputy and this guy Snow rode into town."

"Did you see anyone else come in here after Ben Snow left?"

"No, but there's a back door. Snow or Reilly might have returned that way and killed my brother."

"Why?" Pedley asked, shifting the gun on his hip. "Why should anyone want to kill Len if you were running an honest game?"

"Why did anyone want to shoot Lincoln? Even a guy like my brother probably made enemies. There are a lot of hired guns around this town," he said, shooting a knowing glance at Ben.

"But Len wasn't shot," the sheriff pointed out. "He got knocked on the head a few times. That's hardly the work of a professional killer."

"That's more a brotherly sort of crime," Ben observed. "Like Cain and Abel."

"Like who?" Harry asked, missing the implication.

But Sheriff Pedley was still more interested in Ben. "You make an awfully good suspect, Snow, whatever you say. You might have killed him before you left, or you might have come back here later."

"You goin' to arrest me, Sheriff?"

"I just might."

"Well, you know where to find me," he said. "I'm goin' now."

"Where'll you be?"

"Cathy's dress shop, probably. Look there first." He could feel their eyes on him as he walked out the rear door and around to the street again.

The sky above was clouding up again, and it looked like there might be more rain on the way. He cursed the recent mud on his boots, collected from behind the Golden Swan, and wondered when Arizona ever had all the dry weather he heard about. Certainly it was wet enough this month.

"Hello again, stranger," Cathy said. "The sheriff make an arrest yet?"

"If he had I wouldn't be here. I'm still the prime suspect."

She looked away from him, making an obvious effort to avoid his eyes. "Ben . . ."

"Yeah?"

"This . . . story they tell about you . . . Is it true?"

"You too, huh? You believe it too."

"Not really, Ben," she answered, starting to unpack another dress. "You like this one? It came in this morning from New York."

"It's fine. You believe it, don't you?"

She looked down at him in the chair, at the holstered gun hanging loosely at his side—the gun she'd never known him to draw. "Are you?" she whispered. "Are you Billy the Kid?"

He sighed and looked away. "Billy the Kid's been dead for nine years. Everybody knows that."

"There was a man . . . he rode into town a few weeks after you arrived. He knew Billy, back in New Mexico. He swore you looked just like him, just like he would look at the age of thirty . . ."

"My name's Ben Snow," he answered quietly. "I'm from New Mexico, but that's as far as it goes."

"But this man was so certain. He . . . he said he ran into you in Denver a few months back. Said you shot it out with two of the best shots in the state and killed them both. He said you handled a gun just like Billy the Kid used to."

"I know. I've heard all the stories a thousand times and that's why I keep moving on."

"Did you kill those two men up in Denver?"

"They hated each other as much as they hated me. They were so busy trying to kill each other that I managed a couple of lucky shots."

"And where was it before Denver?"

"Before Denver? With the army at Wounded Knee. Slaughtering Indians."

"And before that? Nine years ago?"

"You really believe it, don't you? What do you think I am, a ghost?"

"No, you're human, Ben Snow. All too human at times. But there are always stories. Some say Billy the Kid never died that night nine years ago in the girl's bedroom."

Ben nodded. "And stories like that have been the curse of my life. That's why I never draw my gun if I can help it. That's why I use my fists."

"Did he . . . really look like you?"

"So they say. And when people saw how I could shoot, the story just naturally got started. This year has been worse than most. The territory seems full of men who knew Billy personally."

She came over to him as he stood up, and she said, "I believe you, really, but you haven't actually told me anything. You still could be . . . him."

"I could be."

"A man like Billy the Kid might have killed Len Antioch under certain circumstances."

"He might have."

"Why don't you leave, Ben? Why don't you get your horse and ride out of Frontier?"

"Because then the sheriff would know he was right. They'd come after me, and if they didn't find me there'd be another story to follow me to the next place."

"So what are you going to do?"

"Well, right now I think I'll try to get back inside the Antioch brothers' office and have a look around. There might be all sorts of interesting things around."

"If it's Harry Antioch, he'll kill you," she said simply.

"I've had men shoot at me before," he told her. "See you later."

He went back into the street, under clouds leaden with the threat of rain. A passing horseman spattered mud on his pants, and in some towns that would have been a shooting offense. Things were a bit more friendly in Frontier, though. He'd not heard a gunshot during the two months he'd been there. Pistol butts made quieter weapons.

Reilly, the deputy, was standing by the alley door to the Golden Swan, checking the bullets in his revolver. "Thinkin' of shooting somebody, Reilly?" he asked.

"Maybe you, wise guy. It would give me quite a name if I gunned down Billy the . . ."

"Name's Ben Snow. Remember that. Now step aside while I go in."

"I'm here to keep people out, mister."

"Go tell your boss I'm inside, then." Ben pushed past him and entered the office. Reilly followed right behind him, hand on gun.

Ben wasted no time. He'd dealt with gamblers wiser and older than the Antioch brothers many times, and he knew just where to find what he sought. A quick look through the three regular desk drawers yielded nothing, and he pulled the gun from his holster.

"I'm ahead of you," Reilly said, drawing his own weapon in a flash.

"Don't worry, I've never fired since I got here, have I? It's just that I happen to know this desk. I saw one just like it in Kansas City once. Look here." And with a quick motion of his gun he smashed into one of the ornate panels that ran along the side of the massive desk.

"What in hell you doin', Snow?"

"Here, unless I'm all wet, are the books and records for Len and Harry's gambling activities in this town. You run and tell Sheriff Pedley I've found them."

Reilly hesitated only another moment. "He won't like your being here."

"He'll like it a hell of a lot less if you don't tell him right away."

With that the deputy was gone, his gun back in the holster. And Ben was flipping through the pages of the first big ledger he'd taken from the secret drawer. There were pages covered with notations and brief abbreviations, and one especially kept appearing more than the others.

And then, in the half second his eyes were off the other door—the door to the bar—it opened, and Harry Antioch was with him in the room. As swiftly as a trapped fox his hand had gone for the little Derringer under his arm. "Hold it right there, Snow."

"Well! This is a pleasure."

"Drop the gun on the floor. Quick! You might be a fast shot, but you're not that fast."

"I know everything, Harry. It's all here in the books."

He twisted his upper lip into a sneer. "Then you'll have to die, won't you?"

Ben was still hanging on to the gun, pointed at the floor, hoping for the chance, the split second he needed. And then the back door opened, and Deputy Reilly came hurrying in.

"The sheriff says—" He saw Harry Antioch and the gun just an instant too late. He clawed at his own holster in a sudden reflex motion, but Harry was much too fast. He whirled and the tiny Derringer coughed once and Reilly fell backwards, blood spurting from his right eye.

Ben knew it was now or never, knew he'd already waited a second too long. He started to bring the gun up, mentally gauging the angle as he had a thousand times before. But Harry Antioch had dropped his gun arm to his side. He stood staring at the fallen body as if he'd never seen one before. "I didn't mean to kill him," he mumbled.

Ben held the gun steady, but he did not fire. He couldn't kill this man now. Perhaps later, but not now. "He was just an eager kid deputy, Harry," Ben said quietly. "He didn't have to die."

"Now what do I do?" he asked, half to himself.

Ben motioned with his gun. "I'll give you a five-second head start, Harry. Then I'm coming after you."

Harry Antioch looked deep into his eyes—and saw that he meant it. He opened the door behind him and went out, fast. Ben counted five and then went after him.

Harry was behind the bar, shoving cartridges into a shiny silver revolver. He dropped down out of sight as Ben appeared in the doorway. "We can make a deal, Snow," he shouted. "I'll cut you in."

Ben glanced around to make sure no one was there to take a stray accidental bullet in the stomach. But the Golden Swan was closed to customers. Through the front window he could see only Sheriff Vic Pedley hurrying out of his office down the street. That gave him maybe a minute at most.

"A deal, Snow! This town has enough for both of us."

"What about Pedley?" Ben asked quietly.

"I'll handle him."

"No go, Harry."

"Then die, damn you!" Harry Antioch shouted. He fired once, wildly, over the top of the bar. Ben knew he could have taken him without firing a shot, but the memory of the dead deputy in the next room was still too fresh in his mind.

He dropped to one knee and carefully fired five shots into the wood of the bar, just about where Harry's head had appeared. There was a choking scream, and cough, and then Harry Antioch's head rose above the bar again. Ben could see he was hurt badly.

"Damn," he coughed. "Lucky shot . . . damned lucky."

"Drop the gun, Harry. Maybe the Doc can still save you."

But the gambler was on his way out, on his way to join his brother. "Tell . . . me one thing, Snow . . . Are you really Billy . . . Billy the Kid . . . ?"

Ben looked at him with sadness and silence in his eyes. He took a step toward the tottering man, but already it was too late. Harry Antioch was dead on his feet, just as Sheriff Pedley came through the swinging doors . . .

Later, they were sitting around in Gus's place, eating lunch—Ben and Cathy and Sheriff Pedley. The sheriff was frowning into his soup, perhaps thinking of his dead deputy, and of the three bodies that would travel up to the graveyard on the hill.

"So, Antioch killed his brother, huh?" he said, as if seeking confirmation in his own mind.

Ben looked at Cathy, grim and silent with her food, and somehow he hated himself for what he had to do. It would have been so easy just to let things go.

"No, I don't think so, Sheriff," he answered, looking away.

"You don't think so? What in hell you mean?"

"Harry Antioch was a gambler, but not a killer. You didn't see his expression when he gunned down Reilly, but I did. I think that was the first man he ever really killed in his whole life. He certainly didn't kill his brother."

"Well, hell, then who did?"

Ben's eyes came back slowly to meet and lock with Pedley's. "I think you did, Sheriff . . ."

"What the hell!"

Behind him, Ben heard Cathy gasp. "I found their secret set of books, Sheriff. They showed large payments to you from the gambling. You were apparently a secret partner in the Golden Swan right from the beginning."

"Maybe I was. That doesn't make me a killer."

"No, but a lot of other things do. Len tried to hire me to kill Reilly, but he didn't seem at all concerned about you. I suppose he figured he could always keep you in line. But you two battled about something—maybe about your deputy—and you bashed his head in with your gun. Afterwards, you made the mistake of mentioning that he'd been hit over the head several times—a fact you could hardly have told from the condition of his skull. Maybe some of them big eastern docs could have counted the number of blows, but not you, Sheriff—unless you were there."

"No jury will believe that, Snow."

"There's more. I'm willing to bet the mud on your boots is a perfect match to the mud by Len's back door . . ."

"I walk that way lots of times. So what?"

"And before he died, Harry said he could take care of you and apparently keep you from bothering him. What do you think he meant by that? Blackmail, probably, because he figured you for his brother's killer."

The sheriff twisted his mustache with nervous fingers. "There's no proof there. No proof for a jury."

"What about the books?"

"Things are like that in Arizona. You think the people will send me to prison because I had an interest in a gambling house and bar?"

"We could try it."

But the sheriff had one more trump card. "They'd as soon lynch you right now, if I let the word get around that you killed the Antioch brothers and my deputy. They're already convinced you're some sort of ghost of Billy the Kid, and folks in these parts don't like things they can't understand."

"So where does that leave us?"

"You get out of town by tomorrow and we call it a draw. The woman goes with you because she knows too much." Cathy gasped at this, and turned toward Ben.

"I'm not in this," she said. "I've got a business on Frontier Street, a good business. I'm not going anywhere."

Sheriff Pedley shrugged. "There's no other possibility, is there?"

"I can think of one," Ben said quietly. "You get out of town and sign a paper before you go turning over the Golden Swan to me. You're the sole owner now, you know."

Pedley laughed out loud. "Give it to you? *Give it to you?*"

"That's right."

"You think I'm out of my head?"

"Then where are we, Sheriff?"

"You leave."

Ben frowned at his coffee. "If I don't?"

"I shoot you and say you killed them all. Maybe I shoot the woman for good measure too." He kept his voice low, so that the words didn't carry to the counter where Gus was working.

Ben sighed finally and stood up. "If that has to be the answer, let's settle it now. Outside. In the street."

"Oh, no. You're a gunman. I wouldn't stand a chance against . . . Billy the Kid."

Ben took out his Colt and laid it on the table. "There's one live cartridge left in here. I used the other five on Harry. You can check that."

Pedley frowned in hesitation, then checked the cylinder of the gun. "OK, so what?"

"I'll spin the cylinder, so I don't know where the live cartridge is. Then we'll draw at the same time. I'll have to pull the trigger from one to six times to get off my shot. That should give you all the advantage you'll need."

Pedley was beginning to smile, for the first time that day. "Sounds fair enough," he said. "Of course, you know even if you kill me the townsfolk would never let you leave alive. They'd pounce on you and tear you apart before my body hit the ground."

"That's the chance I'll take," Ben said. "Outside, in five minutes?"

Sheriff Pedley nodded. "Five minutes. Right out in front."

He got up slowly and went out into the street to wait, and Cathy's hand came out to grip Ben's arm. "You fool! What kind of a fight is that? You'll get off maybe one shot before he fires. The odds are five to one against you."

"Maybe," Ben said. "Wish me luck."

"You crazy fool," was all she could say.

He waited another moment, then holstered his gun and got up. Outside, a cool breeze was blowing down Frontier Street, and Sheriff Vic Pedley stood alone in front of the Golden Swan.

"Here I am, Snow."

"I see you."

"Spin the cylinder."

Ben carefully took out the gun, held it pointed toward the sky, and twirled the magazine with its single cartridge. One out of six. Then he dropped the weapon back in his holster.

"Count of ten, Sheriff?"

"Count of ten's OK."

Ben started to count. "One . . . two . . . three . . . four . . . five . . . six . . ."

And Pedley joined him for the last four numbers. " . . .seven . . . eight . . . nine . . ."

A pause ever so slight.

". . . ten . . ."

Ben's gun was out of the holster before the final word had left his mouth. His finger was squeezing the trigger.

Once.

Twice.

Pedley's gun was coming fast, his eyes glistening like a tiger's.

Ben's finger tightened a third time and got only a click.

Pedley smiled and paused a split second for a careful aim.

And Ben's gun roared on the fourth try.

Pedley spun around with the bullet's impact and went down in the dust, and his finger jerked spasmodically on the trigger. Then he was dead.

Ben sighed and holstered his gun. He didn't look at the sheriff again, but walked away instead, back toward the doorway where Cathy waited.

"Ben! How . . .?"

"I've done it before, back in New Mexico," he said quietly. "I can always get off five before the other man fires, so really the odds are on my side. They always take their time because they figure they've got me."

"Oh God, Ben!"

"Pedley was wrong about one thing, though. These people don't care whether he's dead or alive." He motioned toward the body, where a crowd of quiet people was collecting.

"You'll be leaving now, Ben?"

"I might as well. Let someone else fight over the Golden Swan."

"Ben . . . you are a gunfighter, aren't you?"

"You might say that."

Her voice dropped to a quiet whisper. "Are you . . . Billy the Kid?"

"Was anybody?" he answered. "Was he ever just one man, or was he just a collection of legends?"

"Are you?"

"Ben Snow's the name," he answered with a smile. "Remember that."

And presently he rode away from the town called Frontier, and all was at peace once more . . .

THE VALLEY OF ARROWS

Ben Snow wiped the sweat from his forehead and hunched over his saddle, gazing down into the peaceful valley before him. In another year, another age, this might have been farmland, or a sea of grazing grass for the great herds to the east. It might have marked the birthplace of a town or an empire. But right now there was only the fort, pale in the morning light, seemingly asleep.

Fort Arrowhead was a handsome place from up there, stretching across the valley like some great wooden throne. The men who manned it were mere ants, moving in and out of the gates, carrying on their various functions in a world all their own.

Ben sighed and turned his horse down the narrow grassy trail into the valley. This was the place he sought, a tiny dot on all but the newest maps. A city in the making, perhaps, or possibly just a last outpost against the red man. Fort Arrowhead.

They had seen him coming from a great distance, and a dozen rifles glinted in the morning sun, following the slow movements of his horse. He didn't blame them for their caution. At that distance he could have been an Indian as easily as a white man. When he'd ridden a bit closer he saw some of the rifles disappear from the top of the wooden wall. An officer and two soldiers appeared at the gate, motioning him to stop.

"Pause and state your business," the officer commanded.

Ben brought the horse up short, keeping the smile on his face. "Ben Snow's the name. I'm here to see your commanding officer."

"What about?" the officer asked suspiciously.

"Indians," Ben answered simply.

"Dismount and lead your horse." Ben obeyed and followed the man inside the compound, across an area of stained and dusty grass that told him Fort Arrowhead had not been too long in this location—not long enough to wear the grass from underfoot, at least. The people, most of those who clustered around for a look at this new arrival, were soldiers—though he was surprised at the number of women at the fort. The distant cries of children told him that whole families apparently made it their home. Hazardous as it was, perhaps there was more safety here than out among the dark hills where any rock or bush could hide an enemy with a flaming arrow.

Presently the officer paused before a long wooden cabin with a flag rippling gently before it. "Wait here," he said, and motioned to the two soldiers to make certain Ben did just that. He entered the building and spoke a few words to some unseen person, then returned to the door and motioned Ben inside.

The commanding officer of Fort Arrowhead was Colonel Noakes, a tall rangy man with a white mustache that reminded Ben of Custer. He spoke only occasionally, preferring a monosyllabic reply to the longer messages of other men. Ben had heard of him, because army men like Colonel Noakes brought a legend with them wherever they went. He'd fought in the Civil War a year after West Point, at Bull Run, and marched through the south with Sherman. He'd gone west in the seventies, to fight Indians with the rest of the war-trained troops. He'd been promoted to captain under Custer, and had only missed the Little Big Horn because he'd been on leave, back in Chicago. After that he'd risen swiftly to major, and then to colonel, leading the great revenge raids that tore the Indian from his land and splattered the west with years of blood.

Colonel Noakes was a man the Indians hated. It could be said that he did not likewise hate them, but that detail did not change the situation at Fort Arrowhead. Whereas Noakes felt with all his heart that he was only doing a fighting man's duty to his country, the Indians who now ringed the valley unseen had other ideas. To them, Noakes was another Custer—a man to be killed in the heat of battle, or knifed in the silence of sleep. Noakes was in command at Fort Arrowhead, and that was why this outpost had been picked for the attack both sides knew was only days or hours away.

"Colonel Noakes, my name is Ben Snow . . ."

He looked up, nodded. "Heard of you. Well?"

"Could I speak to you alone, sir?"

Noakes waved the other officer away and repeated, "Well?"

"Sir, I have come upon information that could be of vital importance to you . . ."

The colonel grunted. "What?"

"Someone at Fort Arrowhead is in league with the Indians."

Had he expected the statement to take Colonel Noakes by surprise, he'd have been disappointed. The tall man took the news without turning a hair. "Very interesting. Who?"

"That I don't know, sir, though it may very well be one of your officers. I picked up a trail yesterday, up in the hills. Two Indians had met with someone —someone who rode a shod horse. I followed the horse back to the fort. Since you have rigid security measures in force, it's my guess that only an officer could have gotten out alone."

Colonel Noakes cleared his throat. "Quite right. Thank you." His gaze returned to the papers on his desk, as if Ben had merely told him the time of day.

"But, sir . . ."

"That's all, Snow."

Ben turned and went outside. So the trip down into the valley had been for nothing. The man who sat behind the desk was not interested in betrayal by one of his officers. He looked up at the sky and cursed the dark gray clouds that warned of rain in the distant mountains.

"You all through?" a voice asked, and he saw the officer who'd admitted him.

"I guess so."

"You're Ben Snow, huh?"

"That's the name."

"Heard about you, from some people in Frontier. You're pretty fast with a gun."

"I rarely use it," Ben answered honestly. "I believe any dispute that can't be settled with fists shouldn't be settled with guns."

The officer merely smiled. "They say you killed two men back in Frontier. With your gun."

Ben frowned at the man, ignoring the last statement. "I didn't catch your name, Captain."

The officer bowed slightly. "Captain Roberts, sir, at your service."

"Glad to meet you, Captain. But I do think I should be getting along now, before the storm breaks."

"One moment, if you would be so kind, Mr. Snow." He laid a hand on Ben's shoulder. "There's someone who wants to meet you."

"To meet me?" Ben followed him across the central yard to one of the houses on the far side. Could there be someone here from his past, from those years of wandering and doubt?

"In here," Captain Roberts said, holding open the door. It was obviously an officer's residence, belonging to Roberts or one of the others.

Ben walked in, adjusted his eyes to the dimness, and made out finally the shadowy figure of a young woman. He had only a second to dive to one side before she fired the revolver she held in her hand.

And she would have fired again had not Roberts leapt in at her, pinning her arms to her sides. "Anita, you crazy fool!" he shouted out. "You'll have the whole garrison down on us!"

Captain Roberts pulled the gun from her hand and rushed back outside to meet anyone the shot had attracted. Ben picked himself up from the floor and took a better look at the woman who'd just tried to kill him. She was about his age—perhaps thirty or thirty-one—with tired eyes that reflected too many years west of the Mississippi.

"To what do I owe the honor?" he asked quietly.

"I . . . You don't look like him . . ." Her expression was puzzled, unbelieving.

"Like who?"

"Billy the Kid," she answered quietly. "I heard he wasn't dead. I heard . . . that you were Billy the Kid, come back from the grave . . ."

Ben sighed and sat down. Everywhere it was the same. Everywhere the same story. "Do I look like Billy the Kid?" he asked her.

"No, not really. The . . . the face is the same, but you're taller, stronger."

"You knew him?"

She nodded, a slight jerky movement of her head that he barely caught. "Nine years ago, just before he died. In a little town in New Mexico . . ."

"And you thought it was me. You thought he was still alive."

The nod was firmer now. "They said he was alive. They said he was in Frontier, using the name of Ben Snow. And that's you."

"Which only goes to prove you can't believe everything you hear." He paused and studied her a bit more intently. "Are you Mrs. Roberts?"

"Yes," she answered. "Three years now. He's a good man but he doesn't understand me."

"Did Billy?"

The eyes flickered shut a moment. "Sometimes. That was a long time ago." Then the eyes came open. "What brings you to Fort Arrowhead, Mr. Snow?"

"A useless mission, I'm afraid. I stumbled upon some information I thought might be of interest to your commanding officer. I was wrong."

The door behind him opened and Captain Roberts reappeared. His face was white and his voice trembling. "God, Anita—some savage has gotten in and killed Colonel Noakes . . ."

The effect of his words on Ben was not as startling as it might have been. The Navajo horsemen were waiting just beyond the hills, and it was not impossible that one of them had somehow penetrated the walls of Fort Arrowhead to kill the man they hated so much.

"How?" Ben asked, because it seemed a likely question.

"An arrow. Through his throat. The men outside never heard a thing. Major Schult just found him."

"Who's in charge now?"

Roberts thought a moment. "Why—Schult is second in command."

"I want to see him—right away." They hurried away, leaving Anita Roberts alone in the dim quarters that were her home. Outside, the distant playing of children could still be heard—but now Ben noticed another sound, or absence of sound. The headquarters building he'd left such a short time before was now a magnet of silent activity. A dozen uniformed officers were clustered around, their voices dulled as if in deference to the dead.

Major Schult was shorter than the others around him, and he conveyed the impression of a latter-day Napoleon. Now, with the mantle of leadership suddenly draped around his shoulders, he seemed calm and efficient, issuing orders with the same subdued tone that the others used.

"Major Schult? My name's Ben Snow. I'd like to speak to you, sir."

"Snow? Snow?" he repeated, seeming to search his memory for some past knowledge of the name. "Can't you see I'm busy, man?"

"I'm afraid it's about Colonel Noakes, sir. And the Navajo."

"Well . . . come in here." He led the way into the office, carefully looking away from the crumpled thing behind the desk. But Ben looked, and saw the body of Colonel Noakes, a Navajo arrow protruding from the left side of his neck. The arrow was slanted downward, as if it had been fired from above, and Ben's eyes went automatically to the ceiling of the little room. His gaze met only the brown beams of the solid wooden roof, without an opening in it.

"I spoke to the colonel as soon as I arrived," Ben began when they were alone in the room with the dead man. "I told him I'd stumbled on hoofprints up the valley, showing that someone from the fort had met with two Navajos. There was something funny—secret—about the whole look of it. I knew at once that this was no peace meeting or truce talk. Someone from this fort— probably an officer since he was out alone—had met the Indians for a purpose I could only guess."

"You told the colonel this?" Schult asked, a frown beginning to crawl across his wide forehead.

"I told him."

"You really believe this?"

"I believe there are a half-thousand Navajo braves waiting just beyond the hill. Perhaps they're waiting for a signal."

Major Schult thought about this a moment before replying. "You're aware of the situation here? You're aware that it's him they're after?" He motioned toward the body almost at their feet.

"I've heard stories," Ben admitted. "He was an old Indian-fighter."

"Ever fight Indians yourself?"

"I was with the army at Wounded Knee earlier this year."

Schult's face reflected a brief expression of disgust. "I mean fight them, not massacre them. Indians are human just like you and me. There are ways of dealing with them."

Ben's mouth twisted in a hint of a smile. "What deal would you suggest in the present circumstances?"

Major Schult thought about it for only a brief moment before replying. "You and I could ride out there and tell them the colonel is dead. It might stop the attack. We could even give up his body if necessary."

"Don't you think they know?"

He shook his head. "I'd stake my life that no Navajo entered this compound. Something, someone else killed Colonel Noakes."

"And you think this would turn back those Indians? You think we could get within a mile of them without being shot down?"

"I think they'd respect a flag of truce, Mr. Snow."

"Why me? Why do I get picked for the job?"

"Two reasons. It'll get you out of here safely, and it'll give me someone I can trust. If your story is true, any of my men might be the traitor."

Well, that was it, and Ben saw no way out of it for himself. He didn't trust the waiting Navajo, but it seemed at least as safe as remaining here at Arrowhead, in the company of an unknown traitor, a murdering Indian, and a girl who had tried once to kill him. "All right," he decided. "When do we go?"

"Right now. They're certainly not going to sit out there beyond that hill all day . . ."

They rode out, into the valley, with Major Schult holding high a white guidon signalling their friendly intentions. For the first half hour they saw not a living soul, and the conversation between them was limited to speculation about the great black clouds that still lurked near at hand.

Presently, though, Schult turned to Ben. "I see you're still wearing your gun. Perhaps you should remove it."

"I feel more comfortable with it on," Ben told him. "If you knew more about Indians you'd be wearing sidearms, too."

"Not with a truce flag. Guns poison the atmosphere."

"Yeah."

"Some folks say you look a bit like Billy the Kid used to," the major said casually.

Ben kept his eyes straight ahead. "Billy's been dead nine years. I can't help what stories get started. Talk to Captain Roberts' wife some time. She knew Billy quite well."

"Oh?"

"Anyway, there are the people we came to see," Ben said, motioning toward the rocky bluff ahead. A party of Navajo scouts, perhaps nine or ten of them, had appeared over the ridge. They stood simply watching, waiting, making no move to challenge or stop them.

"What now?" Major Schult asked.

"They'll have a leader somewhere," Ben said. "If they don't kill us they'll probably take us to him." And even as he spoke the Indians began riding down around them, forming a silent circle as if at the command of some unseen chieftain.

"They seem to have us," Schult said.

"At least we're still alive. You keep your hand on that white flag and I'll keep mine near my gun."

Presently the surrounding circle of Indians paused, and down a narrow gully rode a single Navajo warrior such as Ben had never seen before. The man was tall, over six feet, and his hair was pure white even in youth. He carried himself upon his horse like some Greek god and wore only a single feather in the band around his forehead. But the most amazing thing about him was that he carried not a weapon. Not even a knife hung by his side as he rode toward them.

"I am called Running Bear," he said. "These are my people."

"You are Navajo?" Major Schult asked.

The great head shook. "I am from the north. I have met your Colonel Noakes on the plain of battle before. He killed many braves."

"Colonel Noakes is dead," Ben told him, "slain not an hour ago by a Navajo arrow."

The eyes flickered, but no other expression crossed the face of Running Bear. "Are these words true?" he asked Schult.

"They are. We will surrender the body if it will ensure safety to the people of the fort."

Running Bear's eyes flicked shut an instant, then opened. "No, a single life will not avenge the death of my people. I was promised the lives of one hundred men."

"Promised?" Schult exploded. "Promised by whom?"

"I was promised," Running Bear repeated, and that was all he would say.

"What of the women and children?"

"If possible we will not harm them."

"You be damned," the major shouted. "We'll meet you at the gates with bullets and sabres."

The Indians tightened their circle around them, and Ben saw one fitting an arrow into his bow. Another held a rifle ready.

"Remember," Ben told Running Bear, "we come under a flag of truce."

The Indian nodded slowly. "You come, and you go. I hope you reach the fort in time. Go now, and be ready to meet us." His words carried a note of menace that made Ben's hair tingle. The circle opened for them and he spurred his horse around.

"Come on, Major. Let's get out of here."

But Schult held his ground. "Hand me your gun," he said. "I'll settle this war right now." He let the truce flag fall to the ground.

Ben could wait no longer. He slapped Schult's horse into motion and led the charge out of the circle of braves. Behind them, he heard Running Bear's voice raised in some ancient command.

An arrow bit the dirt a few feet ahead of Ben's galloping horse, and another whistled past his head. "We've had it now," he shouted back at Schult.

"Any day I can't outrun Navajo arrows!"

"What about bullets?"

"They won't chance the noise if they're riding to attack the fort. This way they can be into the valley before my men see them coming."

Ben drew his gun and twisted in the saddle, but there was no sure shot open to him. The warriors of Running Bear were all around them, but well out of pistol range. He cursed himself for not bringing a rifle.

"Well, at least I can get off a few shots in the air," he said.

"Save them. We might need every one."

Their horses were sweating with the strain now, hoofs pounding the dust. And around them Indians on horseback were swarming down into the valley, like the melting snows of spring. One warrior, his painted naked body glistening, drew up not a hundred feet away, raising his bow in silent challenge. Ben twisted in his saddle and shot the Indian dead.

"Where the hell did you learn to shoot like that?" Schult gasped out, beginning to fall a bit behind.

"When people think you're the ghost of Billy the Kid, you've got to be able to shoot."

Ahead, perhaps two miles down in the valley, the guarding walls of Arrowhead rose suddenly into view. They might just make it, he thought. And then the sky was filled with a great tide of arrows, falling from either side like a summer cloudburst.

"Schult!"

Behind him the major's horse went down, sliding in the dirt. Schult staggered to his feet as a painted brave charged in on them. Ben wheeled his horse around and fired twice as the Indian met Schult's body with a feathered spear. At that range he couldn't miss and the enemy's skull seemed to blow apart under the bullet's impact.

But the major had fallen now, bleeding from the side where the spearhead had scraped and cut at flesh. "Come on," Ben shouted, pulling at him. Somehow they made it onto the single horse, riding on down the valley. And the arrows followed them down.

Schult, riding behind him, grunted once—and Ben knew an arrow had found its mark. "Hang on," he said. "Not much farther now."

The doors of the fort were opening before them, and the bark of rifles was sending an answer to enemy arrows. They'd made it, somehow.

Ben slid to the ground as Roberts and another captain came running over. They helped Schult out of the saddle, trying not to look at the blood and mess of his torn uniform. There was one arrow still in his back and Ben pulled it out, bringing a new gush of blood.

"He can't last," Captain Roberts said.

"Bandage him up," Ben said. "He's not dead yet. And who's next in command?"

"I guess I am," Roberts told him.

"Well, get up to that wall and feast your eyes on more damn Indians than you ever saw before. They're comin' like the wind and nothing's goin' to stop them."

Roberts looked briefly frightened. Then he ran off to issue orders to the men who would defend the fort. It was the women who took up the task of caring for the wounded major, and Ben saw Anita Roberts unrolling a clean bandage for him. It surprised him somehow, to see her out here in the daylight with the other women.

"Mrs. Roberts . . ."

She looked up at him. "I'm glad you're back."

Overhead, a single arrow cut the air and clattered harmlessly off a tin roof. "Everybody under cover," someone shouted. "Here they come."

Ben pulled her under cover as the air was suddenly torn with sound and fury. Two men hurried to carry the wounded major inside.

"Oh, God," Mrs. Roberts gasped at his side. "Will they kill us all?"

He didn't bother to answer. High on the wall a soldier toppled backwards in death. The arrows kept coming, and now there was rifle fire from the Indians too, as they began risking their small supply of ammunition.

"Your husband's in charge now," Ben said. "He'll hold them off."

"But that's just it," she gasped. "He won't. He likes them better than white men. He . . ."

Ben stared. Her words dug into his brain and he moved. Of course! Captain Roberts . . .

"Where are you going?"

"I'll be back," he shouted. "Stay under cover."

The arrows thudded into the ground around him as he ran, and he could see that some of the Indians had already gained the top of the wall, battling hand to hand with the defenders. But Ben kept going, bursting through the door of the post headquarters.

Captain Roberts was there, alone, sitting very still in the colonel's old chair. "This is where I find you while your men die out there," Ben said.

"What is this, Snow? What are you doing here?"

"You're the one who betrayed the fort, Roberts. You rode out yesterday and met with Running Bear. When I followed your tracks here and told the colonel, you had to kill him. That arrow was never fired from a Navajo bow. You used it as a dagger to stab him. That's why you rushed out after your wife tried to kill me. That's when you did it—in those few minutes before Schult found the body. You overheard what I told the colonel and tried to lure me to my death too. You knew Anita would try to kill me."

Captain Roberts rose from behind the desk. He was holding his service revolver pointed at Ben's chest. "It doesn't matter now what you know. Running Bear is knocking on the gates. The fort will be his within an hour."

"Why?" Ben asked him. "Why?"

"Because I like Indians. Because I hate every damned man in this outfit. Because just for once I want to play God."

"Put down the gun, Roberts."

"Oh, no. You won't talk me out of this. Nobody will."

The door behind Ben burst open and a sergeant rushed in. "Captain— they're massing for a final charge. What'll we do?"

"Do?" Roberts brought the gun around slightly to cover them both. "We'll surrender. Pass the word to surrender."

"But Captain . . ."

"That's an order, Sergeant. Surrender!"

Ben made a move toward his gun but the captain's weapon was back on him at once. "No moves, Snow. This is my day."

And so they waited like that, while the sergeant passed the order to surrender. Gradually the firing on the walls grew less, and then suddenly there was the terrible squeak of the great gates being thrown open. The fort was in the hands of Running Bear.

Roberts motioned Ben outside with his gun, and Ben saw the Navajo braves charging through the open gates with unrestrained shouts of victory. And in their midst rode the triumphant, fantastic figure of Running Bear, his white hair flowing behind him, unarmed yet somehow the strongest of them all.

"Greetings, Running Bear," Roberts shouted from the steps of the building. "I have delivered the fort into your hands as promised." There was an angry murmur from the men at this, but already the forces of Running Bear were in control. Arrows and rifles covered every man and woman.

At a motion from the Navajo chief, a warrior took up his position directly behind Ben, his bow bent and ready. "Now," Running Bear said. "A single movement and you die. An arrow can be quite effective at a range of six inches."

"It can be quite effective at any range," Ben agreed. "But I don't think you want to kill me."

Running Bear moved his horse a bit closer. "No? All adult white men here will die. You among them."

"I will fight you for their lives," Ben said. "Just you and I. If I win, everyone lives." It was a dangerous move, but he figured a fifty-fifty chance with knives and better than that with guns.

But Running Bear shook his head. "I carry no arms. I fight no man."

"You just watch while your men do the torturing and killing, huh?"

"No torture. The deaths will be swift and as painless as possible. I am not a savage."

"If you won't fight me, let me fight your friend Roberts here," Ben said.

But the officer took a backward step. "No! Don't listen to him, Running Bear. Kill him!"

"Yes," Running Bear agreed suddenly, and motioned to the warrior who stood behind Ben.

This is it, Ben thought, tensing his back for the bite of the arrow. But instead there came the crack of a pistol, and the Indian toppled, his arrow zinging into the ground.

They turned as one man and saw Anita Roberts in the window of one of the buildings, gripping her pistol with both hands. And Ben supposed there was something right and just about her saving his life after trying to kill him.

But already a Navajo brave was raising his rifle to the window where Anita stood. Ben tensed for a leap across the ten feet separating them, but at the last second there came a scream from Roberts.

"No!" he shouted. "Not Anita!" And the army pistol he still held barked twice. The Indian dropped his rifle and toppled to the ground, but before his body hit, five arrows thudded into Roberts' chest and back. He twisted, clawing at them, a look of amazement written across his face. Ben looked quickly away, because he did not want to see this man die.

The Indians brought Anita to her dead husband, and stood by quietly as she sobbed over him. Through it all Running Bear sat motionless on his horse, moving only to raise a hand of command against a brave who gestured with his knife toward Anita. "We have killed her husband," he spoke. "That is enough."

And so they stood there, Ben and Running Bear facing each other across the sobbing woman and the dead traitor, with two hundred soldiers and four hundred Indians waiting for the word, the command, that would mean death to so many.

"Now what?" Ben asked finally.

And Running Bear spoke. "Show me the body of Colonel Noakes," he said.

Ben led him inside, with two armed braves following, and in an inner room they found the colonel's body stretched out on the floor, covered with a blanket. "Here," Ben said softly. "Captain Roberts killed him."

And Running Bear bent and lifted the dead eyelids, and stared for a long time into those unseeing eyes. "Yes," he said finally. "Yes."

And then, with his long white hair trailing behind, he left. He mounted his great horse and spoke a few brief commands to the warriors. Then he turned one last time toward Ben, standing on the steps. "We will meet again," he said, and it was not a threat but rather the words of one warrior to another.

Then they were gone, riding back through the gates of Fort Arrowhead like the very wind that rose in the west. And as they rode, a gentle rain began to fall from the gray clouds over the valley. And everywhere the soldiers of the fort began to pick up their weapons and care for their wounded.

And Ben Snow went with Anita to tend to Major Schult's torn body. And presently a burial detail took away the body of her husband to the graveyard outside the walls.

And there, in the rain, a great peace settled over the valley . . .

GHOST TOWN

B en Snow had been riding for half a day when he spotted the lonely sheepherder and his flock, blots of white against the gray of the valley. He spurred his horse a little faster, and saw the man look up, startled, fearful with the age-old terror. Whether gunman or cowpoke, a strange rider most often meant an enemy of sheep.

But Ben Snow was hardly interested in the bleating creatures that now ran from his path. Night was fast approaching over the eastern hills, and he would be needing a camp for the resting hours. "How far to the next town?" he called out to the sheepman.

The man on the ground, a pale youth still in his early twenties, eyed Ben uncertainly. "Raindeer's just over the next hill," he said finally. After a moment he added, "But you don't want to go there."

"Why not?" A night in a hotel was better than one under the cold stars anytime.

"Raindeer's a ghost town."

"That doesn't bother me. Sometimes I like to be alone."

"You don't understand, mister," the sheepman said slowly, as if addressing some St. Louis dandy. "It's a ghost town with a ghost. It's haunted. No one goes to Raindeer anymore . . ."

Ben smiled down at the man. "Well, I guess I can risk a ghost for one night. Thanks a lot." Then his horse was under motion again, scattering sheep before it.

The wind was turning colder as he rode. It was the hour of dusk, a dismal one on the plains at any time, but especially bleak this night when he rode alone. It wasn't as if he was riding toward anything—that would not have been so bad. But he was riding away from something. He'd been riding away from something for as long as he could remember.

The sheepman had spoken the truth. A town stretched out before him, a town of shacks with only a semblance of a street. It might have been a deserted mining town, except that there were no mines within a hundred miles. As he rode down along the dusty trail he passed a weather-beaten sign that might have been standing for a century:

> **WELCOME TO**
> **RAINDEER**
> **The Town That**

The last words, whatever they were, had long ago faded and rotted away. There was a date, too, that looked like 1866. Perhaps the town had been born in that first brave year after the War, when men still thought the worst was behind them.

Ben Snow hardly remembered the end of the War. He'd been barely alive at its beginning. A book about it, *The Red Badge of Courage*, had just been published back east, and Ben had found a copy that had drifted into Santa Fe somehow. He could have been a young man then, and perhaps he wouldn't have acted much differently from the young man in the book. He didn't know. Instead, he'd been born a generation later, two thousand miles further west, in a country where men were only now beginning to hang up their guns.

Welcome to Raindeer . . .

Ghost town in a valley that time had passed over.

He tied his horse to a wobbly hitching post and went into one of the darkened buildings, searching for a lamp. There was nothing but dust and sand and sagebrush. And memories. The big mirror and the place where the bar had stood (for this had been a saloon). Bars were valuable west of Texas, and they were often moved from one place to another.

He wondered where the name of Raindeer had come from.

"Stand right there, mister."

Ben turned around slowly, his hands carefully away from his sides, and looked into the barrel of a rifle. That didn't surprise him half as much as the person who held it—a dirty-faced girl with a kerchief wrapped around her head, wearing a sweat-stained blouse and tight jeans. She was standing in the doorway, caught in the fading dusk, and she must have had eyes like a bat to see him in the darkness.

"I was told the town was haunted," he said, taking a step forward.

Without changing her expression she fired a bullet into the wall a close two feet to his left. "I said to stand still."

"I heard you. Be careful with that thing."

There were riders outside now. Two, no, three, and they'd been riding hard. She didn't seem surprised to hear them. "Come on in," she called out. "We have a visitor."

They had lamps and these were quickly lit, bathing the scene in a sort of red glow. And by this light Ben first saw them: the Indian, wearing white man's clothing but carrying a knife instead of a gun on his belt; the Beard, a foul-mouthed old man who constantly chuckled to himself, who wore his gun down on the hip and chewed tobacco; and lastly the Preacher, whose gun was almost hidden by his black suit. Almost but not quite.

It was the Preacher who spoke first, and he spoke as their leader. "Toss your gun over here, mister, and she'll put down the gun."

Ben shrugged and unstrapped his belt. "I was only looking for a place to spend the night," he said. "I thought this town was deserted."

"It is deserted, mister," the Preacher replied. "We're only spending the night too. Who are you?"

"My name is Ben Snow."

The name meant something to the Beard. His hand went for his gun in a flash, until he remembered that Ben was unarmed. But even then he kept it resting on the butt. "That's Billy the Kid," he croaked.

The Preacher frowned. "Billy the Kid's been dead a long time."

"I'm glad you agree," Ben said. "I've been trying to convince people for years."

"Don't let him fool you!" the Beard said. "I saw him kill a man back in '90."

"Is that right, Snow?"

"I've killed a few men. Who hasn't?"

"I haven't," the Preacher said. "But that's beside the point. We're going to have to tie you up and leave you. Can't take a chance of your causing trouble."

"What kind of trouble?"

But the black-suited man ignored him. "Girl—tie him up. Good and tight."

She set down her rifle and came toward Ben. "It'll be a pleasure."

"I'll take a look around," the Beard said. "He might have friends." The Indian followed him out, and the girl came around Ben to start her work. At that moment there wasn't a gun on him, but he had a feeling the Preacher could be awfully fast on the draw, even with that coat on.

The girl pulled his arms roughly behind his back and tied the wrists while the black-suited man watched. Then she tied his legs at the knees and ankles and toppled him over on his side. "I'm sure you'll stay there," she said. The Preacher nodded and went out to join the others at the horses.

"You must have some name besides Girl," Ben said, now that they were alone.

"Laura. Does my name interest you?"

"You interest me." His eyes were on the tight jeans, worn at the buttocks from heavy riding. "How'd you get mixed up with those three?"

"Harry's my brother."

"The one in the black suit?"

"Of course! It wouldn't be the other two creeps, for God's sake! That bearded one, Jason, gives me the creeps. And the Indian's not much better. Where my brother dug them up, I'll never know."

The bearded Jason returned at that moment, and walked over to Ben. "You damn killer! Your fast draw don't help you now, does it?" He aimed a kick at Ben's ribs, but Laura stopped him, blocking it with her foot.

"Lay off, Jason. Get lost."

"Damn tramp! Gettin' ready to sleep with him already?"

She slapped him across his bearded cheek and he went away mumbling. "It's like that all the time," she told Ben, not seeming too upset.

"What are the four of you up to?"

She shrugged, too innocently. "Just riding. Tell me about you, Ben Snow. He said you were Billy the Kid."

He rolled over on the floor, trying to get comfortable. "A lot of people say that. Doesn't make it true, though. Billy Bonney was born in '59 and killed in '81. I wasn't born till '61 and I'm still around, a mighty live 34 years."

"Then why do they say it?"

"Too many rumors that Billy lived after '81. I guess the people wanted him to be alive or something. Hero worship, you know. I was fast with a gun and the story got started. It was one jump ahead of me all across the southwest in '90, and it's still around now. I've had five years of living down a legend, and I've killed some men trying to do it. Trouble just seems to follow me."

"You talk like an educated man."

"I guess I've had a bit of schooling."

She sat there on the floor beside him for a moment, thinking her own thoughts. Then she hopped lightly to her feet. "I'll be back. I want to look around some too."

H e lay there alone for a moment, then started working on his bonds. She sure knew how to tie knots, but he thought maybe in time he might get one hand free. He'd been at it about five minutes when he heard the scream.

It was a terrifying thing that echoed through the old building, but the most awful part of it was the way it was cut off in the middle, as if some giant hand had closed down forever. There were running footsteps somewhere above him, and after a moment the girl Laura entered from outside. "Who . . . ? God, what was that?"

"Untie me and we'll go see."

She ignored him and ran off toward the back room, which seemed to have been the source of the scream. "What's this, water?" she mumbled from the darkened doorway, and reached for one of the lamps. At the same moment Ben managed to get a hand free. He was already ripping the thongs from his legs when she dropped the lamp and stumbled backward with a choking gasp.

The Indian and the black-suited Harry had appeared from somewhere. In the sudden confusion they hadn't even noticed he was free. They were clustered around the doorway, where the flickering light from the fallen lamp shone in on a scene from hell.

The bearded Jason was in there, pinned to the wall like some giant butterfly with a shaft of wood and metal. His eyes were open and staring in death, and to Ben it looked as if almost in that last second of life before the shaft pierced his chest he'd seen some great unexpected truth. But the horror of Jason, awful as it was, could be only a part of it. At least a body was something solid, physical. But around the body, covering the floor in irregular puddles, was more water than Ben Snow had seen in days. It was almost as if here, in the middle of the desert, some creature of the sea had appeared to strike down this man.

"What's that thing through his chest?" Harry gasped out.

Ben took a step closer to examine it, carefully avoiding the puddles of water. "It's a harpoon," he answered at last. "Like they use on whales."

And they stood there, looking, not really understanding, because death can never really be understood by those who have yet to experience it. Ben took advantage of the moment to slip the pistol out of Jason's untouched holster. When he turned from the pinned corpse he was covering them with the gun.

"*Caah!*" the Indian shouted, his hand going for his knife. Ben fired from the hip and nicked his finger. That stopped him, and it stopped the others too.

"Now let's talk," Ben said quietly. "In the other room."

He followed them in and motioned toward chairs. The gun in his hand gave him the old feeling of power. He lit another lamp and sat down opposite them.

"Did you kill Jason?" the black-suited man asked.

"Hardly. I was still tied up at the time."

"But there's no one else in this damned town."

Ben shrugged casually. "Then it must have been one of you three." He wasn't yet ready to spring the other possibility on them.

The Indian's finger was still bleeding. "No," he said simply. "No kill!"

"See?" Harry said, as if this proved something. "The girl wouldn't have the strength, and I was outside when it happened. Besides, why would we kill him? He was a friend."

Ben scratched his bristled chin. "Maybe I'd be able to answer that one better if I knew what the four of you were doing here."

Harry and the Indian exchanged glances, but neither spoke. Finally, after the silence had become obvious, the girl said, "Well, why not tell him? We've got a murder on our hands now."

"Shut up!" Harry told her.

But she ignored him. "We robbed a train," she told Ben. "Just like that."

"Don't listen to her," Harry insisted. "She's just kidding you."

"Is this kidding?" she asked, suddenly on her feet by the bulging saddle-bags the Indian had brought in. She overturned one and emptied its contents on the dull, sandy floor.

Money, packages of new paper money, tumbled into view. Ben knelt to pick up one, keeping his gun ready. "Big bills," he said. "They'll have the serial numbers listed."

Harry shook his head. "We'll have it spent before they do anything like that. It'll take them a week to get the news across the country. How about it, Snow? We'll cut you in for Jason's share. He sure won't need it."

But Ben wasn't buying. "Sure, it'll take a week! Didn't you damn fools ever hear of the telegraph?"

The Indian said, "We get out now. Split up money."

"In the morning, Redman. That'll be soon enough."

Ben smiled a little. "We may none of us be alive by morning. Unless one of you want to confess killing him."

"Why would we kill him?" the girl asked.

"Money. More money for each of you now. Or perhaps, Miss Laura, he caught you out there and tried to attack you, and you had to kill him."

But she only shook her head, silently. The Indian spoke up again. "Evil spirit kill him. Water spirit."

Ben frowned at the thought. It had to be discussed, at least. "He may not be so wrong. Some say the town is haunted."

"Haunted! By what?" Harry was a true unbeliever. Ben imagined that he questioned anything that wasn't black or white, and that made all the stranger his dress of a Preacher. Or was he a Preacher only when he robbed trains?

Ben shrugged in answer to his question. "We're in a deep valley here. It might even have been a river at one time, emptying into the Gulf of California. Perhaps some time a hundred years ago, a whaling ship made its way this far . . ."

"Don't give me that crazy talk!"

But Ben could see that it wasn't crazy talk to the Indian. He backed away, then headed for the door, unmindful of the gun Ben still held. He didn't go far. At the doorway he uttered another gasping, *"Caah!"*

"What is it?" Ben called out.

"Evil spirit has stolen horses!"

They all went to look, but of course the Indian spoke the truth. The horses were indeed gone. "There must be someone else here," Harry insisted.

"We'll search again. Any of you might have moved the horses," Ben pointed out. "But we'll search. No funny business, though. Remember, I've got my gun back."

"I'll remember that, Snow. You remember my offer of the money. There's still enough for all of us."

"What makes you think I want your money?"

Harry smiled a little, a twisted sort of grimace. "Billy the Kid would have wanted it," he said and walked away.

They took lamps and spread out to search through the ruined buildings for the horses, and Ben found himself somehow teamed up with Laura. "Your brother's a pretty crazy guy," he said as they explored the big barn that might have been a stable once.

"He's all right."

"Sure. All train robbers are."

"He had a hard childhood."

"Didn't you have, too?"

She hesitated. "Yes. I guess girls can take it a little better than boys."

"Why's he wear the black suit?"

"He studied for the ministry once. Really. They threw him out because he drank. He was wearing the suit on the train so he could get into the money car without arousing too much suspicion."

"Did he kill anyone on the train?"

"No. The Indian stabbed a guard, but I don't think he killed him."

"How much money is there?"

"We're not sure. A lot of it. Over a hundred thousand dollars, on its way to west coast banks."

He thought about that. It was a lot. With a quarter of it he could stop running from those who would make him a gunfighter. He could move to San Francisco, or back east to St. Louis. He realized suddenly that Laura was saying something. "What?"

"You and I. We could take the whole thing."

She'd really said it—his ears weren't deceiving him. "You'd double-cross your own brother?"

She shrugged her shoulders. "I don't owe him anything."

"We wouldn't get far without horses." He paused, then added casually, "Unless you hid them somewhere."

"How could I? You're right, of course. It's crazy." She'd been standing close to him. Now, in the shadow, she leaned her body against his and kissed him. Before he could do more than respond briefly, there was the sound of voices from outside.

"They're looking for us," he said, breaking away.

They went out into the darkness, where Harry and the Indian were waiting with swinging lanterns. "The harpoon's gone," Harry told them. "Someone took it out of Jason's body." He was scared.

Ben broke into a trot as he headed back to the building, feeling the reassuring slap of holster against thigh. Whether human or ghost, the murderer had retrieved his weapon. That could only mean he intended to use it again.

The bearded corpse was on the floor now, tumbled there by someone or something. Where the harpoon had been, there was now only a ragged, running wound, and the blood that had held back so long was now covering the floor to mix with the dampness and the puddled water. "Neither of you saw anything?" Ben asked them. "Where were you—together?"

"No. I was upstairs and the Indian was across the street. He came over and found it, then called me."

Ben turned to the red man. "Well? You didn't see anything, I suppose."

The Indian shook his head. "Found water," he said, with a bit of pride. "Water?"

Ben followed him out the back door. Sure enough, a large rain barrel sat there, with an inch or two of water still in the bottom. Rain came rarely to the region, but there'd been a few heavy downpours in recent weeks, enough to explain the water. Now all he had to explain was why the ghost—or Jason—had splashed it over the floor inside. It seemed like a wasted effort if its only reason was to heighten the effect of the harpoon as a weapon. Besides, if the ghost wanted them to leave, why steal their horses and make escape impossible? No, the more he thought about it, the more certain he became that one of them was the ghostly killer, looking for a larger share of the loot.

"Is someone watching the money?" he asked.

"I hid it under the stairs," Harry said. "It's safe."

They went back outside, where the night wind was beginning to pick up. Eddying sand cast strange patterns over the almost-street, and now the stars were beginning to appear from behind the dispersing clouds. Ben thought he heard the distant whinnying of horses, but he could not be sure. It might only have been a trick of the wind.

"O.K.," he told them. "We split up again and keep searching. Laura, go in with the money and sit tight. If anything suspicious happens, start blasting away with that rifle of yours."

"I want to go with you," she said.

"No." He had a feeling he could force one of the others to show his hand if he was alone. With Laura along, the killer wouldn't be likely to appear.

He left them and went off by himself, this time along the back of the line of tottering structures. He held his lantern close to the ground, searching for hoof marks in the sandy soil. But there was nothing that could certainly be distinguished in this light.

He'd been moving along the street about five minutes when he became conscious of someone following him. Laura, perhaps. He doubted if the Indian would make that vague shuffling sound on sand. But he couldn't take the chance. He left the lantern propped on a fallen timber and moved out of its yellow circle of light.

Someone, across the circle from him. Someone, stalking him as Jason might have been stalked. He drew his gun carefully and waited, certain that he was as invisible as the other. But then, hadn't Jason been invisible too?

Suddenly, off to the right, there appeared a tiny spot of glowing fire. It might have been a star fallen to earth, or the frozen burst of a pale rocket. It might even have been the ghost of Raindeer, if Ben Snow believed in such things. He turned his gun to aim at the strangely glowing spot, but the movement now seemed to blur in the darkness to his left. There was the crunching thud of blade against flesh and bone, and the glow vanished before Ben's eyes.

He circled the lighted area, and now with it behind him the stars cast a pale glow over the scene. A thing, something bulky, curled into itself in the dust, and ahead were the running footsteps of a murderer. Ben knelt for an instant in the spreading blood, trying to pull the harpoon free, but it was too late. The man before him was the Indian, and he was dead.

Now Ben was running too, in the direction of the retreating footsteps, down between the darkly dead buildings that sometimes leaned too far out at him. Silently, without a shouted warning or a shot. But Ben kept his gun ready, running with it held high.

The other, desperately, leaped onto a creaking wooden porch, then into one of the buildings where even the stars could not reveal him. Ben followed.

And there, just inside the black door, was the glow of light—the ghost?—again. This time Ben did not hesitate. He fired twice from the hip, and the glow dissolved in a splintering crash.

A mirror! He looked down at his chest, his stomach, and realized suddenly that the glow was upon him! He was standing there in the void, a perfect target for the ghostly killer.

He threw himself to the floor as a gun blazed out, tearing through the loose cloth of his shirt. Ben answered the weapon's flash with his remaining four bullets.

For a long time silence settled like the dust about him. He waited for more shots, his glowing stomach pressed against the protecting floor. But none came. Presently there was the noise of cautious arrival in the doorway behind him. Harry and Laura were there, with lamps. "What in hell happened? You all right?"

"I think so," Ben said, getting to one knee. "Shine the light over there."

"God! You got him, whoever it was."

Ben walked over and kicked at the body with his toe. The face, in death distorted, was still familiar. It was the face of the sheepman who'd warned him about the town only a few hours earlier.

"There's your murderer," Ben said. "He killed Jason and the Indian. He's a sheepman from over the next hill."

"You're a good shot," Laura said. "Even in the dark."

"Especially in the dark. If I'd thought about it, I'd have known it was the sheepman, of course. He's the one who tried to tell me the town was haunted, to keep me away. And the water in the room where Jason was killed—there had to be a reason for it. I thought about it, but that crazy harpoon misled me. The water was simply an attempt to wash the floor, to clean up some possible clue to his identity. Jason found him there, waiting to claim his first victim, and the sheepman killed him with the harpoon, just as he killed the Indian a while ago."

Harry shrugged. "The Indian is no great loss. It's just one less cut on the money. But what clue could the sheepman have left on the floor?"

"Something he feared any of us would recognize. Probably dirt and manure, the odor, the stink of sheep. I don't say I would have recognized the smell, but he must have feared we might. Those sheepmen have queer ideas sometimes about us, like we belong to a different world."

They left the body there, and went back to the building which had once been a bar. "What about the horses?" Laura asked.

"I imagine they're over the hill, with his sheep. We'll go look."

"First we split the money," Harry said, kneeling in his black pants by the Indian's saddlebags. "This'll be easy money for you, Snow, damned easy!"

"I'm not taking any money," Ben said.

"Hell, I didn't mean you haven't earned it. You killed that sheepman if nothing else. Killed him before he killed all of us. What was he—crazy or something?"

"Crazy with an odd form of insanity, I think," Ben answered slowly. He picked up the lamp and carefully blew out its flickering blue flame, plunging them into darkness. Across the pile of stacked-up currency, another fiery spot glowed brightly. This time it was not a reflection.

"What in hell'd you do that for?" Harry gasped out.

"I had to see if you had one too," Ben sighed into the unseen.

A revolver exploded next to his ear and the burning spot went out, like a star blotted by clouds. Harry the Preacher screeched once and fell against Ben, knocking his already-drawn gun out of line.

Then Laura was lighting the lamp again, covering Ben with the steady gun of a girl who has just killed her brother. "You're smart," she said. "Too smart."

"I've got a gun too, Laura," he said, keeping it pointed at her, remembering even as he did that he hadn't reloaded it since killing the sheepman.

"How'd you know?" she said, keeping her weapon where it was as they faced each other kneeling, a few feet apart, with the lamp and the money and her brother on the floor between them.

"The sheepman had to have a motive. He wanted me away, but that was before you people arrived. If he was expecting you, someone must have told him. Someone must have told him about the money. He killed Jason in the dark with that harpoon—where'd he get that, in one of the buildings here?—and it was a good weapon for scaring people away. But he did kill him in the dark, and he killed the Indian in the dark, but not before I'd seen a glowing spot on the Indian's shirt, making the target like a light—and there was one on your brother. It's a little dab of phosphorous, a chemical that glows in the dark. If I wasn't developing a spreading stomach, I'd have noticed it at once on my belt buckle. Since the sheepman could hardly have put it on us all, he must have had an accomplice who did—the same person that told him about the planned train robbery and the money. You, Laura."

"Why me?" Her face was hard in the glow.

"None of the others had the opportunity. You tied me up—but I imagine it was when you kissed me that you dabbed my buckle."

"Put away your gun and we can talk," she said. "They're all dead now. There's just you and me."

He shook his head. "The gun stays out. Maybe you think you can shoot me before I get off a shot myself. Maybe you'd like to try."

"The money's there for both of us."

"And now that your boyfriend's dead I'll do for a companion—is that it? No thanks I'm sure you wouldn't value me any higher than your own brother, and look what happened to him."

"I never owed him anything."

"No, but you gave him something. A bullet."

She was staring into his eyes now. "Put down that gun. You wouldn't shoot a woman, would you?"

"That depends on whether or not I'm really Billy the Kid. Under the circumstances, I think Billy would shoot a woman."

She thought about this a moment longer, then said, "All right, we'll throw down our guns together. Then we can talk about the money."

"Agreed," Ben nodded. The two guns hit the floor with a clatter together. "Now what?"

"If you won't come with me, we can split the money here and go our own ways."

But now Ben shook his head. "I'm taking the money into town, to turn it over to the sheriff. I think you'd better come too."

She cursed softly and made a dive for the gun, but Ben had it first. She grabbed up his, squeezed the trigger twice, then hurled it at his head when nothing happened. "Damn you, cowboy! Shoot me if you want!" Then her hand clutched the lamp, and she hurled this too. It shattered against the far wall, and in a moment the bone-dry timbers were ablaze.

"You little fool!" Ben holstered her gun and tried to catch her, but she was too quick, rolling away from him, jumping lightly to her feet and running toward the stairs. The entire wall was now ablaze, lighting the place with a sort of dangerous, flickering daylight. Hot, like the desert sun.

She must have been trying to reach an upstairs window, where she might have dropped to the ground and escaped in the night. But she couldn't know that the fast-rushing flames had already weakened the ancient timbers. The whole stairway started to go at once, and the flames received it like wood on a campfire. She screamed, and then vanished into the spreading inferno . . .

Ben just had time to pull the saddlebags full of money into the street. Then, by the light of the leaping flames, he made his way back over the hill to the place where he found the missing horses, tied among the restless sheep. He took his and turned the others free, and rode back for a time the way he had come, until the first rays of morning could guide him on a route around the ghost town.

Somewhere, far ahead, he'd find a town and a sheriff, and leave the money without explanation. And keep riding. Let others find the burnt-out ruins of the town, and the five bodies scattered there.

It was really a ghost town now.

He wondered where it had ever gotten the name of Raindeer . . .

THE FLYING MAN

The summer of '96 had not been good to the people of Twisted River. Too hot, too dry, too lonely, surrounded by nothing but a desert which no one ever crossed and a line of high hills which few wanted to cross. It was a perfect place for a man like Ben Snow, who wanted to be forgotten, but the motives which kept the other three hundred-odd citizens in a dried-up hole like Twisted River were more difficult to pin down. Perhaps, in one way or another, it was the mine up in the hills that held them, with its promise of gold and enough occasional fulfillment to keep them content.

But outsiders, especially in that September of '96, tended to avoid the town. It was a place where time was standing still, where a few hundred people were rotting in the sun. Not a place to visit, or make a living, unless you enjoyed working down in the mine where the temperatures were sometimes thought to reach a hundred and twenty degrees.

One day was much like another in Twisted River, though, and that was something Ben Snow liked. He could stroll the dusty streets, earn money at occasional odd jobs, even fish in the narrow stream that gave the place its name. There was even a girl named Sue, who worked at the small hotel where Ben had a room. Ben liked her. He liked the town in a crazy sort of way. And only the sheriff wore a gun.

This day—it was a Tuesday—there was an undercurrent of expectation in the streets when he came down from his room. "What's up, Sue?" he asked her, taking in the bright dotted shirt and tight pants that were her working clothes.

"Stranger headin' this way across the desert," she told him, as excited as the rest seemed to be. "He's got a wagon and everythin'!"

Strangers didn't come to Twisted River very often. In fact, this was the first one Ben could remember in the six months since he himself had ridden into town. He went out to the street in time to see a big wagon drawn by two horses just turning into town. The people had already surrounded it on all sides, crowding quietly close, and even from where he stood Ben could read the large garish sign which must have been the focus of interest at that moment: *Doc Robin, The Flying Man!*

Ben had seen quacks and medicine men all over the West, but at first sight this seemed something quite different. The man himself was tall and white-haired, though with a youngish face that made one suspect the hair. He spoke in a booming voice that carried from one end of the street to the other. "Gather round, gather round! Doc Robin, the Flying Man, has come to town to thrill and amaze you." And they gathered.

Ben stayed on the porch of the hotel, where he had a perfect view of the white-haired man as he went into his well-rehearsed speech. "Folks, I come to your fair town bearing the greatest invention the world has ever seen, an invention that at this moment is sweeping the East and Midwest. No longer need man be grounded to the earth like the snakes and lizards—now he can *fly*, like the eagles and the hawks, *fly* like he was meant to! Here," and he tugged at a cord that released a whole side of the wagon's canvas covering, "here you can feast your eyes upon *it!*"

Ben feasted, and the thing he saw was a contraption like a giant set of wings, or rather a double set—one above the other. They had a span of perhaps fifteen feet, with a metal bar in the center of the lower pair, where a man apparently could hang on. "You mean those things fly?" someone shouted from the crowd. Ben recognized Frank McCoen from the livery stable. "Maybe you can put some on my horses!"

But Doc Robin was apparently used to the heckling. Already he was passing out handbills among the crowd. Ben took one and saw at once that it was indeed an impressive thing. There were pictures—actual photographs—of a man flying through the air supported only by the double pair of wings. And there were articles from a number of big Eastern papers, including the *New York Times*. The man in the pictures was a German named Otto Lilienthal, who'd made more than a thousand successful glides with a series of "hanging gliders" which he'd built.

"Yes, my friends," Doc Robin was saying again. "You see it, but you still doubt. I recognize the doubt in your faces. Well, tomorrow morning on that hill yonder I'm going to show it to you in the flesh. I'm going to fly off the hill with this set of wings! And when I land, when you're all convinced that man at last can fly with the birds, I'm going to give each and every one of you an opportunity to place your orders for these wings. Laugh, laugh now if you want—you won't be laughing tomorrow. Why, right now these things are so popular back in New York that the police are considering special traffic regulations. The people are gliding right off the *buildings*—I've seen it myself!"

He went on like that for the better part of an hour, and Ben could see he was beginning to convince even the more doubting members of the crowd. If nothing else, he would have a big turnout in the morning. Through it all, Ben noticed Sheriff Hanson leaning against the bank building across the street, taking it all in, the badge and the gun at his side occasionally catching the sunlight's glint when he moved. Apparently he was as interested as anyone else, and not at all about to run Doc Robin and his wagon out of town.

After a time Ben grew bored and drifted away, down toward the stream now almost dried to death at the end of the scorching summer. There'd be no fish to catch for quite some time . . .

H e ate supper at the hotel with Sue, as he'd been doing most every night for weeks. Some nights they'd saddle up their horses and ride out across the desert for a few miles, where there was nothing but the stars. Tonight, though, he felt unaccountably restless, as if somehow the coming of Doc Robin had disturbed the peaceful equilibrium he'd been so long building.

"No ride tonight, Ben?" she asked.

"No. Little sleepy. Guess I'm getting old."

"At thirty-seven? I never heard you say that before."

"Sometimes I think I should go East, Sue. Maybe to New York."

"Where the men fly off the buildings?"

He laughed and started to roll a cigarette. "I doubt that, somehow. But . . ."

"There he is!" she whispered suddenly. "He's coming toward our table!"

And indeed it was Doc Robin, tall and snow-haired, moving between the tables toward them. "Ah," he said when he'd reached their side, "do I have the honor of addressing Mr. Ben Snow?"

"Don't know as it's much honor, but I'm Ben Snow all right. What can I do for you, Doc?"

"A slight business matter. Could the charming young lady excuse us?"

"Sure," Sue said, slipping out of her chair. "I'll be over at Frank's stable with the horses, Ben, if you change your mind about that ride." She smiled a bit uncertainly at Doc Robin and was gone.

"What's this all about?" Ben asked.

"Could we talk somewheres private—maybe up in your room?"

"I guess so." Ben led the way upstairs, wondering what had prompted Robin to find out his name and where he was staying. "Here we are."

His room was hardly a place for entertaining, with a brass bed, wash bowl, lamp, chair, and a dull gray wallpaper broken only by a faded portrait of General Custer. But Doc Robin seemed not to mind. He motioned Ben to the only chair and sat down on the edge of the bed himself. "Ah! Fine. Now to business."

"What kind of business?" Ben asked suspiciously.

"Let me start by saying I know who you really are."

Ben felt the old terror rising inside him. Not again, God. Not again. "I'm Ben Snow. Nobody else."

Doc Robin smiled. "Don't try to fool me. I was an old friend of General Lew Wallace. Used to have dinner with him. Fought with him in the Civil War. Don't look fifty, do I? Except for the hair, but that's good for business."

Ben cut in on the rambling with, "Only Lew Wallace I know of is the man who wrote that book, *Ben Hur*. And I never met him."

"Maybe you didn't meet him in person, but that's the man I'm talking about just the same. Governor of the New Mexico territory he was, back in '79 and '80 when Billy the Kid was shootin' up the place. He was working on his book then, I guess. I was out there to visit him, and I heard all about Billy the Kid."

"Then you heard he was killed by a sheriff in '81."

"Maybe Lew Wallace and the rest of the lawmen thought he was killed, but there's those of us who know better," Robin said slyly. "There's those of us who know he's been alive all these years, traveling around the west—using the name of Ben Snow."

"Get out, Robin. I don't like your sort of business."

"But it *is* business, Billy—Ben—and there's money in it for you. I want to hire your gun for tomorrow, for a hundred dollars."

"Oh?" Ben settled back in his chair. This was beginning to sound interesting. "Who do I have to kill?"

"Probably no one. That's why it's so damned easy. After I make my flight in the morning I take orders for these things. A hundred dollars apiece—ten bucks now and the rest when I deliver 'em. In a town this size, full of gold-mine money and all, I'll probably sell close to a hundred sets of wings. That's a thousand dollars all told cash in the hand. You get a hundred of it for makin' sure nothing happens to me."

"Like what? Like Sheriff Hanson arresting you?"

Doc Robin smiled. "We understand each other. That, among other things. Someone might try to take the money away from me, in one way or another."

Ben sighed, feeling tired. "You're nothing but a confidence man. You have no intention of delivering wings to these people. You'll take their ten dollars each, all right, but they'll never see you again. You want me to cover you while you slip out of town tomorrow night."

"And you'll do it, Billy."

"Like hell I will! And the name is still Ben. Do your own shooting!"

"I'm too old to gunplay. Bad eyes. Flying that thing is dangerous enough."

"If you can really fly with it, why not really sell them? Some people are crazy enough to buy them. Why turn it into a confidence game?"

Doc Robin looked a bit sad at this. "There are complications. For one thing, the German Lilienthal was killed last month, flying one of the things. But I didn't bring those clippings along."

"He was killed and you're still going out there and glide off a cliff in the morning!" The man amazed Ben more with every statement.

"A thousand dollars is mighty good pay for two days' work. It's well worth the risk. I've hit three towns in the last two weeks, and I got the next one all picked out. Going to work my way to California and retire on a fortune. Beautiful country out there."

"Why did you pick this place?"

"Because of the gold mine. The folks must have money. I cleaned up in Texas, in the cattle country. Hundred twenty-two orders in one place."

"There's not much money here. Take my word for it and clear out tonight. I'm not handling a gun for you. I don't even have a gun anymore."

Doc Robin shrugged. "Guess I'll have to get someone else then. The peace of mind's worth the hundred it costs me. Never did like gunplay."

"What if I tell the folks you're a swindler?"

The white-haired man smiled. "Then I tell 'em you're Billy the Kid. Wouldn't like that, would you?" He slid off the bed and picked up his hat. "See you in the morning?"

"If I don't sleep late."

Doc Robin smiled and went out. After a moment Ben latched the door and unhitched one of his saddlebags. He came up with a dull bronzed Derringer he hadn't loaded in months. It only took two .45 slugs, but that would be enough. He wasn't about to start guarding swindlers from the law, but he might need the weapon for other purposes now . . .

The morning was sunny, with a bit of a breeze from the direction of the western hills. By the time Ben reached the street he could see that most of the town was already up there, waiting to see the Flying Man. Sue had waited for him and they walked up together, along with Jethro Aarons from the bank. Sheriff Hanson was already on the scene, standing with his foot on a convenient rock, seeing everything and everybody. And Frank McCoen, come perhaps to see the twilight of his beloved horses in the glory of this new flying device. And Sue's brother Tommy, an unfriendly youth no doubt hoping to see some sort of tragedy. They all came, and gathered close around Doc Robin and his remarkable wings.

"I want to go closer, Ben," Sue said.

Jethro Aarons was resting on a rock. "You two go ahead. This climbing's bad for my leg."

But in a moment Ben had lost Sue in the push of the people. There was only the crowd, the mob, wanting to see a man perform a miracle. And Doc Robin was not about to disappoint them. He was poised on his toes, with the great double wings above him as he gripped the bar and tensed his tall body for the run. Ahead of him, the hill fell suddenly away to the desert floor below, and a few of the townspeople had gathered there, to see his landing. Then, with the breeze at his back, he started to run.

It was a moment Ben Snow would never forget. His feet left the earth as if plucked by a giant invisible hand, and Doc Robin was airborne. Outlined against the morning sky like some giant bird from prehistory, swooping down over the desert floor, carried by the same wind that caressed the tumbleweed and shifted the rippled sands. Doc Robin, the Flying Man.

And then, when the sudden roar of the delighted crowd had reached its peak, something happened. The white-haired man seemed abruptly to loosen his grip on the wings. He hung there another moment, held by the system of bars and struts, then detached from the life-giving wings like an eagle's victim being dropped in flight. With no controlling weight the wings themselves began an eccentric final glide to earth, but Doc Robin's body hit first, bouncing a bit as it collided with the sandy desert floor. Behind Ben someone screamed, and then everyone was running at once.

Sheriff Hanson reached the body a moment before Ben and several others. He turned him over, feeling for his heart, but the hand came away sticky with blood. "Dead," he said simply.

"From the fall?" someone asked.

Sheriff Hanson shook his head without looking up. "Appears to me he's been shot. Murdered . . ."

"Who killed Doc Robin?" Jethro Aarons was asking, his leg resting stiffly out in front of him as he recovered from the exertion of the climb. "I guess that's the question, all right." They were gathered in the main lobby of the little bank, for no good reason except that Twisted River's leading citizens had taken to gathering there of late, perhaps in unspoken recognition of the fact that it was difficult for Aarons to walk very far elsewhere.

Sheriff Hanson was there, of course, and Frank McCoen from the stables, and a number of others Ben knew by sight. No one had excluded him, so he'd remained, on the fringes of the crowd while the town fathers talked. The body had been removed to the local undertaker's dwelling, and Robin's wagon sat lonely and abandoned before the hotel. "Well, I think McCoen shot him to keep the horses in business," Coxen the mine owner said, but no one laughed.

"You just shut up," McCoen answered. "How in hell could I hit a man with a pistol at that range?"

Sheriff Hanson cleared his throat. "I don't think anyone could hit him with a pistol from the ground."

"You think maybe the killer was up there with him—invisible?"

"No—I think he was killed with a rifle. It looked to me like a rifle would make that sort of wound."

Jethro Aarons got carefully to his feet and hobbled across the room. "That's even more fantastic. No one had a rifle up there today."

"No one even had a pistol but the sheriff," Coxen added, pointedly.

"I've got my deputies up there now, searching the rocks for the weapon. I think the killer took it up there and hid it early this morning, so it would be all ready."

"But he didn't even know where Robin was goin' to take off from, did he? How could he know where to hide it? And what motive could he have for killing Robin?"

It became a general exchange of opinions then, and Ben decided there was no more to be learned here. He slipped out the door into the noonday sun, looking casually up and down the street for Sue. She was nowhere in sight, but her brother Tommy slouched against the unused hitching post in front of the tavern.

"Where's Sue, Tommy?"

"How should I know? I don't keep a chain on her. Maybe I should, though, huh?"

Ben started to ignore him, but the temptation of his foot blocking a portion of the wooden sidewalk was too much to resist. He swung his boot and caught Tommy just behind the knee, collapsing him in a heap. "Damn you, Snow! I'll get you for that!"

"Sure," Ben said, walking on. "You do that."

Sue was at the stables again, which didn't really surprise him. With McCoen more interested in the murder, someone had to take care of the horses. She looked up as he entered, smiling. "Where were you, Ben?"

"Around. Want to go for that ride now?"

"It's hot out there in the afternoon sun."

"I was thinking we might ride up into the mountains. I want to ask you a few things."

Her expression was curious but unquestioning. "Sure." She started to saddle up her horse, a great powerful bay who could have been a racer back

East. He'd told her once they should go to Kentucky for the Derby, but of course they hadn't, and he'd heard a horse named Ben Brush had won the race that year. Since then, when Sue was being funny, she called her bay *Ben*— whether for Brush or Snow he'd never asked.

They rode out of town the back way, avoiding the tensions of Main Street and the scattered groups of gossips and speculators. The sun was as hot as she'd said, but up among the foothills there were shady stretches where the horses could graze while Ben and Sue talked.

"You and your brother have been here all your lives. Tell me a little about some of these other people."

"About them? What about them, Ben?"

"The sheriff, for instance. Has he just always been here?"

She laughed a little, sadly. "Tommy and I are about the only ones in town who've *always* been here. Sheriff Hanson came when I was fifteen—six or seven years ago. He's a good man for the job, I suppose, though until now we never had any crime to speak of. A drunk or two, that was about all."

"What about some of the others? Aarons and Coxen? And McCoen?"

"I don't know much about Coxen. He just all of a sudden appeared and became manager of the mine. Jethro Aarons has been here a few years. He had a bank in Kansas City but decided to go further west. On the trip a band of outlaw Indians broke out of a reservation and shot up his train. His knee was shattered by a bullet and he hasn't walked right since. And Frank McCoen— well, you know him pretty well yourself."

"I know he loves horses. I don't know whether he'd kill for them or not. Doc Robin might have been an enemy to him."

"That's silly! Frank wouldn't hurt a fly."

"Maybe."

"We'd better be getting back, Ben. We didn't really tell Frank we were going, and someone should be watching the horses. Besides, Mr. Komar at the hotel will think I deserted him."

"What about him?"

"Ben, stop it! Are you trying to be a detective or something?"

"Someone has to get to the bottom of this business."

"Well, not you. That's the sheriff's job."

They rode back in silence, and found the town much as they'd left it. Someone had brought Doc Robin's wings in from the desert and put them in front of the undertaker's place, like some weird appendage to be buried with the corpse. But now things were quiet at the bank and Ben wondered where the village fathers were.

He found out quickly enough. As they rounded the corner in front of the stables, he saw Jethro Aarons towering over a little group of them. Sheriff Hanson was at their front, and his hand was resting too casually on his gun butt. "What's up, Sheriff?" Ben called, already somehow knowing.

"Going to have to ask you some questions, Ben. Get down off the horse."

He could feel the hard pressure of the tiny Derringer in his pocket and he wondered if this would be his last chance to use it. No, he couldn't risk killing innocent people. This was a time for answering questions. "Take my horse, Sue."

"What is it, Ben? What do they want? Sheriff, what's the meaning of all this?"

Hanson motioned with his hand, and Ben saw Sue's brother standing near the edge of the group. "This boy has made some grave charges against you, Ben. Says he heard Robin talking to you last night. Says Robin accused you of being . . ."

"Tommy! How could you?" She went to him, her face a fury of betrayal.

". . . of being Billy the Kid."

The words fell like a rumble of thunder, and even Sue turned ashen. "Ben . . ."

"Billy the Kid's been dead fifteen years," Ben said quietly.

"I heard him! I heard him say it to you. I was right outside the door!" Tommy was in the limelight now, and enjoying every minute of it. This was the revenge he'd so long sought against his sister's lover.

And Frank McCoen joined in. "I heard tell of a man named Snow, out Arizona way. Fast with a gun, and said to be Billy the Kid. Never connected him with you, though. You always seemed such a nice fellow, Ben."

Ben stood his ground, but his heart was beating faster. The urge to run was upon him, the old familiar urge that had followed him across the West. Why should he worry about this little town that had turned on him? Why not pull his gun and shoot his way out of Twisted River and be done with Sue and her brother and the fishing and all the rest of it . . . Why not?

But instead he asked, in a level voice, "Well, Sheriff, have your men found the rifle yet?"

"No, it's not up there anywhere. But you were just out for a ride in that direction, weren't you?"

Sue jumped back into the battle. "That's a damned lie, whatever you're thinkin'. I didn't have my eyes off him the whole ride. He never went near no rifle!" Her tiny breasts were heaving in anger.

"Calm down now, Miss."

"Well, how do you think I shot Doc Robin without a rifle, Sheriff?"

"Don't know exactly how, but you're the only one with a motive. He knew you were Billy the Kid so you killed him."

Something clicked in Ben's mind then, like the final bullet sliding into the chamber. He knew—he knew and he could tell them. But should he? Would it mean only more killing in this peaceful place? Would he be able to stay now whatever he might do? "Let me talk to you alone, Sheriff. I think I can tell you who killed Doc Robin."

"Be careful—it's a trick of some sort." This was Coxen, the man from the mine, a man no one ever noticed until he spoke.

Sheriff Hanson smiled a bit. "I think I can take care of myself. We'll go over to my office, Ben. I hope for your sake you have a good story to tell . . ."

B en sat across the desk from him, feeling already a prisoner as Hanson carefully placed his gun on the scarred wood between them. Hanson was a friendly man, an honest man, but he almost seemed to be daring Ben to try for that gun. Perhaps any small-town sheriff would like to tell his grandchildren he shot Billy the Kid, even if it wasn't true.

"Start talkin', Ben."

"All right. You start listening, because we probably haven't much time."

"What's goin' to happen?" The hint of a smile was back again.

"Just listen. What Tommy says is true—Robin did think I was Billy the Kid. He was nothing but a con man, a guy who'd latched onto this flying invention back East and hoped to make some money off it. The German who made those thousand glides wearing the wings is dead, by the way, but Robin wasn't telling that part. He planned to collect a ten-dollar deposit against the delivery of the wings, then sneak out of town tonight. I was to cover him in case there was trouble, only I refused to go along with it. Anyway, when he left my room he said he'd have to get someone else, and that was the tip-off. You had the right motive, Sheriff, but the wrong killer."

Over his head the clock was ticking loudly. The afternoon was almost gone. "What do you mean, Ben?"

"When Robin left my room he sought out someone else, some other resident of Twisted River that he'd recognized as an ex-gunman. He must have found someone, since he was willing to go through with his scheme today. Only the second person he approached was a man whose position here could not be endangered. This man would have no two-bit con man exposing his past life. Robin had to die, even while he thought the killer had agreed to work with him."

"Makes sense. If you can name names."

"I can, Sheriff. Think about it—Doc Robin spotted me because I was standing on the hotel porch while he talked, right in his line of vision. But he told me he had bad eyes. Would he be likely, after several years, to recognize or even notice a person like Coxen, for example?"

"I guess not."

"He'd notice someone like you, though. A con man would always notice the sheriff." Hanson's hand edged toward the gun as Ben spoke the words. "But then there was the problem of the rifle. Robin was killed with a rifle and your deputies found no weapon hidden up in the hills. Therefore the killer brought the rifle with him, shot Robin while the crowd's attention was focused on the flying man, and then took the weapon away with him."

"Who could have done that? All I carry is a pistol, and no one else in town carries any weapon at all."

"Exactly, Sheriff. A rifle is an obvious weapon, not the kind easily concealed."

"I read somewhere about sawed-off ones . . ."

"They wouldn't have the accuracy at the range in question. No, this had to be a full-sized rifle in the hands of an expert marksman."

"Who?"

"A rifle could perhaps be hidden under a woman's skirts with some difficulty, but Robin would hardly have approached a woman to cover his escape. And what man, of all the men who walked up there this morning, could have concealed a rifle on his person? Only one—the stiff-legged banker of Twisted River, Mr. Jethro Aarons."

"Impossible!"

"Is it, Sheriff? He fits all the facts. An important position to protect, a bad limp and tall stature that make him stand out in any crowd, and a perfect place to conceal a rifle—up his pants-leg!"

"Without anyone seeing him?"

"He hobbled up with us, but paused back among the rocks. He was behind the crowd, and no one was looking when he pulled out the rifle and shot the man who was flying above their heads. Then he simply slid the rifle back up his pants, next to his stiff leg, and walked back down with the rest of you. He's a tall man, remember, with long legs."

"Maybe," Hanson conceded. "Just maybe."

"You know that Aarons rarely walks anywhere because of his leg. You even hold your meetings in the bank for his convenience. Didn't it strike you as odd that he should hobble all the way up there over rough ground—even to see a man fly through the air?"

The sheriff got to his feet and picked up the pistol. "Let's go talk to him."

They went down the dusty wooden steps and started to slant across the street to the red brick bank building. They were perhaps in the middle of the street when the crack of a rifle split through the afternoon quiet. Hanson grabbed for his shoulder, spinning at the bullet's impact, and went down.

"That could have been through the head just as well," a voice spoke from the sheltered doorway of the bank, and Ben saw Jethro Aarons standing there, his rifle pointing like a third eye.

"You've killed one man already today," Ben said, edging nearer. The Derringer was still in his pocket, and useless at this range. "Isn't that enough?"

The sound of the shot had attracted people, and young Tommy was the first to arrive, running into the range of the banker's rifle before he realized what was happening. Aarons shifted his weapon slightly to cover the youth. "All right, boy. You're in it now. See that wagon down the street? You're going to drive me out of town in that, and if you want to live you don't try anything."

Tommy started to back away. "I . . . Mr. Aarons . . . what . . .?"

"He killed Doc Robin, Tommy. He did, not me. And I'll venture that's not the first man he's killed."

"Cut the talk," Aarons growled. "Get that wagon, boy, and drive it right up here in front of the bank. Remember, this rifle has quite a range, and I can even pick off men who are flying!"

"Who are you, Aarons?" Ben asked, edging a step nearer. "A gunman?"

"I was, years back. The fastest shot in Kansas. But Kansas got civilized too damn fast for me. I worked in a bank for a while, and then took a little of their loose money and came West to open up my own. A sheriff's shotgun did this to my knee and I decided to go straight. Twisted River was the place for it till Doc Robin happened along. He might have had bad eyes, but he had a memory for faces. I couldn't have anyone spoiling my setup. Didn't count on a smart guy like you—not till I saw you looking at me back at the stable."

"Let us help Hanson. He's bleeding to death."

"No one goes near Hanson or his gun till I'm out of here in that wagon."

"Our horses could catch you in ten minutes."

"Try it and the boy dies." Tommy had brought the wagon around, his hands trembling on the reins. He was no longer the wise-guy brother hating his sister's lover. Now he was only a frightened youth staring at the threat of death for the first time. And not liking what he saw. He was of a different generation, not the gunfighter or the pioneer, but the first of a new lot.

Ben was near enough now, and as Jethro Aarons started his awkward climb into the wagon, he could have blown his head off with two shots from the Derringer. But the rifle barrel was almost touching the back of Tommy's neck.

Ben owed the boy less than nothing, and perhaps that was the reason, oddly, that he spoke first.

"I'm drawing on you, Aarons!"

The tall man turned, swinging the rifle barrel in an arc that seemed almost slow to Ben's eye. The smile on his lips was the old gunfighter's smile, and perhaps it was because Aarons was a gunfighter that he chose to fire on Ben rather than Tommy. He didn't seem surprised to see the Derringer, or perhaps it was too fast for him ever to see. His own shot buzzed past Ben's cheek to kick up the dust ten feet beyond. Ben fired from the hip in the same instant and killed him with the single shot . . .

Later, when the cool of the night had come sweeping across the plain, Ben and Sue rode out under the stars. He knew he would be leaving soon—there was no longer a place for him in Twisted River now. But for tonight he needn't think about that.

"It was odd," he said, riding slowly beside Sue. "Doc Robin could have earned that money honestly just by charging folks to watch him fly. And Jethro Aarons needn't have feared him at all. And chances are the townspeople wouldn't have done too much if they had known about Aarons."

"They would have drawn their money out of his bank."

"Probably," he sighed. "Money, it's always money. Doc Robin wanted to make it crooked when he could have made it honest, and Jethro Aarons wanted to make it honest when he could have made it crooked. People are pretty strange."

"Were you scared out there, Ben?"

"Scared? No, I knew I could outshoot him."

"Knew it? But how could you?"

He smiled a strange sort of smile, the smile of a wanderer, of a gunfighter. "Doc Robin knew about both of us," he said simply. "And he tried to hire me first . . ."

THE MAN IN THE ALLEY

Ben Snow looked up from the fresh deck of cards at the tall man across the table. The other players had drifted away, cursing the luck of the cards and the skill of the dealer, and this was the only customer now. Ben waited until he'd dealt two hands of blackjack, winning on both, then said quietly, "Find anything?"

The tall man nodded slightly. He was handsome, well dressed, and half French. His name was Claude Musset and he worked out of the New Orleans office of Pinkerton's National Detective Agency. "I think we have him located for you, Mr. Snow."

"Where?"

"St. Louis."

"What name is he using?"

Claude Musset frowned a bit in uncertainty. "I'd rather tell you that in St. Louis. Can you be there by Friday?"

Ben gave only a passing consideration to the job and the girl who'd held him in Kansas City this long. If the man he wanted was in St. Louis, that was where he would be on Friday. "I'll get a train out of here tomorrow night," he told Musset.

"Fine. Meet me at the new Art Building in Forest Park on Friday morning at nine. He's living near there."

"All right," Ben said. "Another hand?"

The Pinkerton man shook his head. "A couple more and you'll have won enough for our fee. Goodbye, Mr. Snow."

Ben waited until the other dealer relieved him on the hour. Then he strolled slowly through the gilt-edged palace of splendor, searching for the head man. The bar was filling slowly with the weeknight's usual crowd, mingling East and West, city and frontier, with a scattering of war veterans. "I was right behind Teddy going up San Juan Hill, and now he's the Vice President!" Ben smiled a little and kept on going. For as small a war as it had been, there sure were a lot of veterans around these days. And they all knew Teddy Roosevelt personally.

Back in his room, a little place that never pretended to be home, he started packing a suitcase. He'd told the boss he was leaving, and now Jane was the only one left to tell. There was no one else in Kansas City who would care.

She came in while he was packing. "Going somewhere?"

"Away for a few days. To St. Louis. I'll be back."

"What's in St. Louis?"

"Business."

"The Frenchman?" He'd told her about it one night, told her more than he should have.

"Yes, if you must know. He's found my man."

"Does it mean so much to you, Ben? Does it mean more than your job . . . and me?"

He sat down on the bed and pulled her to him, feeling the smoothness of her familiar flesh beneath the dress. "Jane, Jane—look at me. I'm forty-one years old, and what have I done with my life? Cowboy, army scout, bartender, dealer in a gambling house—a different job, a different town, every year. I settle down and lead a normal life until someone happens through who knows the name, or the face, or the story. Ben Snow, sure! The fastest shot in the West, the man who's really Billy the Kid because everyone knows Billy isn't dead"

"Ben . . ."

"In every town it was the same. Either I ran or I stayed. And when I stayed I ended up killing someone. They all wanted a shot at Billy the Kid. Or they wanted to hire my gun for their own purposes."

"But that's gone now, Ben! This is 1901—the twentieth century! The West is tamed. No one wears a gun anymore, at least not in Kansas City."

"This was about as far east as I could go, but even here it wasn't far enough to outrun the stories. I tried changing my name, but it didn't help. Nothing helped, until I hired the Pinkerton man. You see, I got to thinking that all these stories couldn't just be rumors. Maybe Billy the Kid didn't die in 1881 in New Mexico. Maybe he was still alive, and if I found him it would end my troubles."

"And now the Frenchman has found him?"

Ben shrugged. "He's been looking for six months. He found something —someone—in St. Louis, but I don't know just what. Don't you see that I have to go there?"

"I see. I suppose I see what it means to you, Ben."

He kissed her gently. "I'll be back."

"Unless you find him. Unless you find him, Ben, and he kills you."

"Don't worry your head about that. I'm too young to die."

"If Billy's alive, he's the same age, Ben. Maybe he thinks he's too young, too."

"Maybe . . ."

S t. Louis sprawled in the August heat. And at the western edge of the sprawl was Forest Park, a rambling wild place which now hummed with the toil of man. The Louisiana Purchase Exposition was still nearly three years off, but already the place was beginning to take shape. Over 1200 acres of ground were being cleared, with scores of holes marking the early stages of temporary and permanent construction. The Art Building was little more than another hole in the earth when Ben finally located it, and he sat down under a nearby tree to wait for Musset.

He didn't like the heat, and never had. Here, along the great Mississippi, there was not the dryness of the desert trail but rather a sort of humid mist that clammed his skin. He felt in one pocket for the little Derringer he always carried, and then took a copy of *Plenty's Weekly* out of the other pocket. From Kansas City eastward, everyone read Arthur S. Plenty's sharp-tongued views on politics and world affairs, and it hadn't taken Ben long to acquire the habit. *President Vacations in Ohio While Supreme Court Denies Citizenship to Puerto Ricans,* one subhead read, and though it wasn't strictly accurate, it made good reading for Plenty's people.

Ben was plowing through an editorial about the year-old assassination of Italy's King Humbert when the tall Pinkerton man came into view through the trees. "You're late," Ben greeted him. "I was beginning to think I had the wrong place."

Musset smiled. "A lovely park, isn't it? Your first trip to St. Louis?"

"My first. Where's our man?"

"Well, I fear I have some bad news for you, my friend. He's gone."

"Gone! After I came all the way here?"

"Listen, please. Just listen. Our man, using the name of William Kidd—"

"That's him! William Kidd—Billy the Kid!" Ben could feel his heart beating faster.

Musset smiled his slow smile. "Don't jump to conclusions. That is what people have been doing about you for nearly twenty years, remember. Unfortunately, the name is our strongest piece of evidence. William Kidd is the right age, and he has lived in the West, but that's all I can tell you. Here in St. Louis he's been doing odd jobs, and associating with some most interesting people."

"Who, for instance?"

"He has a wife—or mistress—named Sadie, who travels with him. They had an apartment just beyond the park until yesterday. And he frequently associates with a woman Anarchist named Emma Goldman, who has quite a reputation. She's from Rochester, in New York State, and she travels about the country making speeches for the cause."

"If she's still here can't we question her as to where Kidd might have gone?"

"Oh, I know where he's gone. He and Sadie bought train tickets for Buffalo."

"Buffalo!"

"It's near Rochester, and it might mean some sort of Anarchist meeting. On the other hand, perhaps Kidd just likes fairs. The Pan-American Exposition is on in Buffalo now and a number of St. Louis people are up there looking around, getting ideas for 1904, you know."

"Could we go there?" Ben asked. "I've come this far."

The Frenchman smiled. "I anticipated you. I have already notified my office that we'd be traveling to Buffalo."

Ben laughed and they started out of the park together. "You really think this man might be Billy, Claude?" he asked, using the detective's given name for the first time.

"Who knows, my friend? Perhaps he is only the descendant of Captain Kidd . . ."

The train to Buffalo was crowded and hot, and even a summer cloudburst on the way did little to comfort Ben. It was more than a year since he'd been on a horse—perhaps this was progress, but the new modes of transport didn't excite him. Trains seemed to Ben to be built more for travel by animals than humans, and as they journeyed northeast his dislike of the conveyance and the countryside only heightened. Chimneys and mills and streets crowded with carriages, people and more people. Kansas City and even St. Louis seemed lovely by the time they reached Pittsburgh, a hulk of a place.

Buffalo was smaller, but the crush of humanity seemed even more intense. Everywhere there was talk of the Exposition, and visitors—both American and Canadian—were pouring into the summer place. "I don't see any buffalo," Ben said, though he hadn't really expected to.

Musset shrugged. "Used to be called Buffalo Creek. Named after an Indian or something."

"How do we find Kidd and the girl in this mob?"

He gave Ben his slow smile. "That is my job. Stay near the hotel and I'll contact you in a day or so."

Ben didn't like it, but there wasn't much he could do. He spent the next day roaming the streets, where newsboys on busy corners sold day-old copies of the *New York Times*, and *Plenty's Weekly*, and the Buffalo papers. He stopped for a beer in a new bar equipped with electric lights, then wandered back to the hotel. At six o'clock, Musset joined him.

"It was less trouble than I expected," the detective told him. "Kidd's friend Emma Goldman lectured in Cleveland last May, and while she was there she met a man named Leon Czolgosz."

"What in hell kind of a name is that?"

"Polish. He's been hanging around the fringes of these Anarchist groups for some time. But the point is that he's living now in West Seneca, just outside Buffalo. He has a room in a boarding house there, and Kidd visited him this afternoon."

"Where's Kidd staying?"

"Here in town, with Sadie. They have a room over John Nowak's saloon on Broadway. 1078 Broadway. He may be the man you're looking for, but he's certainly not suspicious at this point. I followed him all the way back from West Seneca without attracting attention."

"Thanks, Claude. That's all the information I need." The Derringer in Ben's pocket felt suddenly heavy. After all these years he was about to meet this man—William Kidd, William Bonney, Billy the Kid—who'd been only a name till now.

"Don't get your hopes up, my friend," Musset cautioned. "For all we know the real Billy might be in that New Mexico grave."

"I just want to talk with him. I'll be careful."

"He has friends. But I can tell you this Czolgosz will be out of town. He received a telegram while I was watching the place, and with a bit of a bribe at the Western Union office I managed to get a glimpse of a copy. It was from New York, from someone calling himself *The Asp*. He instructed Czolgosz to take a boat to Cleveland tonight, and return here Saturday."

"The Asp? You're sure you haven't been reading those Nick Carter books, Claude?"

The detective smiled. "Anarchists are an odd lot. They like all this intrigue and chasing about. But there seems to be something big in the wind."

"Well," Ben said, thinking out loud, "this is Thursday. If Kidd's friend is away till Saturday that should give me time to see him. Maybe I could be heading west again by the first of the week."

"Monday's a sort of holiday—Labor Day. We could stay over and take in the fair."

"Even holidays I never heard of! These eastern cities have everything."

"They even have laws against killing people, my friend. Different laws from the West."

Ben chuckled easily, but his hand went again to the pistol in his pocket. "Don't worry, I can't use him dead. If he's Billy I want him alive and kicking."

He left Musset in the lobby of their hotel about eight o'clock and went to the little Broadway hotel where Kidd was staying. But neither he nor the girl was in their room, and after a three-hour wait Ben gave it up for the night. He went back to his room, a bit discouraged, wondering what Claude Musset had found to do in this strange city so far from home.

Friday was warm, with scattered white clouds that seemed about to converge into a solid cover. Musset was still off on some mysterious mission, so Ben went again to the hotel over Nowak's saloon. This time he was in luck. The room clerk cast a tired eye around the little room that passed for the lobby and pointed. "Sure. That's Mr. Kidd and his wife just going into the bar." Ben thanked him and followed.

William Kidd was a little man who looked younger than the forty-one years he should have been. But then Billy had always looked like a boy, which explained the nickname that had followed him for so many years. The more Ben watched him from his vantage point at the bar, the more convinced he became that here surely was the man he sought, the man who could give him a life of peace after all these years of flight and violence. He'd been so interested in Kidd that he'd hardly noticed the girl Sadie. She must have been ten years younger, with a face at once pretty and hardened. She was a Western girl, from farther west than St. Louis. Ben had seen her type before, in the bars and even on the trails. A mining camp girl, an army post girl—wherever there were men with money to spend.

He was about to join them on some pretext when he noticed Claude Musset at the door, scanning the faces along the bar. Ben downed his beer and strolled slowly over to join him. "Looking for me?"

Musset gave a brief nod. "I thought you'd be here. Talked to Kidd yet?"

"No. I was just about to."

"Be careful. We're getting into something big. Too big. They're dangerous men."

"How dangerous?"

Musset wasn't smiling today. "I went back to Czolgosz's boarding house. He paid for his room with a defective revolver he no longer needed. I assume he has another weapon.

"You worry about Czolgosz. This Kidd's my man."

Musset nodded. "I'll see you back at the hotel."

Ben went back to his place at the bar and ordered another beer. When he turned toward the table again he was startled to see that Kidd was gone. Sadie sat alone, fingering her empty glass. Well, maybe he'd just stepped into the men's room. Ben decided it was the perfect opportunity to move in. He picked up his glass and walked over to the table.

"Lonesome?" He knew the approach would neither surprise nor anger a girl of her type.

"Beat it, mister."

"Just thought you might like a drink."

"Blow!"

"That man you were sitting with looked familiar."

"He's my husband, and he'd like to rattle your skull if he caught you talking with me."

"I'll take that chance." He pulled over an empty chair and sat down. "The man I know is named William Kidd. That your husband?"

Her eyes narrowed with suspicion. "How do you know him?"

"Back in New Mexico, long time ago."

"I never knew he came from New Mexico. You sure?"

Ben retreated a bit. "Well, we can ask him when he comes back. Where'd he go?"

"You got me," she said with a shrug. "But he probably won't be back for a while."

Ben finally talked her into having another drink, and they sat for a time in uneasy conversation. Sadie apparently had met Kidd some two years earlier in Texas. They'd traveled to St. Louis, been married there, and settled down to —what? Ben didn't miss the fact that Sadie carefully avoided mentioning her husband's occupation. Toward midnight it became obvious that Kidd would not return, and she excused herself to return to the room. Ben had one more beer, then headed home himself.

There was some sort of commotion in the street before the hotel—a growing crowd of nighttime people milling in a widening circle. As Ben started to press his way through, a woman toward the center of the crowd screamed. "He's dead!" someone else shouted. Ben's heart beat a little faster, as if he knew what he would find even before he saw it. Stretched in the gaslight's glow, his face not twisted nor even pained—more surprised, if anything.

Claude Musset, a detective and almost a friend, a man who shouldn't be dead. But was. With the knife still deep in his chest. "I saw him staggering. I thought he was drunk." Just a few minutes sooner, five minutes, ten minutes, and Claude might have been alive. "Has someone called the police?" Ben turned away, feeling sick, feeling useless, as if all this searching, this trip halfway across the country, had been all for such an ending.

The violence was still pursuing him. Even here among the Easterners there was only death. And death was the same anywhere.

Ben didn't sleep that night. He sat up instead at the hotel room window, watching the comings and goings in the dim street below, occasionally rolling a cigarette and smoking it to a half-inch butt. With luck the hotel staff wouldn't link him to Musset, and he wasn't about to volunteer anything to the police. He was a stranger in a far country, and all he knew of Eastern police were the universal stories of the "Third Degree," the "Sweat Box," and the rubber hoses, used indiscriminately on men and women alike. He had no hankering for that sort of thing, and if anyone was to avenge Musset's murder it was certainly up to him. He'd hired the Frenchman, brought him to Buffalo on the trail of a man perhaps twenty years dead.

But Musset then had mentioned something "big," something apparently even bigger than the discovery of a living Billy the Kid. Ben puzzled over that for some time, trying to fit together the pieces of what he'd seen and heard. The detective's killer, it seemed, must be one of three persons—Kidd, Sadie, or Czolgosz—since these were the only ones he'd had any contact with in Buffalo. Those three—and the mysterious name in the telegram, *The Asp*. But Ben himself had spent the evening talking with Sadie in a bar, and Czolgosz was supposedly in Cleveland for the day. That left Kidd as the best bet for the killing, and now Ben remembered all too well how he'd left the bar right after Musset. Had he noticed the detective lurking around earlier in the week, and followed him from the bar to knife him in some shadowed place within sight of the hotel? And what had Musset discovered that made his death necessary?

It was dawn when Ben finally settled down on the bed, with the breeze from Lake Erie cooling the room so that he needed a blanket. He slept . . .

The Saturday papers were full of the murder, though Musset had not yet been identified as a Pinkerton detective. Ben anticipated another rash of headlines when that fact reached the newsmen. It was early evening when he made his way back to the Broadway hotel, half expecting that Kidd and Sadie would already be gone, in flight like the autumn birds to some distant, uncertain location. But they were still registered, though not present at the moment. Ben waited around a while and then went back to his hotel. If they were still in town they apparently were going to ride out the storm of the murder. Perhaps, if he was lucky, they hadn't even noticed him speaking with Musset at the bar.

On Sunday his luck was better. It was the first of September, and the following day was the semi-holiday, Labor Day, which Musset had mentioned. It was hot in the city that afternoon, with shirt-sleeved men watching longingly as bartenders rolled barrels of beer into dim caves of coolness. Ben was having a beer at the bar beneath the hotel when he saw Kidd in the little lobby, greeting a slender man with slightly stooped shoulders and a smooth, round face. He strolled casually over to the door until he was within earshot.

"You get in last night, Leon?" Kidd asked.

"Yeah. Took the boat back," said the dull-eyed man, who must have been Czolgosz. "How are things?"

"Good. We're meeting him at ten tonight."

Czolgosz nodded and they went past Ben into the bar. If Kidd recognized him as Musset's companion, he gave no sign. Ben waited until they were seated over their beers, then went out to the sweaty room clerk. "See that little brown-haired guy in there?"

"Yeah."

"He staying here?"

"Yeah."

"What's his name?"

"John Doe."

"You kidding?"

"Look, mister, you asked me his name. He's registered as John Doe and that's all I can tell you. We don't ask questions."

"Thanks," Ben said with a sigh, turning away. And what did it all mean? Czolgosz had used his real name just a few days earlier without apparent worry. Was this new secrecy connected somehow with Musset's killing?

He thought about it most of the evening, and that night at ten he was standing in the shadows across Broadway from the hotel. They came out together, Kidd and Czolgosz, walking purposefully down the nearly deserted street. About a half block from the hotel they paused at the mouth of a narrow alley, looked both ways, and entered it. Ben crossed the street after them, his right hand curled lovingly about the cool metal of the Derringer in his pocket.

The gaslight was far enough down the block so he entered the alleyway in deep shadow, moving his left hand along the rough brick of the wall to guide him. The alley ran through to the next street, and there the gaslight was almost at its entrance, so that the three figures were silhouetted to his eye. Three—Kidd and Czolgosz and a third man, much bigger. Their conversation was low, but something changed hands—an envelope, perhaps, for Kidd and another for Czolgosz. Something on the big man's hand, perhaps a diamond ring, caught the light and sparkled a moment. Then it was over. The big man looked over his shoulder at a waiting carriage under the gaslight. Ben drew the little gun from his pocket, knowing he must act now or not at all.

But what could he do? Shoot them down in an alley for a crime they might know nothing about? Perhaps Musset had been the simple victim of an attempted robbery. No, for now the gun had to stay silent. Ben backed carefully out of the alley and ran silently up the block to a convenient doorway. In a moment Kidd and Czolgosz were visible, heading back in the direction of the hotel.

But now the hunt began in earnest for Ben. As he had once tracked Indians across the western plains for the Army, he now tracked these two through the streets of Buffalo. He was back at the hotel early Monday morning, ready to stay with the first one who came out. This day it was Kidd, who did nothing more than wander aimlessly about the downtown area. But he had better luck next time, when he followed Czolgosz to a Main Street shop and stood only a few feet away while the little man bought a .32 Iver Johnson revolver with an owl's head stamped on either side of its hard rubber handle. It cost four dollars and a half.

On Wednesday evening there was a stir of activity through the city with the arrival of the President to attend the Exposition the following day. His wife's illness had caused him to miss the original date back in June, but now the city was giving him a regal welcome, complete with the booming of cannon in the evening air. Kidd and Czolgosz were up in their rooms, but Ben found Sadie once more alone in the bar.

"Hello, there," he said, sitting down without an invitation.

"Oh! You again."

"Not down greeting the President at the station?"

"Not me. I leave that politics stuff to my husband."

Ben signalled the bartender for a couple of beers. "I'm still trying to see him."

"He's around all the time. Him and his friend."

"Do they have a job here?"

"Who knows? As long as there's money coming in, I don't ask questions." She lifted the beer and downed half of it without pausing for breath. "Good. I was thirsty."

"How much longer you going to be around? I'd still like to catch your husband."

"He said something about leaving the end of the week."

This time Ben didn't stay long with her. It wouldn't do for Kidd to find them together, not just then. But soon, before the end of the week, Ben was going to have to act.

On Thursday Czolgosz traveled, with fifty thousand others, to the Exposition where President McKinley delivered a surprising speech modifying his views on reciprocal trade. Ben paid little attention to the speech, but the place itself fascinated him. There were pavilions and displays everywhere— bearing such wondrous names as the Temple of Music, and the Fountain of

Abundance, and the Court of Lilies. There was, toward evening, the giant cream-colored Tower of Light, more than four hundred feet tall and lit by thirty-five thousand electric light bulbs. The buildings for the most part had the massive Spanish look of mission architecture, in keeping with the Pan-American theme. And everywhere there were these wonderful electric lights, powered (in some manner unfathomable to Ben) by the waters of Niagara Falls some fifteen miles away.

As the lights were starting to go on, Czolgosz left the Exposition and wandered back downtown, where he sat alone in the park until ten. It was a dull sort of a night, warm and dull, but to Ben—the silent watcher—it had the muggy feel of impending doom.

On Friday morning, with Kidd's hours in the city growing shorter all the time—at least according to Sadie—Ben knew he must do something. Still, perhaps this would be the day they'd reveal themselves somehow. He chuckled to himself, thinking that his indecision reminded him of a fellow named Hamlet in a play he'd seen in Kansas City.

So he followed Czolgosz again. The slender man seemed to move with purpose this morning. He bought a cigar at the bar, then strolled a few blocks till he came to an open sewer. He paused a moment, dropped a bundle of papers down it, then kept walking. In a small side-street restaurant he ate breakfast, then paused at a barber shop for a shave. He boarded a streetcar for Niagara Falls, but soon changed his mind and returned to downtown Buffalo. All the time he seemed to be preparing—for what?

In the afternoon, at a little after two, he returned once more to the sprawling grounds of the Pan-American Exposition, with Ben not far behind. Presently he joined a line waiting outside the Temple of Music, standing patiently beneath the sculptured heads of composers which looked down upon the scene. Ben stood a little apart, watching, and presently he asked a passing policeman, "What's the line for?"

"Shake hands with the President. Four o'clock. Better get your place."

"Thanks." Ben watched the line with a puzzled frown and began to roll a cigarette. Somehow Czolgosz hadn't seemed the type to stand under the hot sun waiting to shake the President's hand. Then, as his eyes scanned the crowd, he picked out Kidd, lounging casually near the cooling Fountain of Abundance. Both of them, here together!

At four o'clock the lofty doors of the Temple of Music swung open, and the Presidential reception had begun. The line of waiting public moved between a double row of police and soldiers, toward the President in his black frock coat and white vest A few men, apparently Secret Service agents, stood by him. It was hot under the hundred-and-eighty-foot dome of the place, and a number of people were wiping the sweat away with their handkerchiefs.

Ben watched it all from the doorway. He watched Kidd, casual in the heat, watched Czolgosz produce a bulky handkerchief from his pocket, watched a man with a bandaged hand now greeting the President.

And then he saw it.

Czolgosz was not using his handkerchief to wipe away the sweat—he was holding it against his body, as if his hand too were bandaged. But there was nothing wrong with Leon Czolgosz's hand!

Nothing wrong. Something wrong. Everything wrong!

Czolgosz was in front of President McKinley now, being urged along gently by one of the guards. Ben's hand dropped to the Derringer in his pocket. Only seconds. God, seconds . . .

Czolgosz fired twice through the handkerchief.

McKinley shivered, straightened in astonishment, and began to fall, falling as soldiers and guards flung themselves upon the assassin and clubbed him to the floor, his handkerchief ablaze from the powder, fists and rifles beating at him. "Be easy with him, boys!" McKinley called, bloody from the stomach but alive.

"I done my duty," Czolgosz muttered as they dragged him away still beating him, slapping him, punching him.

Ben watched it all with a sort of disbelief chilling his spine. When he looked around for Kidd he was gone, into the madness of humanity that surged and screamed and scrambled on all sides. What was there to do now? What was there to do, now that he knew the thing Claude Musset had died knowing . . . ?

A President does not die unnoticed in America, and though it took McKinley eight days to breathe his last, the shock waves had already gone out across the nation. Czolgosz admitted under the third degree that he was an Anarchist, though he constantly refused to implicate others in the plot. But the very word Anarchist was enough to inflame the countryside. Arrests were made from New York to New Mexico, and in Wyoming a Czolgosz sympathizer was tarred and feathered. In New York, *Plenty's Weekly* rushed a special edition through the presses while the police were still trying to get the facts from Czolgosz, and thundered editorially: "A two-bit Anarchist with a four-fifty pistol has plunged the nation into turmoil, and as President McKinley lies between life and death in a Buffalo home, the eyes of America are on Theodore Roosevelt, who might at any moment become the youngest man ever to serve as President of these United States."

After days of questioning, Czolgosz admitted his connections with Emma Goldman, though he denied she'd had a hand in the crime. A warrant was issued for her arrest in St. Louis, but she fled the city before it could be served, fearing harsh treatment by the police there. She finally surrendered a few days later to Chicago police, but she fared no better with them. One officer punched her in the face, and she must have learned that the third degree was much the same in every city. Back in Rochester, meanwhile, her father was being excommunicated from his synagogue.

And in Buffalo, Ben Snow read all the papers, listened to all the talk, and waited. William and Sadie Kidd hadn't quite made it out of the city in time. They'd been picked up for questioning and held by the police for several days, though it seemed certain they'd be released soon unless Czolgosz broke down and told everything. At first the police had confidently asserted that others were involved in the assassination plot, but as the September days drifted on and Czolgosz maintained his silence, it seemed more and more likely to Ben that these others would escape. He thought about the shadowy man in the alley, with his flashing diamond ring, and wondered if they would ever meet.

McKinley died on September 14th, and Theodore Roosevelt became President. Two days later, on Monday, the Buffalo police released Kidd and his wife for lack of evidence. Ben followed them to the hotel while they packed, with a sense of impending doom building up within him. They were going, the police could not hold them, he could not hold them. If he went to the police with his story, what would it prove? Could he even connect the assassination with the murder of Musset a week earlier? With every tick of the clock Kidd was walking out of the scene, out of Ben's life.

And if he was Billy the Kid?

There was one thing, one way of knowing. One thing that had haunted Ben down all these years. They'd thought he was Billy because of his fast draw. Billy had been the fastest gun in New Mexico back twenty years earlier. He'd still be fast—faster than Ben maybe—but it would be a way of knowing. If Ben could get him to draw, then nick him in the shoulder or elbow, he might have the admission he needed. And if Billy couldn't swing for McKinley's assassination, there were still those twenty-one killings waiting back in New Mexico.

Ben followed them through the dark streets at a narrowing distance, seeing only a short man with a suitcase, a woman with a hatbox. He waited until their passage to the station took them along a deserted areaway, where there was no one to disturb what would happen. The doubts were still in his mind, the uncertainties, the hesitations, but he realized it was now or never. He must act or Claude Musset would have died for nothing.

"Billy!" he shouted from fifty feet away.

They turned, startled, and in the flickering of the single gas streetlight Sadie recognized him. "That's him! That's the guy was asking me the questions!"

A little closer, so the Derringer could cover the gap. A little closer, but not too close . . . "I've followed you across the country, Billy. Draw!"

"What the hell . . . ?"

"*Draw!*"

. . . Aim for the shoulder . . . or the elbow . . . fast, as soon as his hand comes out with the gun . . . as soon as . . .

Ben saw it coming, almost faster than the eye could follow, and felt the hairline of pain as the blade sliced through his shirt. The Derringer roared in reply, true—too true—to its mark. The shock of the knife, instead of the expected pistol, had made his brain reject the carefully planned shot, and the habit of a lifetime had asserted itself. Kidd staggered once, then fell on his face, his hand already groping for a second knife.

"You've killed him!" Sadie screamed. "He's dead!"

Ben walked up slowly, wiping the blood and pain from his side. "I'm sorry. I only meant to wound him." How many times had he spoken those words before, if only in his heart? The eternal lament of the gunfighter. He reached into his pocket and pulled out a few bills. "Take this. Get out of town, Sadie . . ."

But she only kept on screaming to the lonely street, and he realized with a sort of shock that she'd really loved this man crumpled now at her feet. He turned, sadly, and walked away fast—and though he remembered now the knife in Claude Musset's chest it somehow didn't help. Kidd, whoever he was, had paid for his crimes, whatever they'd been.

Away from there, away from the screaming woman and the dead man, he paused out of breath and tried to collect his thoughts. There was still one person who could tell him what he wanted to hear, one man who might know the true identity of William Kidd. The man in the alley . . .

The offices of *Plenty's Weekly* occupied the entire ninth floor of a thin building in lower Manhattan. New York, everything about it, was unbelievable to Ben and so he simply ignored it. He had one goal in coming to the city, and when he'd risen in the ornate open grillwork elevator and waited the proper length of time he finally found himself face to face with the legend itself.

Arthur Plenty leaned back in his oversized chair and gestured toward the pitcher of beer on his desk. "Help yourself, kind sir. No one can survive New

York summers without lots of beer—*plenty* of beer, you might even say! Ha, ha, ha!"

"Thank you," Ben said quietly.

"And what was your business again? Busy, you know. Getting out a weekly is busy business. Ha!"

"I read your special edition on McKinley's assassination."

"Horrible thing, horrible! I only pray this man Roosevelt can hold the nation together." He poured himself a beer and scooped the sweat from his beefy face.

Ben Snow smiled thinly. "I was surprised at your concern, since you had criticized McKinley so often in the past. And you even ran an article on assassinations a while back . . ."

"Yes, yes, we did. Amazing coincidence."

"Amazing. You know, I was a sort of acquaintance of Czolgosz's up in Buffalo."

The big man's manner began to change, subtly. "You knew him?"

"Him and a few others. William Kidd, a girl named Sadie . . ."

"Yes. Well, Czolgosz received a fast but fair trial. It is all over now."

Ben nodded, unsmiling. He would have liked a cigarette, but he needed both hands free. "Czolgosz dies the end of October. But it's a shame he'll be dying alone. The man who hired him to assassinate McKinley is still at large."

"You must be mistaken, Mr. Snow. No one hired Czolgosz. Heaven knows the Buffalo police tried hard enough to implicate others, but they were most unsuccessful."

"They just didn't look in the right places, Mr. Plenty. They didn't look, for instance, in the alley off Broadway when Czolgosz and Kidd were being paid for the assassination. Ten o'clock, the Sunday night before the shooting."

"You should write fiction for me, Mr. Snow." Plenty's hand went to the beer pitcher, but this time it shook a little as he poured.

"Not fiction, fact. I saw it myself. I saw a big man with a ring on his finger, very much like your ring, Mr. Plenty."

"Who are you, sir? What is your business with me?" The beer was forgotten now, and behind his head a sudden afternoon breeze was disturbing the curtains.

"I already told you my name, Mr. Plenty. My occupation might be listed as a justicer. I had a bit of justice for your friend Kidd last week."

"Kidd!"

"I killed him."

"I know no Kidd."

"I think you do. I think you paid them both to assassinate the President. I think you're just about the leading Anarchist in the country, Mr. Plenty."

"I could have you arrested for making charges like that, Mr. Snow. Charges without a shred of evidence to back them up." He opened a desk drawer and started to reach inside.

"The gun that killed Kidd is aimed right at your fat middle, in case you have any ideas."

He brought out a box of cigars, and the harmless gesture seemed to renew his sagging strength. "No ideas, Mr. Snow. Only a cigar—not poisonous, not exploding. I am hardly a violent man."

"You spoke of evidence a moment ago. I think I have some, in addition to my eye-witness identification. You were so anxious to get out your special edition on the assassination that you slipped a bit in your editorial. You mentioned that Czolgosz paid four dollars and fifty cents for the gun."

"I believe other papers have mentioned the fact."

"But they hadn't then—that's just the point. When you went to press Czolgosz hadn't talked yet. I knew the price of the gun because I was standing next to him when he bought it. But how did you know it, Mr. Plenty? It proves you not only had contact with Czolgosz the night I saw you together, but that you had contact with him or Kidd later in the week—and that the subject of the gun was specifically discussed."

"My reporters bring me these things!" he screamed, pounding the desk. "Someone told me it cost four-fifty!"

"Then there's the matter of the telegram. A friend of mine, a detective, saw a telegram from someone called *The Asp*, giving instructions to Czolgosz a week before the assassination. Sadly, my friend was too much the detective. He couldn't have really seen the words *The Asp*, because *the* is rarely used in telegrams. I haven't seen many of them, but I know too that they're printed with all capital letters. So instead of *The Asp* what my friend must have seen really were simply the capital letters ASP, printed together. ASP for Arthur S. Plenty."

"You call that evidence?"

"Some of the Lincoln conspirators were hanged for far less."

It got to him then, and he stopped shouting. He just sat there, gazing across the desk at Ben. "All right. How much do you want?"

"Only justice, Mr. Plenty, that's all. It's my country, too."

"McKinley was no good. He deserved to die if anyone ever did."

"I'm no judge of that. And neither are you." He paused, then asked the big question: "But tell me one thing about it. This man Kidd—who was he, really?"

"I don't know—a drifter, someone Emma Goldman picked up in St. Louis." He dismissed it with a wave of his hand. "She found Czolgosz in Cleveland."

"Was she in on the plot?"

He shook his big head. "Not really. I sent Czolgosz to Cleveland to recruit more people, but he came back empty-handed. He and Kidd were the only ones. He had lists of other Anarchists, but I made him destroy them so the police wouldn't find them in his room."

"All right," Ben said. It was another dead end. William Kidd was a buried issue.

"Do you want money?"

"No."

"What are you going to do—tell the police?"

Ben looked at him, feeling pity and revulsion mingle in his mind. "I don't know. I don't really know. I suppose I'll have to think about it." And he got up to leave. "Goodbye, Mr. Plenty."

He walked out of there and waited for the slow elevator down, really not knowing what he would do. Perhaps an unsigned letter to the police . . .

At the entrance Ben found his passage blocked by a gathering crowd of curious, excited people. A woman was screaming and another seemed to have fainted. He fought his way through to the center of the crowd, much as he'd done that night in front of the Buffalo hotel. But this time it wasn't Claude Musset with a knife in his chest.

"He jumped! I saw him go!"

"God, what a mess. Anyone know him?"

"It's Plenty, the magazine publisher. He ate in my place every noon."

Ben walked away, feeling sick. It was a sort of justice, he supposed, but one he hadn't figured on. Still, a man who felt he could take the life of the President of the United States would probably feel no qualms about taking his own life if circumstances dictated it. There'd be no need for a letter to the police now. Czolgosz could die alone for his crime and no one would be cheated.

Except maybe the history books . . .

THE RIPPER OF STORYVILLE

Ben Snow met Archer Kinsman in a little Texas town near the Gulf Coast. It had been a year of wandering for Ben, and with the coming of winter he'd headed south ahead of the snow and cold. Here, near the Mexican border, there was still a scent of the old West in the air, still a blending of horseflesh and longhorns and gunsmoke. It was Ben's sort of town —at least till Archer Kinsman found him there.

Kinsman was old, not so much in years as in appearance. He was a man with one foot in the grave, and the fancy carriage, the pearl-handled pistols, the expensive cigars would not keep him out of it. He found Ben in the back room of the Rio Cafe, and settled down across the table from him with an air of troubled haste. "You're Ben Snow, aren't you?"

"That's right," Ben said, taking in the trappings of wealth, the ashen complexion that aged the hard lines of the face.

"I'd like to hire you for a job," he said, "I'm Archer Kinsman. You may have heard the name."

"Sorry. I'm a stranger in these parts." Whatever he wanted, it would probably be good for a free drink at the very least.

"But your fame has preceded you, Mr. Snow." And there was the knowing smile again, that look which had followed him across the West.

"You want to hire a gun?"

"I want to hire the fastest gun in New Mexico."

"Wrong state, Mr. Kinsman. This is Texas."

"But you're from New Mexico, aren't you?"

Ben sighed and drained the bottom of his beer glass. "Yes. I'm from New Mexico."

"Let me buy you a beer." He signalled to the bartender out front. "I've heard stories, you know. About your little adventure in Mexico, and the others. You're quite a man."

"Let's be frank, Mr. Kinsman. You've heard stories that I'm Billy the Kid, not dead after nearly twenty years but very much alive, wandering the West with a fast gun for hire. The stories aren't true."

Kinsman brushed it aside. "Of course not—didn't believe them for an instant! But you're still the man I want to hire. There is absolutely no killing involved. In fact quite the opposite. I want you to bring my daughter back from New Orleans."

"Then why do you need a fast gun?"

"I need a man who can protect himself against some tough customers. My daughter . . . well, perhaps I should tell you the whole story." He passed a handkerchief across his face, and his skin was as white as the cloth. "There were the three of us—my wife, my daughter Bess, and myself. We lived up north a ways. After years of nothing I'd managed to get together enough money to buy a small ranch, and things were looking pretty good. But I suppose I wasn't a very good father. I certainly wasn't a very good husband. One night I found my wife in bed with my foreman. I shot him, of course, but she jumped in front of my gun and they both died. Bess was eighteen when it happened, and I guess it was an awful shock to her. I never knew whether she blamed me or her mother more, but I suppose we were both destroyed that night in her eyes. Anyway, she left the ranch—walked out on me—and I haven't laid eyes on her in six years."

Though his eyes had blurred a bit in the telling, it was still more than obvious that Archer Kinsman was carved out of stone. His wife and daughter had gone, and for all his words the fact didn't really upset him. The only thing that interested Ben was why, after those six years, he was suddenly taking some action. "You say she's in New Orleans?"

Kinsman nodded. "At first she wrote to me occasionally. Not so much to reassure me as to add to my torment, I think. She'd drifted along the coast to New Orleans and become . . . well, a common prostitute. I think that's the worst thing a father can say about his daughter, but damn it there's no other halfway polite name for it. She wrote me that she was following in her mother's footsteps, and it was a letter near tore my heart out. I went looking for her a few years ago, got as far as that section—Storyville, they call it now— and I turned right around and came back home. I guess I was afraid of what I might find."

"And you want me to go there, to find her?"

He nodded again. "I'll pay you well to bring her back to me, Snow. I know you're a man can do it."

"Why is it so important, after six years?"

His hand shook as he reached for his drink. "Look at me, just look at me! There's death in these eyes, on this face. I've been to the best doctors in the state and they all tell me the same thing. A blood disease of some sort. No cure, no hope. I'll be a dead man in a month, two months, three months at most. It's an awful thing to know you're going to die."

"Everyone has to die, Mr. Kinsman."

"But do you really believe that? Don't you think, deep down inside, that you might be the exception?"

"I might have when I was younger," Ben admitted. "I think every youth has dreams of immortality." And then suddenly, hardly knowing he'd spoken the words, or why, he added, "I'll get your daughter for you, Mr. Kinsman. I'll bring her back."

"God, I want to see her worse than anything else in the world. To see her before I die. I've written her, sent her a hundred dollars every Christmas, and on her birthday . . . I'm a rich man now, Mr. Snow. It was almost as if complete success followed on the tragedy of my life. A year after she left me, a year after I killed my wife, oil was discovered on my land. Imagine— damned black stuff that kills off the grazing land! And yet it's made me a millionaire. I'd kept it a secret for a long time, not daring to tell Bess when I wrote her, fearing that she'd come back just for the money. But last month I told her, because with death staring me in the face that was her money, all of it."

"Did she answer your letter?"

"No. As I said, at first she wrote fairly regularly. Lately, during the past two years, I've hardly had a word from her. A simple *Thanks* scrawled on a post card in response to my Christmas gift. And a cheap greeting card for my birthday. At least she still remembers that. But nothing, not a word, when I told her she might soon have a million dollars."

"Do you have her address?"

"No. I write to General Delivery and she picks them up there. I have a picture, a photograph, taken when she was fifteen, if that's any help."

Ben studied the photograph, and saw a girl with long blonde hair. A pretty girl who might now be beautiful. In the picture she still clung to the wisp of innocence about the eyes, but that would be gone now. The face would be changed. And the body.

And the mind.

"All right," Ben sighed. "But you still haven't explained it all. Why me? Why not just a lawyer to bring her back?"

"I don't know. I suppose it's the murders that have added to my anxiety."

"Murders?" The word sent a familiar chill down Ben's spine.

"I imagined you'd read about it in the papers."

"I rarely read papers."

"Three weeks ago one of these women was killed in Storyville. Slashed to death with a knife. Last week there was another identical killing. Some of the papers have hinted there'll be more. They think it's him."

"Him? Who?"

"That English fellow. What was his name? Jack the Ripper . . ."

Storyville had come into being in the heart of New Orleans only a few years earlier, in '97, as a result of a city ordinance sponsored by Alderman Story. Although prostitution had been legal in the city since before the Civil War, this was the first attempt to limit it to a specific section of the city. It was a large hunk of the area, too—bounded by Iberville Street, St. Louis, North Basin, and North Robertson Street. In it were to be found the houses, saloons and casinos which made up the dark side of New Orleans life. Street after street, here was the Arlington Palace, the New Mahogany Hall, the Poodle Dog Cafe, Pete Lala's Cafe, and more. White and Negro, working together, playing together. The houses themselves ranged from marbled, elevator-equipped palaces like the New Mahogany to tiny one-room "cribs" just off the street. It was a city in itself, and over it all hung the muted beat of a new music, muffled only by the closed doors and shuttered windows now that winter had shuffled south.

Ben Snow heard the music on his first afternoon in Storyville, as he wandered down Basin Street on the flimsy trail of the girl named Bess Kinsman. He wore his gun under his coat—not the tiny Derringer he sometimes carried but the old .45 he hardly knew the heft of any more. New Orleans was Eastern, but it was still .45 country. At least this week. It was four days since he'd left Kinsman in Texas, long enough for another girl to have died horribly in the shady back alleys of Storyville. The morning paper had told him all there was to know: her name was "Sadie Stride, Negro," about thirty years of age. She'd been found face down in a shallow fountain in front of one of the more elaborate houses. There was no doubt that the same knifer had killed all three girls.

Ripper Prowls Storyville! one paper screamed. And maybe he was prowling. Ben didn't really care at that point, so long as he kept his knife off one girl named Bess Kinsman. But the heavy gun felt good at his side.

"Bess Kinsman."

"Bess Kinsman? Don't know her. Nearly six hundred girls in the district this winter. Look, go over to the Arlington Annex and buy a *Blue Book* for a quarter. If she's a Storyville girl she's listed in there."

"Thanks. What's that music they're playing, anyway?"

"That there's called jazz sometimes. It's real music."

At the saloon called the Arlington Annex there was a single black piano player, and he too was running through the rhythm and beat of it. The customers, a mixture of races, seemed to have caught the feeling of the music. A dark girl at the bar was moving her body a bit in time to it, and one couple was doing a fast dance in the back. Ben followed instructions and purchased a *Blue Book* for twenty-five cents, then sat down at a table to study it with growing amazement.

Here, in carefully alphabetized lists, were the women of Storyville—white, octoroon (though only a half-dozen of these), and "Negro." There were ads for the bars too, and for some of the available musicians. They were piano players for the most part, colored almost exclusively, and several prided themselves on their ability to play jazz. But just then Ben was more interested in the listing of girls. *Kinsman, Bess*—there it was, as big and bold as life. All right, Bess, we've found you.

He walked the three dusky blocks to the address that had followed her name, not really knowing whether he'd find a mansion or a crib. The place, when he reached it, was somewhat between the two extremes, a pale gray house that needed painting. It was not the typical New Orleans place, with scrolling ironwork on the second-floor balcony. No, this one looked more to Ben's inexperienced eye as if it might originally have been built by a Northerner —perhaps one of the post-war wave that swept over the disaster of the Southland.

"I'm looking for Bess Kinsman," he told the colored girl who answered the door.

"Sorry. We don't open till seven."

"I'm here on business. But not your kind, exactly. I want to talk with her."

"She ain't here. I'll call Countess Lulu for you."

Ben shrugged and stood waiting on the doorstep, trying to conjure up a mental portrait of the woman named Countess Lulu. He would have been way off—she was white, somewhere past forty, with a look of quiet dignity which must have accounted for the name. At one time she might have been heavier than she was now, for the flesh of her face seemed strangely folded in spots, aging her certainly beyond her years.

"Yes? You are looking for one of my girls?"

Ben nodded, removing his hat because it seemed the thing to do. "That's right, Bess Kinsman."

"You police? About the Ripper?"

"No, nothing like that. I just want to speak with Bess. I'll pay for her time, if that's what's bothering you."

Countess Lulu seemed uncertain. "She's out right now. But if you want to wait . . ."

"I'd like to. Thanks." He followed her into a parlor hung with drab velvet drapes that seemed designed to shut out every vestige of light or sound. There was only one person in the parlor, a huge pale-skinned man chewing on an ugly damp cigar.

"This here's Piggy, our piano player. Every house has to have jazz these days to be any good."

Piggy munched on the cigar and mumbled a half-hearted greeting. He was slumped over a battered upright piano, almost embracing it with a sleepy sort of desire. It might just then have been a woman in his arms.

Countess Lulu seated herself on a heavily pillowed sofa, letting her body sink within the folds of silken splendor as she spoke. "Come sit by me, sir. Bess will be back shortly."

"Has she been with you long?"

"Ever since I came to Storyville. Nearly two years now. Fine girl, and very popular with the customers."

"Does she ever talk about her father? About her life back in Texas?"

"Sometimes. Not often. The girls don't live much in the past."

Ben was carefully rolling a cigarette. "Are you from New Orleans?"

Countess Lulu shook her head. "Tampa, Havana, Mexico City. I move around. Right now this is the place to be."

"Is New Orleans that sinful a city?"

She gave a vague shrug. "Prostitution's been legal here for almost fifty years. And during the Civil War a Northern commander actually issued an order that any Southern lady insulting a Yankee soldier in New Orleans could be treated as a common prostitute. Things like that have done little to uplift the city's standing. Men come to New Orleans expecting a wide-open city, and we give it to them. Wait until the Mardi Gras tomorrow night and you'll really see something!"

Ben had heard about the pre-Lenten festival, when all of the city swarmed into Storyville to forget the staid life of the other fifty-one weeks. Often with masks hiding their faces, the wealthy ran wild among the poor in a near orgy of drunken revelry. He hadn't realized the time was almost upon them, but it was mid-February and Lent would begin on Wednesday.

"Perhaps I'll stay over for it," Ben told her. Behind him, Piggy gave a chuckle at the piano and started running through a tune Ben didn't know.

"We'd put you up here if we had an extra room," Lulu offered. "Sometimes between girls we're near empty. Girls move around a lot. Here today, gone tomorrow. I came to town just after one of the houses burned down, and I was lucky to latch onto some loose ones. Well . . . I think this is Bess now." She'd risen as the front door opened and closed. Two girls and a man entered, and he knew at once which of the ladies was the one he sought.

Her hair was the blonde of the photograph, and if the face was different it was only the difference that aging and hardness could bring. She would be about twenty-four now, nine years older than the picture he carried in his pocket.

"Hello, Bess."

She eyed him with a hard, suspicious look. "Do I know you?"

"I'm a friend of your father. He sent me to find you."

She glanced uncertainly at the two who had entered with her—a handsome dark-haired girl with a look of the South about her, and an alert young man with a chipped front tooth and a thin black mustache. The girl was already going on up the stairs. "I gotta change my clothes, Bess. I'll be in my room if you want me."

"O.K., Dotty. Now, mister, we can talk in here." She motioned back toward the parlor.

"I was thinking of someplace more private."

"For five silver dollars you can come up to my room. The price includes a shot of whiskey."

Ben hesitated only a moment. "Fair enough. Does your friend here come along?"

The man with the mustache grunted and Bess said, "I'll see you later, Hugo. Business before pleasure, you know."

She led the way up stairs carefully quilted with thick carpeting, down a narrow hallway lit by the uneven flickering of gas lamps. And Ben followed with a growing feeling of uncertainty. A simple job was becoming more complex all the time. As he entered the room she indicated, he knew the door across the hall had opened a bit, knew the girl named Dotty was watching through the crack.

"Nice room you have," he told her when she'd closed the door.

"It'll do. Now what do you want?"

He walked over and carefully sat down on the bed. "I thought I told you. Your father sent me."

"What does he want after all these years?"

"I think you know. He wants you home, back in Texas. He's dying."

"I got his letter," she admitted.

"Will you come back with me?"

The expression on her face was difficult to read. It might have been hesitation, it might have been fear. But she answered, "I can't. It's been too long."

"He still loves you."

"Did he tell you why I left? Did he tell you what happened?"

Ben nodded. "He told me."

"And you think I can go back? To the man who murdered my mother?"

"The man is your father. He's dying."

She lit a cigarette. It was the first time Ben had ever seen a woman smoke. "I can't go back. That's all there is to it."

"He's a wealthy man, Bess. A millionaire. And it's all going to be yours. Couldn't you even go back for a million dollars?"

"You don't understand," she said. "You don't know what I've become." He knew, but he didn't say it. Somehow the words didn't fit her face.

"These killings have your father worried. You must be able to understand that much, at least."

"I live here for six years, lead this kind of a life, and he worries now that I might get killed!"

Ben sighed and got to his feet. He could see that further conversation would be useless. "All right. Perhaps I'll see you again. I plan to be around for a few days." Then, as an afterthought, "Who were the people you came in with?"

"I don't see that it's any of your business, Mr.—?"

"Snow."

". . . Snow, but I'll tell you anyway. Dotty has the room across the hall. I've known her for five years, almost since I first came here. Hugo is a good friend. I might even marry him someday, though I'm sure my father would never approve. Satisfied?"

"Satisfied," he said with a smile. "See you around. And think about it, huh? He really cares about you."

"Goodbye, Mr. Snow."

"Aren't you forgetting the five dollars?"

"I was being nasty. Forgive me." For the first time there seemed something beneath the hard outer shell. He smiled as he went out the door.

Downstairs, Piggy was playing the piano and a couple of colored youths had drifted in off the street to listen. Countess Lulu was nowhere to be seen. Ben went outside into the twilight and started aimlessly down the avenue. Already, around him, the sounds of night were swelling up, strange sounds. Happy, vibrant sounds, but still strange.

B en saw the man before he was near enough to speak. He came out of the gaslit gloom with a steady, certain pace, and his hands were deep in the pockets of a greatcoat oddly warm for the climate, even in February. The man smiled slightly and stopped dead in Ben's path. "Don't go for that gun," he said quietly. "I mean no harm."

"Who are you?"

"Police. Detective Inspector Jonathan Withers, at your service, sir."

"Oh?"

"You're a stranger in the area. A stranger in the midst of a rash of murders needs questioning. Agreed?"

"Agreed." The man was obviously English, but with a touch of the South in his speech. He would have been there a number of years.

Inspector Withers smiled. "We're getting along fine. Now I've already had some reports on you. Name, Ben Snow. Correct?"

"Correct. I was hired by a Texas oilman to find his daughter and bring her back home, which I am attempting to do." He went on to sketch in some brief details of his visit and the day's movements around Storyville.

Withers nodded and seemed satisfied. "Come in here. I'll buy you a beer. We have more to talk about." And a few minutes later, over their drinks, he leaned forward and asked, "Have you ever heard of Jack the Ripper?"

"A little. A mass murderer over in London a few years back."

Withers nodded. "In 1888, to be exact. He killed seven women, all prostitutes, and he's never been apprehended. There was a story he'd come to the United States, killed a couple of women up in New Jersey."

"You're English," Ben said, giving words to the obvious.

Inspector Withers smiled thinly. "I was a London bobby in 1888. I suppose in one way or another I've been on the trail of the Ripper ever since."

"You think this is the same man?"

"The crimes are amazingly similar. Prostitutes, struck down in the streets and alleys of the red-light district, horribly hacked with a knife. And of course if I'm right there'll be more killings. He'll get his courage up and go inside again, as he did in London. Right into their rooms."

"Who were these three women?"

The detective counted them off on his fingers. "First, a few weeks back, was a reformed prostitute named Jane Swann. She sang at one of the bars. Killed in an alley. Then, just the other night, Sadie Stride, dead in a fountain a few blocks from here. The Ripper's fifth victim, by the way, was named Elizabeth Stride. Maybe just a coincidence, maybe not."

"Could it be something else? Could there be a racial angle?"

Inspector Withers shook his head. "The first two were white, the latest one colored. We've found no connection among them except for the fact they were all prostitutes at one time. Of course, it's difficult to go back very far—so many people coming and going all the time."

The beat of a jazz piano rose and fell at intervals, like the piquant pounding of some distant surf. "You don't really think I'm involved?" Ben asked.

"Probably not. At least I know you're not Jack the Ripper. There are some reports, though . . ."

"That I might be Billy the Kid? One's as ridiculous as the other."

"You carry a gun under your coat."

"Don't you think it's a good idea, with a mad killer at large?"

Inspector Withers shrugged. "I naturally take the attitude that the police are able to provide sufficient protection."

"Did they provide it for the Stride girl the other night?"

The detective stood up, signifying the conversation was ended without an answer to Ben's final question. "I'll be in touch with you," he said. "If you learn anything, I can always be found."

Ben watched him leave and then ordered another beer. He sat for a time listening to the piano, watching the city of night awaken, stretch, and go off to live. Finally, as he knew he would, he found himself wandering back to the house three blocks from Basin. It was alight now, with all the sad joys of darkness, loud with the music and the laughter that signalled a kind of escape to the world of Storyville. It had been escape, at least, for Bess Kinsman.

Countess Lulu was at the door. "Decided to come back as a customer?"

"Not exactly. I wanted to see Bess again."

"Cost you cash this time. To me."

He handed her the money and started upstairs. The place was quiet for the moment, then he noticed that Piggy was away from his beloved piano. A black man passed him on the stairs, looking away, hurrying to be out of the place. Ben knocked on her door and entered when she gave the word. If she was surprised to see him again she made no sign of it, but only sat waiting on the bed in an air of innocence that must have started with Eve.

"Hello again, Bess."

"You're back soon."

"I was wondering if you'd thought about it. Going back to Texas."

"I've thought about it."

The hardness was there, in her eyes, on her lips. This would not be the same girl Archer Kinsman had driven away, six years earlier. "And?"

"I told you my answer earlier. I haven't changed my mind."

Hardness, even with that innocence which still clung like a veil. She had to be an amazing actress, but which mood was the act? "I was hoping . . ."

He never finished the sentence. A scream had started, rising like the wail of the damned, to be cut off as suddenly as it began. Bess Kinsman was on her feet in an instant. "It's Dotty, across the hall!"

They were into the hall, pounding on the door, forcing the lock, because somehow the sudden silence was more terrifying than the scream. Countess Lulu had appeared from somewhere, and Piggy and the other girls, and on their faces was written the single fearful thought. And the door shivered and splintered under Ben's shoulder and they were looking in on it.

At first it didn't seem so bad. At first she looked almost alive, sitting on the floor with her back to the wall looking at the great red gash where her stomach had been. Then, as they watched, her head started to fall to one side and they saw the thin red razor line on her throat.

It was then that Bess screamed . . .

Inspector Withers was unhappy. He paced the downstairs parlor like a caged tiger, waiting while his men completed the task in the upper room. "A fourth one," he said, "and the day before Mardi Gras. Can you imagine what that madman will do tomorrow, when he's free to wander masked and unnoticed?"

Ben had settled onto Piggy's piano bench, listening, watching, his hand never far from his gun. He had met many murderers before, but this one, so near and yet so unseen, had unnerved even him. "How did he get in?"

Withers shrugged. "Through the window, across the roof. It would seem that the choice of Dotty Ringsome as the victim was dictated simply by the location of her room and the fact that she was alone at the time."

But Ben was thinking. "Her scream was cut off so quickly, though. She didn't start screaming when she saw him coming through the window. He must have actually had the knife in her stomach before she yelled. Then he silenced her with a slash at her throat. Wouldn't this indicate it was someone she knew? Someone she trusted?"

"She might have been dozing on the bed with her eyes closed."

"I suppose so," Ben conceded.

He waited for a time longer, answering questions about what little he knew, watching while everyone in the house underwent the inquisition by Withers and his men. Finally, some time after midnight, they allowed him to leave. He walked the few blocks to the Arlington Palace and found there a room for the night.

Sleep came quickly, but he kept his gun under the pillow, close at hand. His last thought was that somehow he had to get Kinsman's daughter out of that place. The evil that had struck down four girls was very close to her . . .

In the morning he found the Storyville blocks strangely transformed, wearing in the midst of their hidden terror the colorful streamers and gay trappings of carnival time. It was Mardi Gras, the day before Lent, and already there was a scattering of masked, costumed figures in the streets. Down the block a newsboy shouted the latest on the Ripper murders, but even this went unnoticed or unadmitted on a day set aside for gaiety.

The Arlington Annex adjoined the hotel lobby and in the mornings provided a reasonable place to eat breakfast. A bartender was polishing glasses and one of the girls brought Ben a plate of bacon and eggs with an early morning air of bustle. At this hour the only other customer was a vaguely familiar young man with a mustache and a chipped tooth. It took Ben only a moment to place him—Bess's friend, Hugo.

"Hello, there," he offered through a mouthful of food.

"Snow, isn't it?"

"That's right. Ben Snow."

"I'm Hugo Dadier. I hear Bess's old man hired you."

"I guess that's right. He wants her back in Texas."

Dadier had remained standing at the bar. Now he walked over to Ben's table. "I've known Bess from almost her first day in New Orleans. I like to think I can take care of her."

"Can you protect her against the Ripper? Can you get her away from this kind of life she's leading? Can you give her a million dollars?"

"I can try," Dadier said, the eternal answer of the eternal young man, even here among the sins of Storyville.

"Do you think you're right for her? What are you—a pimp, a drug peddler, maybe?"

"Bess and I are two of a kind. We understand each other."

"I'll bet. You should take an ad for her in the *Blue Book*. It might help her business." The remark angered Dadier, but before he could reply Ben had a thought. "Say, do they keep back issues of the *Blue Book* here?"

"I don't know," Dadier said with a shrug, controlling his anger. "Ask the bartender, not me."

Ben walked over to the long polished bar and interrupted the glass-wiping task. "Back issues of the *Blue Book*—do you have any?"

The bartender eyed him oddly. "What good are back issues? The current one's got all the girls listed. The girls not listed aren't around anymore."

"I just wanted to see some."

"Didn't start publishing it till '95."

"All right. Do you have them from '95 on?"

"Guess I could find you a set, back in the office. Just a minute." Ben waited and presently the bartender returned, bearing five dog-eared copies of past *Blue Books*. "You can look at 'em here, but I gotta have them back."

"Fine."

Hugo Dadier had resumed his position at the bar as Ben sat down and began paging through the first of the booklets, not knowing exactly what he was seeking, yet feeling somehow that he would find it here. The books had grown in size with each passing year, and in '97 they had proudly proclaimed the official birth of the Storyville district. Gradually the ads for piano players had begun to appear, though the word "jazz" was not yet used in them.

But right now Ben was more interested in the names. He scanned the lists, making an occasional note, and found what he wanted in a sudden flash of brilliance. The book was two years old, but it seemed to be there. Perhaps, just perhaps, the key to the Ripper murders.

"You seen Inspector Withers around this morning?" he called out to the bartender.

"Not yet. He usually comes by about noon, but today's Mardi Gras."

"I know."

Ben stuffed one of the *Blue Books* into his pocket and made for the door. "Say, I told you I had to have those back!" the bartender called after him, but he was already into the street, swallowed up by a constantly-growing crowd of masked, painted revelers.

It took Ben two hours to track down Withers, and when he found him the Englishman was helping to break up a crowd that had gathered outside one of the houses on North Robertson. A girl, obviously drunk or drugged, had climbed out onto the roof in a brief beaded costume and was attempting to do a French cancan, much to the delight of the crowd below.

"Well," he said, finally noticing Ben in the midst of them, "enjoying the show?"

"I've been looking for you. Can we talk?"

Inspector Withers studied his set face for a moment, then motioned down the street. "At the station house. Come on."

Over a cigarette-stained table in an almost bare office, Ben produced the two-year-old *Blue Book*. He saw the spark of interest in the detective's eyes at once, and he said, "I think I'm onto something, but I need a bit of your knowledge of the district."

"Go on."

"This book lists the girls, with their current addresses, as you know. Well, two years ago all of the dead girls were living at the same address."

"The hell! Let me see that!"

"They were all at Pearl's Pleasure Palace. Now you tell me the rest of it, Inspector."

Withers frowned, then leaned back in his chair. "Of course! I know one or two of them had worked at Pearl's, but after two years I'd forgotten about the others. Pearl's is the place that burned down."

"How many girls were there?"

"At the time of the fire? She had six, I think."

"No piano player?"

Withers shook his head. "Not then. That's a recent addition to these places."

"All right." Ben picked up the book again. "Here are the names I found. Sadie Stride . . ."

"The Ripper's third victim."

"Jane Swann . . ."

"The first victim. She got out of the business right after the fire."

"Laura O'Toole . . ."

"Forget her. She was killed in the fire."

"Mary Quinn . . ."

"The second victim."

"Dotty Ringsome . . ."

"Victim number four, just last night. As you know."

"And Pearl herself?"

Withers frowned at the memory. "Pearl was a middle-aged bum, a heavy drinker. Some even said her drinking caused the fire that night. Last year she killed a man with a broken bottle and fled to South America. She's still there, living in Brazil."

Ben sighed at the list before him. He turned the page and stared down at the final name he'd checked. "The sixth girl in Pearl's house . . ."

"And the Ripper's next victim, if you're correct."

". . . was Bess Kinsman."

The Inspector's face hardened. "Come on," he said . . .

But it wasn't to be that easy. The streets, now in late afternoon, were crowded with the noise and color of carnival, filled to overflowing with masked men and painted women who had forgotten or never cared about the Ripper who had already killed four girls. They were out for pleasure, a physical representation of the "pursuit of happiness" that the Constitution guaranteed. The Constitution—no, Ben remembered, it was the Declaration of Independence—had put it nicely, but they hadn't said anything in there about murderers. There was no law saying people had to suddenly turn off the happiness just because there was a killer in their midst.

He watched the costumes passing in front of Countess Lulu's house, noting especially one fellow dressed as a policeman. It looked like Piggy, but he couldn't be sure. He couldn't be sure of anything just then.

Withers came out of the house, his eyes sweeping the passing crowds. "Well, she's all right. So far, at least. I'll send an officer down to keep an eye out."

"Make sure he doesn't wear a mask. There's a phoney cop out in the crowd."

Withers spotted him and started edging through the crowd. In a moment he was gone, swallowed up in the colorful flow. But Ben stood his ground in front of Countess Lulu's. He knew Archer Kinsman wouldn't be paying much for a dead daughter. A jazz band of sorts went by, the first he'd seen, led by a trumpet-blowing black man dressed like the devil. And as the evening's early shadows began to lengthen in the street he went inside to see how things were.

"What a night!" Lulu was chirping. "Every girl's busy and there are three birds waiting!"

"Where's your music?"

"Piggy's drunk, parading out there someplace." She left him and vanished through a hall doorway.

He stayed a few moments, watching the costumed men who waited in the parlor. Then the thought of it all began to sicken him and he turned away, heading back to the street. His hand was on the doorknob when he heard something crash to the floor above his head. Somebody screamed—it might have been Bess Kinsman.

Ben took the stairs three at a time, his hand already brushing aside the coat to get his gun free. Her door was locked but as he rattled the knob she screamed out again, *"Ben, help! It's the Ripper!"*

His shoulder hit the flimsy door. He was remembering Dotty Ringsome's door the night before, remembering what he'd found there. But Bess Kinsman was very much alive, struggling with a masked figure dressed in a checkered harlequin costume. His right hand clutched a curving knife that flickered with reflected light as they struggled by the bed. *"Shoot him, Ben! He's killing me!"*

But her body was between Ben's gun and the masked killer. As he moved in on the struggling figures the knife plunged downward, slashing at Bess's stomach, darkening her pink housecoat with a sudden splatter of blood. She screamed once more and toppled to the floor, and as Ben caught her falling figure the Ripper hurled himself at the bedroom's sole window, smashing through it in a headlong dive to the roof below.

Ben tore away the housecoat and tried to stop the flow of blood with his handkerchief. Then, as others crowded into the room behind him, he went out the window after the costumed figure.

The roof slanted upward from the window, then ended suddenly with a five-foot gap before the adjoining house. Ben took the leap without thinking twice, landing clawing at the slippery slate. Above him, against the blue night sky, the harlequin costume paused in flight to hurl a shingle of slate down at his gripping fingers. He felt the bits of rock nick his cheek, then he was up, stripping the impeding coat from his shoulders, checking the feel of the gun still in his holster as he climbed. Ahead, the enemy had swung down, hand over hand, to cling flylike to the ornate iron railing of the housefront.

Ben followed, feeling the rusty metal under hand, seeing now the very eyes of the enemy inches away, close enough almost to reach. And the knife blade dull now with darkness, moving like a cobra as the killer hung with one hand clinging. The blade shot out, slashing, as Ben lost his footing, and hung by his fingers above the street twenty feet below. And now the slasher moved in for the kill and the sweep of the knife came closer. Dangling, Ben risked one hand, dropping it to the holster at his side, pulling the gun free, firing as he hung swinging in the air against the iron grillworked balcony.

It was not the best shot of his life, but it sufficed. The masked figure shuddered as the bullet tore into his side, and relaxed his grip on the metal. He fell slowly, like a deflated balloon, and landed on the paving below with a sick thud of finality.

Ben climbed down and fought his way through the gathering crowd. He bent to the bloody, broken figure and ripped away the mask. It was the face of Bess's friend, Hugo Dadier . . .

The following day was Ash Wednesday, the beginning of Lent, and even in Storyville there were those who went to church this day. But for Inspector Withers and Ben Snow there were other things to be done. At the hospital they found Bess Kinsman resting comfortably in a narrow white bed. She was smiling, even though she'd been told a few hours earlier the identity of her attacker.

"It's hard to believe, I know," she told them, "but at times there was a bit of strangeness about him. To think that he killed those four girls so horribly . . ."

"There is no doubt he did it," Withers said. "The knife was the type used in all the killings. Of course he's too young to have been Jack the Ripper, but he must have been just as insane."

"Perhaps not," Ben said quietly. "Or at least not quite as insane as he might seem."

Bess turned to him with difficulty. "You know why he did it? Why he killed the others and tried to kill me?"

"I think so." He turned away from her. "I imagine it will all come out at the trial."

"The trial!" she said, startled. "But he's dead!"

"Not his trial—yours. Inspector Withers is here to arrest you as an accessory in those four murders."

"But . . . but that's crazy! He tried to kill me too! Why would I want those girls dead?" She was sitting up in the bed, her face as white as the sheets.

Ben sighed, feeling tired and a bit lonely. "You wanted them dead because your name is Laura O'Toole. You wanted them dead because the real Bess Kinsman was killed in a fire two years ago . . .

"You were clever," he went on, "very clever. In fact, you made no real mistakes. But I was curious as to why you, of all people, hadn't mentioned the connection among the four murder victims. The police and most everyone else might have forgotten they were all at Pearl's Pleasure Palace at the time of the fire, but certainly you would have remembered. And then of course there was the attempt on your life last night. When I found that the Ripper was your friend Hugo Dadier I was baffled for a moment. He of all people would never have attacked you last night, because he was actually at the Arlington while I was looking over back copies of the *Blue Book*. He knew I had found the connecting link between the victims, and he knew I would be expecting an attack on you. Also, of course, he was in a position where he could have killed you at any time—so why risk everything with his half-hearted attempt of last evening, at the very time I was expecting it and guarding the house? The answer of course was that the attack was a fake. He never meant to kill you, but he had to attempt it last night solely because he did know I was expecting it. Otherwise I might begin to suspect you."

"You call this a fake?" she shouted from the bed. "My stomach ripped open with a knife?"

"I think in that last instant you had an idea all your own. I think you decided Hugo had served his purpose in killing the girls. So you shouted for me to shoot him, which wasn't in the plan. He saw your double cross and jabbed a little deeper than he'd planned. Of course I was on my guard as soon as you called my name through the closed door—it meant you'd been watching me enter the house."

"And why in hell did I do all this?" She was not the same girl anymore. The hard, cold calculation had taken over completely now.

"Well, those four girls were at Pearl's when it burned down, so I asked myself what they might know that made their deaths so important. And I remembered something. I remembered that Bess Kinsman's long letters to her father stopped about two years ago. That's when it came to me. Bess was the one who died in the fire, and you were the other girl—Laura O'Toole. You must have looked enough alike to fool occasional customers and casual acquaintances, but the other girls in the house would have known you took Bess's place after the fire."

"Why? Do you know that too, smart guy?"

"Why? Well, I imagine in the beginning it was only for that hundred dollars her father sent her every Christmas and birthday. Of course you would have known about it, and with Bess Kinsman dead in the fire you must have seen how easy it would be to change places with her. It meant two hundred dollars a year, and you were reasonably certain her father would never try to visit her here. The four girls knew about the switch, of course, and Pearl, and your friend Hugo. But people come and go so fast in Storyville, it was easy to fool the rest. Countess Lulu, for example, didn't show up till just after the fire —so to her you were always Bess Kinsman and no one else."

"So why did I decide to kill the girls after two years?"

"They hadn't minded a little two-hundred-a-year racket, but when you got that letter last month saying Bess's father was dying, telling you for the first time he was worth a million dollars in oil lands, you knew you had to remove the witnesses to your impersonation. Those girls would want their cut—a big cut—to keep quiet. Pearl was already far away in South America, and would never return with a murder rap waiting for her, so you had only the four to remove. Hugo did it for you, not knowing you'd take the first opportunity to dispose of him too. And of course the Jack-the-Ripper idea made a natural cover-up for the true motive."

"That's a good story," she said, calmer now. "You think you can prove it?"

"The murders started a week after you got Kinsman's letter about the million-dollar inheritance. It's not evidence, but it's a fact of the kind juries like to hear."

Inspector Withers interrupted her. "We can easily prove you're not Bess Kinsman—by handwriting, among other things. And now that we know what we're looking for, I'm sure we'll turn up other witnesses who knew both you girls. If necessary we can bring Archer Kinsman here to meet you."

"If he lives that long," she challenged.

Ben sighed and ran his hand along the white railing of the bed. "That was my first clue of something wrong—the fact that you wouldn't go back to Texas to your dying father. The fact that Bess had kept writing to him at first implied she still cared a little for him, yet you refused to go back, even with a million dollars waiting for you. You couldn't, of course, because though you looked a little like a picture of Bess at fifteen, you'd never fool her father. You had to gamble on getting the money anyway, knowing old Kinsman had no other relatives. I imagine you would have produced Lulu and scores of other recent friends to convince the lawyers you really were Bess, once Kinsman was dead."

"I'm not saying a word," she mumbled. "We'll see what a jury says."

"Yes, we will," Withers agreed. "We might not convict you of the murders, but the fraud charges and your general character will put you away for a good many years."

When Ben left the room she had started to cry. The hardness was dissolving, and he wouldn't have been surprised if Withers obtained a full confession before too many days.

But for Ben now there was only remaining the short trip back to Texas, back to the waiting Archer Kinsman with the sort of story he'd hate to tell any father. He almost wished, deep in his heart, that death would beat him to Kinsman's side. That would be the simplest way . . .

SNOW IN YUCATAN

It was some nine hundred miles by land from Brownsville on the Rio Grande to the vast unknown wilds of the Yucatan peninsula, and by horse it had taken Ben Snow the better part of two weeks to make the trip. He'd begun to regret the journey as soon as he was south of the Tropic of Cancer—at Tampico—where both the climate and the populace had turned suddenly ugly. While buying a new horse from a sleepy-eyed Mexican just outside Tampico he'd found himself set upon by a little band of drink-hardened bandits. He'd killed one, wounded another, and escaped the rest only by dint of some hard and fast riding across the shallow waters of the Rio Panuco. And all this with two-thirds of the trip still ahead of him.

He was riding in search of a man named Chancer—Wade Chancer. Just then it was a name and a story told in a San Antonio bar. Little enough to send Ben Snow riding nine hundred miles. Still, there were times when a story told in the barroom dusk was enough to move a man. This was such a story . . .

There'd been three of them, hard and bitter men with the unmistakable look of ex-soldiers. And it hadn't taken Ben long to verify that assumption—they'd served in Cuba with Teddy Roosevelt's Rough Riders. Three ex-soldiers, spreading a pile of rumpled bills and gold coins on the table before him.

"Two thousand dollars," the biggest of them said. "We all chipped in. Others, too."

Ben Snow eyed the money suspiciously. "What's it for?"

"We want you to kill a man for us."

"I think you've got the wrong man."

The big one—his name was Ventnor—shook his head. "You're Ben Snow, aren't you?"

"Yes."

"Then we got the right man. Two thousand to kill Wade Chancer."

"You men look quite capable of carrying out the assignment yourselves. If it's that important, why try to hire me?" He was interested. There was something here that touched the nerve of curiosity always just beneath the surface.

"Because Chancer is a thousand miles away, down in Mexico."

"And I'm supposed to ride all the way down there to kill him for you? Why?"

Ventnor spread his hands flat on the table. "He enlisted with us when the Rough Riders were formed. Most of the men were from the West—Indians, cowpunchers, stage drivers, miners, trappers—and if I say so myself we formed a pretty tough fighting unit. We went down there with Teddy and we beat the hell out of them Cubans . . ."

"Spaniards."

". . . Spaniards! They're all the same. Anyway, we'd have been down there yet if the Yellow Fever hadn't gotten us."

Ben Snow cleared his throat. "What about this man Chancer?"

"Yeah, I'm getting to it. Well, Wade Chancer was with our troop when we went up San Juan Hill. He was with us and he deserted—and because he deserted, my brother and a few other real men died. The Spanish fire got them, at a point on our flank that Chancer was supposed to be covering. It took us a while to trace the rat, but we finally discovered he'd booked passage on a tramp steamer bound for Central America with its first stop at Yucatan."

"You think he got off there?"

"We know he did," Ventnor said. "The Rough Riders came over from Florida on a ship called the *Yucatan,* and I remember him telling us he wanted to go there someday. Anyway, we heard just recently that he's down there, all right. Organizing the Indians to take over the whole damn country. Guess he made himself a general or something."

One of the other two men uttered a blunt curse. "Being a private was never good enough for the likes of him."

Ben leaned back in his chair. "And you want him killed for this?"

"We want him killed because he's a yellow no-good deserter, that's why. If the Army caught him they'd kill him, so we're just saving them the trouble."

Ben cleared his throat and spoke softly, not wanting to antagonize the men. "I didn't think the Rough Riders were actually a part of the regular Army . . ."

"We were the First United States Volunteer Cavalry, mister, even if most all the horses did get left in Florida. We were Army, all the way."

"Teddy hated the name of Rough Riders at first, but it stuck."

They went on like that, three old soldiers, not so old, reliving a brief moment of glory only just passed into history. United now perhaps only in their quest for vengeance. Ben listened for a time and then asked, "Why did you come to me? Who told you I was a hired killer?"

Ventnor smiled slyly. "You're Ben Snow. Some say you're also Billy the Kid . . ."

"Billy's been dead almost twenty years."

"Sure, sure. So you're just Ben Snow. You've still got quite a reputation around the country. We heard of you as far away as New Orleans, on the way back home. You're a killer."

"Maybe. But not your kind of killer."

Ventnor rose to his feet, and the other two followed. "Think it over. Sleep on it. We'll talk again in the morning."

"You can save your breath. I don't like Mexico anyway."

"Think about it."

Ben thought, but not very hard. It was almost by coincidence, later that night, that he found himself in the company of a federal marshal he knew slightly. The talk had drifted to Mexico, and the growing menace of roving bandits, when Ben dropped the name of Wade Chancer into the conversation.

"Chancer. Down in Yucatan. Yeah, I've heard some stories in recent months. He's lots more than a bandit chief, though. He's a regular king down there, or a general at least. Wears medals and everything. Showed up there just after the war, and I guess he's really got the Indians buffaloed. Biggest thing since Cortez."

The news interested Ben more than he showed. It interested him and raised questions in his mind. "Don't you think those stories must be exaggerated? How could any one man so influence hundreds of Indians in just a few months?"

"I'd like to know myself," the marshal chuckled. "I'd try the technique at home." Ben remembered that he had an Indian wife.

"I might be traveling down Mexico way soon," he told the man, not really knowing what had changed his mind, knowing only that it was a spark of the unknown, a quest for a sort of knowledge that had shaped his whole life. The army deserter who deserved to be murdered had become somehow a far more sinister character, a man of power. Men of power were always sinister to Ben, especially when the source of their power was clouded in mystery.

And so the next morning, before dawn, he packed his horse with the necessary supplies and headed south toward the border. He didn't bother telling Ventnor he was going. The ex-soldier would never understand why he was undertaking the trip on his own when he'd refused to do it for two thousand dollars. And perhaps Ben Snow didn't exactly know himself. Certainly he had no intention of acting as the assassin Ventnor wanted to hire. Killing was something for other men, in another age. Usually . . .

South of Tampico, where the country grew gradually more rugged as he approached the mountains around Mexico City, Ben seemed to find the going easier. He covered more miles each day, seeing fewer natives and none of the roving bandit bands he'd encountered further north. He passed through Veracruz, seeing in the distance the ancient Fortress of San Juan De Ulua which overlooked the harbor. This southernmost portion of the Gulf of Mexico became suddenly the Gulf of Campecho, named after a town on the Yucatan coast which he reached on the second last day of his long journey.

It was while he was changing horses for the last time, outside Campecho, that a Mexican horseman approached him, riding slowly but purposefully. "Ah, Señor! You are from the north?"

"Texas," Ben admitted. "And New Mexico before that."

"A long ride. Many horses away." The Mexican climbed down from his beast and walked over, resting his hand casually on the holstered revolver at his hip. Though Ben wore one too, it was still a bit startling to see an armed man approaching with seeming friendliness. Sidearms had vanished from most Texas streets some years before, and only the cowhands and lawmen were likely to carry them now.

"It is long. Perhaps I should have come by boat. The maps show it to be a little more direct."

The Mexican nodded. "You seek someone here?"

"I seek Wade Chancer."

"He is another day's ride across the peninsula. I can take you there if you wish."

Ben held out his hand. "Name's Ben Snow. Be happy to ride with you."

The Mexican nodded. "I am Antonio Yallahs. I am in the employ of Wade Chancer."

Well, Ben decided, if he'd made a mistake in revealing his destination, it was too late to correct it now. But if Chancer was really as powerful as the stories said, Ben would hardly have found him unannounced anyway. They drank together, in a little shack by the stables where a dirty Mexican served warm rum from a dusty amber bottle. Then, afterward, they rode—with Yallahs leading the way up a trail to the east.

They'd been riding for some hours when the scattered brush began distinctly to take on the appearance of a jungle. The weather was warmer, and the trail they followed was all but obscured in places by the unfamiliar vines and overgrowth of a tropical climate. Ben had known nothing like it in his life, and already he was finding his heavy shirt uncomfortable against the skin. Sweat glistened on his forehead, and riding was so uncomfortable that he was almost thankful for the occasional stretches of thick underbrush where they were forced to dismount and lead their horses slowly on foot.

"Is there much more of this?" Ben asked Yallahs at one point.

"Not too much," the Mexican answered. "We are nearing some of the ruins."

"You know the country well."

"I have lived here in Yucatan all my life. Thirty-eight years now. And my father and grandfather before me. My father used to say our family went back all the way to Bartolomeo Columbus, Christopher's brother."

Ben nodded. "Up north, in my country, there are those whose ancestors came over with the Pilgrims. It's an honor, I suppose, to be descended from the brother of Columbus."

Yallahs shrugged. "He was not a very good man. Christopher made him acting Governor of the West Indies, and his main achievement was the introduction of bloodhounds to track and kill any native who opposed his rule. He stole their gold and made slaves of them."

"You're an educated man."

The Mexican laughed. "I learned about Bartolomeo on my father's knee."

"But you speak good English."

"I was educated in Mexico City, and I have traveled to your country. It is a good land."

"Tell me, what is Wade Chancer trying to do down here—build an army of Indians?"

Yallahs shrugged, and as they came out of the underbrush he remounted easily. "I believe he is only attempting to restore the glory that was the Mayan civilization. He is a great leader, a great general."

"He's a deserter from Teddy Roosevelt's Rough Riders." As soon as he'd spoken the words, Ben realized he'd made his second mistake of the day. Though the Mexican seemed friendly enough, there was no way of knowing just where his loyalties stood.

But all further conversation on that subject was cut short as the trail widened suddenly before them. Here, blocking the path as surely as some Spanish army of old, was a great vine-covered pyramid which might have been submerged in this jungle for a thousand years. A flight of crumbling stone steps led up the very center of it, and Ben remembered stories he'd read somewhere of high priests and human sacrifices to a god unknown. "Amazing," he breathed. "Really amazing!"

"There are many such ruins in Yucatan," Yallahs told him. "They are the only remains of what once was a highly advanced civilization. I wonder sometimes as we enter this twentieth century what ruins our civilization will leave."

They rode on, for some hours, until finally a hint of salt air twitched at Ben's nostrils. "We're near the water."

"Correct. And near the end of our long ride. Soon you will meet Wade Chancer for yourself."

The jungle thinned out to nothing as they entered upon a level plateau that stretched perhaps a mile to the sea. On the very edge of a rocky cliff stood a number of ancient and modern structures—another Mayan pyramid and an equally old flat-roofed building of stone. Among these ruins a few shacks and houses had been built, and as they traveled nearer Ben saw the Indians coming out to meet them. Many of them carried modern rifles. With Chancer as their general, they would already know how to use them.

Ben followed Yallahs past the watching Indians and into the ancient stone building next to the pyramid. Below, far below, the pounding of the surf on rocks reached up with a fine salt spray to envelop them, and he imagined that the wind must always be strong here.

The interior of the building was amazingly modern, with evidence that the crumbling stones had been reinforced with handsome timbers of polished wood, probably brought out of the nearby jungle. They passed through two outer rooms and then Ben was left to wait a few moments while Yallahs went off in search of Wade Chancer. It was not a long wait, though, and the Mexican soon reappeared—followed by the man Ben Snow had traveled some nine hundred miles to find . . .

W ade Chancer was a tall young man, just barely out of his twenties, who looked more like a lawyer than a general or a gunfighter. Even the tiny beard on his chin and the three glistening medals on his chest did nothing to dispel the illusion that here was only a masquerade character, a play actor in the costume of the moment. But there was the Army pistol swinging from his hip, and the dangerous look in his yellowish eyes, and when you noticed those things you tended to revise your conclusion of only a moment before. At least Ben did, standing there before this man almost ten years younger than himself. Wade Chancer could be dangerous, simply because he looked so harmless at first glance.

"You've traveled a long way to see me," he said, holding out a hand in greeting. "What can I do for you?"

Ben gave him a smile meant to be friendly. "Oh, I was riding down this way and I heard the stories about you. I remembered I knew a friend of yours back in Texas and thought I'd stop to give you his regards."

The yellowish eyes hardened. "I have no friends in Texas. Or anywhere else for that matter."

"This man's name was Ventnor."

Wade Chancer smiled, and there was a touch of the cruel about his lips. "Mr. Snow, there are three rifles pointed at your back. If Ventnor sent you to kill me, I assure you you'll never get your gun out of its holster."

Ben pushed his hat back a little on his damp forehead. "I'm no hired killer, Chancer. I came only to see if the stories about you are true."

"They're true."

Yallahs appeared from somewhere with three heavy glass mugs. "I believe we could all use a cool drink, gentlemen. Cool drinks for hot heads."

Wade Chancer relaxed and poured the drinks. He settled into a carved wooden chair and motioned Ben to join him. "Excuse me. I wasn't being the proper host. Have a seat."

"Just what are you trying to do down here, Chancer?" Ben asked him.

The bearded young man waved a hand. "Organize a revolution, I suppose. Yucatan, Mexico, maybe all of Central America in a few years. It can be done."

"What is this power you have over the Indians?"

He smiled again. "Only the power of power, and of right. I want to lift them to their place of former glory in this world."

Ben leaned back in his chair, knowing that what he was to say next might bring him three bullets in the back if the rifles were still in position. "Ventnor said you deserted in Cuba."

"Ventnor is a fool. Why should I fight for the private glory of a man like Roosevelt when I can lead my own army, win my own wars?"

Ben sipped his drink and found it a pleasing if unfamiliar mixture. Rum and some sort of fruit juice, he guessed. "Would you kill Mexicans to achieve your goal?"

Chancer grinned. "I would kill Americans to achieve my goal. Wouldn't you?"

Another man entered, a middle-aged balding man with glasses. He was dressed in the European style, the manner now popular in the eastern cities of America, and to Ben he was as out of place here as he would have been on the Texas range. "You have a guest," the man said, a bit startled. "Excuse me."

"Quite all right, Professor Irreel. This is Ben Snow, down all the way from Texas to visit us." Then, to Ben, "Professor Irreel is a famous scientist back in Paris. He has worked with the Curies and many others. As you see, people come from all over to visit the domain of Wade Chancer."

Ben shook hands with the Frenchman. "Pleased to meet you, Professor. Are there any more surprises awaiting me here?"

Chancer laughed. "Only Marge Fisher. She is an American like yourself, a nurse in my employ."

Ben caught the "like yourself." Wade Chancer apparently no longer considered America his own home. He was a true man without a country, and perhaps that was why he felt the need to make his own nation. "Are you employed here too, Professor?" he asked

"Oh dear, no," the Frenchman said, seeming to find the very thought humorous. "You might call this a working vacation. I am here for some months looking into native customs. As you know, the French have always had a deep interest in Mexico."

Ben smiled. "I thought they lost that interest about thirty years ago, with the help of the United States."

Professor Irreel flushed a bit. "We were not speaking of my country's occasional lapses into imperialism."

Wade Chancer was watching the byplay with passive interest, but now suddenly he doubled over and started to cough. He covered his mouth with a handkerchief, and when he removed it Ben caught a glimpse of the red of blood. He recovered his composure almost at once, though, and stood up. "Excuse me. I haven't been feeling well lately." Then he was gone, with Yallahs hurrying after him, leaving Ben alone with Professor Irreel.

"An unusual man," Ben said, lighting up a cigarette from a box on the table.

"Unusual," Irreel agreed, "and dangerous."

"Just how dangerous is he?"

The Frenchman glanced around, his voice dropping to a whisper. "He has quite an organization among the Indians. He talks sometimes of an army to march on Mexico City, and I really believe he means it."

"The Indians would follow him on something like this? After all, he *is* an American."

Irreel shrugged. "But important Mexicans like Yallahs support him. They dream of a return to the glories of the Mayan civilization."

"It takes more than that to control Indians."

"He has a power. There is no doubt about that."

"The thing seems so unreal."

The Frenchman smiled. "Life is unreal. Even I am unreal—my family name even means *unreal*. But these things happen. Certainly the recent advances in science are even more unreal than a man like Chancer. But be careful. I have seen his natives kill strangers here rather than let them leave. None of us are ever quite safe, and especially you with your knowledge of Chancer's past."

"You heard?"

Irreel nodded. "I was listening for a time before I made my appearance. As I said, be careful. Very careful."

"I can manage."

Professor Irreel nodded and left, as suddenly as he'd appeared. It was already dark outside, and presently Yallahs returned to show Ben to his quarters for the night. The place selected for him was in one of the wooden shacks near the ancient pyramid, an odd little room that appeared to be used for storage. He explored the area with some care after he'd been left alone, and was about to turn in when he heard the unmistakable sounds of someone approaching.

Ben's hand was resting on his gun when a candle flickered through the doorway and a girl appeared. She was an obvious American, with a freckled face and blonde hair, and she could only have been the nurse, Marge Fisher. "Hello there—I heard there was another American staying the night."

"Come in," he said, removing his hand from the gun butt. "This place is full of surprises. My name's Ben Snow."

"Marge Fisher. I'm a nurse here, doing what I can to care for these Indians. I suppose it's a part of Mr. Chancer's schemes for conquest to supply them with a semblance of medical care." Her cultured voice had a bit of an edge to it that surprised Ben in a girl who couldn't yet have been twenty-five. He wondered irrationally if perhaps she also served as Chancer's mistress. "You're the second person tonight who's hinted at a dislike for Wade Chancer," he said. "Is Yallahs the only friend he's got?"

"Chancer uses enemies the way other men use friends. Who else have you talked to?"

"The Frenchman—Professor Irreel."

She dropped a little wax on the table between them and set the candle firmly in place. Its flickering yellow light did things to her face that were not unpleasant. "Don't be taken in by Irreel," she said. "He's playing both sides for his own reasons. I'll bet when he was denouncing Chancer he didn't tell you he presented him with a medal, did he?"

"A medal?"

She nodded. "Two of those medals he wears are U.S. Army—I think he stole them off a corpse. But the middle one is French. Irreel brought it from Paris about a month ago and presented it to him, as a token of friendship from the French government."

He took in her firm young body, only partly hidden under the typically Mexican costume she wore. "Why are you telling me all this? What can I do about it?"

"You're an American, like me."

"So is Chancer."

"That's just it! I've known for a long time that the government in Washington wouldn't let this thing get out of hand. I knew they'd send someone to deal with Chancer."

"Well, I'm not the one, believe me. A man named Ventnor tried to hire me to murder Chancer, but I wasn't having any of that, either. You might say I'm just passing through, which is less than can be said for you."

The girl bristled a bit. "I told you he hired me as a nurse. If you don't believe me, come on my rounds with me tomorrow." As an afterthought, she added, "You can meet Old Oake."

"Who?"

"One of the Indians. He's the guiding spirit of them all, really. The oldest man in the world, I suppose."

"How old is he?"

"He says he was a small boy when Cortez landed at Veracruz, in 1518. That would make him 390 years old. I know it's fantastic, but the tribe actually has written records about him dating back more than a hundred years. He was a withered old man already at the time of our American Revolution, and an American historian visited him in 1840."

Ben was beginning to see some light. "And Chancer hired you mainly to look after this old man, right? That was his first move to get control of the Indians—by showing a sort of kindness to their leader, a leader who was directly linked to the past Chancer is trying to revive."

The girl smiled. "You're a regular detective. Of course the Mayan civilization was already in its final days when Cortez conquered . . ."

Ben cut her off with a quick thrust of his hand, tumbling her toward him. "Someone outside!" he whispered urgently, his other hand going for the gun on his hip.

The wooden door was flung open, and two wild-eyed savages threw themselves in, long knives glistening in the candlelight. Under him, Marge Fisher gave the gasping beginning of a scream, but Ben already had his gun out. He caught the first Indian along the temple with his revolver barrel, feeling the cold blade of the dagger as it sliced smoothly through his shirt. Off balance, he toppled backwards, knocking the candle from the table. If it were only him he'd have taken a chance at hand to hand combat in the dark, but with the girl in danger he couldn't risk it. In the last instant of the candle's flicker he fired two quick but careful shots, picking his targets as he had for twenty years—with the unfailing skill of a man who lived by the gun.

Silence. And then, after a moment, "Ben?"

"Lie still. They might not be dead. Can you reach the candle?"

"I think so."

"Good. Light it and keep back out of the way."

The stub of candle leaped to life again, and in its glow Ben saw the bodies of the two would-be killers. He'd caught one in the left eye, but the other was still alive, gasping out his last few seconds on earth as the blood bubbled from a fatal chest wound. Ben knelt beside him, trying to catch the words his lips seemed to be forming. "What?"

"*Nieve . . .*" He spoke the word once more, clearly, and then he was dead.

"Snow," Marge Fisher translated. "He was saying your name."

"Maybe." Ben got to his feet and started reloading his pistol.

"What are you going to do with them?"

He looked around, out the door, and then carefully closed it. "Seems like no one's coming to investigate the shots. I'll dump the bodies off the cliff, into the sea. That way Wade Chancer will know I mean business. If he wants to send some others, I'll be ready."

"You're staying here, after this?"

Ben nodded. "At least till tomorrow. I want to go see this man with you, the one who's 390 years old . . ."

Activity in the morning seemed to be normal to Ben's eyes, with the Indians going about preassigned tasks without visible concern over their two missing comrades. He saw Professor Irreel strolling with Yallahs along the edge of the cliff, but if they were searching for bodies they gave no sign of it. With his wide-brimmed sombrero turning up in the breeze, the Mexican seemed dangerously off balance.

Marge Fisher was at her own quarters, preparing a kit of assorted medicines for her daily rounds among the natives. "I was up early," she said. "Wade Chancer seems quite ill."

"What's the matter with him?"

"I don't know, exactly. Hemorrhages and diarrhea, but I don't know what's causing it. He's still a young man."

Ben glanced over some of the bottles. "You haven't been feeding him poison by mistake, have you?"

"Certainly not! I couldn't anyway—he has an Indian cook taste all the food for him, just like the old Roman emperors.

"Sometimes I think he's a devil, not human at all. See this?" She held up a square black box. "It's a camera, for taking pictures, you know. The Indians are fascinated by it. But a few weeks ago I tried to take Chancer's picture and nothing came out. The film was all foggy, as if I'd photographed a ghost!"

Ben examined the camera with interest. He'd seen them before, but never close up, and the very idea of photography held a boyish fascination for him. "Another of the wonders of the twentieth century," he said. "Someday I suppose everyone will own one of these. Have you taken any pictures of the old man?"

She nodded. "I have some good ones. But come along, and you can see him in person."

Ben followed her as they made the rounds of some of the Indian shacks. She told him there were many more living in the jungle, and it was probably from there that the two now-dead assassins had come. Ben listened to her with interest, and observed the Indians they visited most carefully. About a number of the younger males there was a sameness of expression, a something in the eyes, that both attracted and repelled him, and he wondered about it.

Finally, toward noon, they reached the farthest of the outbuildings, a shack no different from the rest, but one which seemed set apart in spirit if not in actuality. "Here we are," Marge Fisher breathed, as if entering a church.

The man inside was indeed old—his wrinkled, almost mummified face was certainly the most ancient Ben had ever seen—and when he spoke there was about him an unmistakable death-like rattle. He talked in utter disregard to their questions, speaking in a half-Spanish, half-Indian tongue of the glories he had known, of the thunder and clash of armor as the mighty armies of Cortez moved across the land all those many years before. And by his side crouched Old Oake's great-great-great-great-great-great-grandson, already an old man himself. Yes, Ben thought, this was the perfect place for a man with a dream of past glories. What better beginning for Wade Chancer than among a tribe of Indians who daily heard these tales of glorious warfare from the lips of a revered old man?

They remained there for some twenty minutes, drinking in the sight and the sounds of Old Oake. Finally, as the visit was coming to an end, Yallahs appeared in the doorway. "You must come, Miss Fisher," he said somberly. "Wade Chancer is very sick."

"I'll come at once."

They hurried off together, and Ben was left alone with his thoughts. He wandered slowly back, pausing for a time to climb among the worn, weed-grown stones of the great pyramid. There were steps leading to its summit, and Ben climbed them, resting for a while at the top to contemplate the vast panorama of sea and jungle that stretched below him. The climb had made him short of breath, for he was no longer a young man, but up here so near to the clouds he forgot that for a moment. A man could feel the power from here, where everything else seemed so small. From here, a wise coward like Wade

Chancer could imagine himself the ruler of all about him, could sacrifice human lives to his cause just as the Mayans had so long ago.

Ben climbed down reluctantly, and went in search of Professor Irreel. The Frenchman's quarters in a wing of the great stone house were easy enough to find, but the man himself was nowhere in evidence. Ben spent a few minutes glancing about the tidy, nearly bare room, noting the titles of a variety of reading matter on a bedside table. Most were booklets, printed in French, on a variety of scientific subjects. Ben had picked up a bit of French while living in New Orleans, and some of the titles were clear enough: *The History, Products, and Processes of the Alkali Trade*, by C. T. Kingzett, London, 1877; *On the Chemical Effects of Radium Rays*, by Marie Curie and Pierre Curie, Paris, 1899; *Metallurgy: Silver and Gold*, by J. Percy, London, 1880.

Ben picked up one of the booklets and was intent on translating what few words he knew when Professor Irreel returned. The Frenchman was white and trembling. "Wade Chancer has died," he said with a broken voice. "God help us all . . ."

The gloom that hung over the great house throughout the afternoon gradually gave way to a growing sense of urgency as darkness approached. News of Chancer's death had already spread among the Indians, and the sounds of their restlessness reached them in the big room where Ben Snow had met Wade Chancer for the only time in his life. Marge Fisher was there, and Professor Irreel, along with Yallahs and Ben. The Mexican had a rifle out, and paced the floor like a caged lion in some terrible zoo of his own making.

"They'll kill us all," he said. "They're madmen."

"Then let's get out of here," Ben suggested.

"Back through the jungle?"

Professor Irreel cleared his throat. "Chancer kept a small boat at the base of the cliff. That would get us around the jungle and back to civilization."

But Yallahs only waived his rifle. "I'm not going. There's too much here to let slip through our fingers."

"But you just said they'd kill us!"

"Not if we control them," the Mexican said. "Not if we control them the same way Chancer did."

"Through Old Oake?" the girl suggested.

Yallahs shook his head. "That was only part of it. Old Oake only helped create the right mood for a man like Chancer."

Ben decided it was time he was heard from. "Old Oake is a fake, anyway."

"A fake?"

"Of course! Nobody lives to be 390 years old, even down here. Haven't you ever noticed how much old Indians look alike, especially in the dim light? It's just a family plot—when one Old Oake dies, they bury him secretly and the son takes his place. The present son is almost old enough now to take over. If one of the Old Oakes ever dies without children, that will be the end of it. But in the meantime, it's a great legend—even though some of the other Indians must suspect the truth. There was a man in Europe I read about once, called Old Parr, who worked the same kind of thing. He was supposed to have lived from 1483 till 1635, but actually it was a grandfather, a father, and a son taking their turns at the role."

From somewhere outside came the sound of a shot. "The natives are restless," Marge Fisher said, trying unsuccessfully to make a joke of it.

Yallahs made for the door. "I'll stop them," he said. "I have to!"

Ben shouted to Irreel. "Take Marge down to that boat and wait for me. I'm going after that crazy fool."

Outside, a bonfire had been lit over near the edge of the jungle, casting its flames high into the night sky. By its glow, Ben could see a score of armed savages running his way. He fired two quick shots to hold them off and glanced around for Yallahs. The Mexican was halfway up the pyramid, hurrying toward the room of darkness at its top. Ben followed, making the climb for the second time that day. He knew the Indians would not be far behind.

"Yallahs!" he called out. "Stop!"

The Mexican had already reached the top, and was lighting a candle to guide his search for something. "You can't stop me. There's too much at stake!"

"What?" Ben asked, cornering him at last, panting for breath. "What could be worth such a price?"

Yallahs turned, still clutching the rifle. "Understand me, friend. I do not want only power, as did Chancer. I want the glory that goes with power. See here—this is the sarcophagus of a Mayan high priest, a man dead for perhaps a thousand years. What I want is a rebirth of the glories he knew, for Yucatan and for all of Mexico."

"That is why you supported Wade Chancer?"

"That is why I supported him."

"And that is why you allowed him to give drugs to the Indians?"

"Drugs?" The Mexican's eyes were cautious in the flickering candlelight.

"You know damn well what I mean, Yallahs! Those Indians are half insane on narcotics. You can see it in their faces, in their eyes. That's why they followed Chancer's commands so readily—because he'd made addicts out of them. One that he sent to kill me muttered about *snow* before he died. He wouldn't have cared what my name was—he was calling for more of the drug, which I imagine is cocaine. Its white crystalline form must have seemed much like snow to the Indians, who'd know about snow probably only from some of the pictures Marge Fisher showed them."

Yallahs moved his free hand, and the lid of the high priest's sarcophagus slid back on stone rollers. "You're right. He gave them cocaine, and there's more of it in here—a fortune in cocaine that I helped him get from a coca tree plantation in South America. I'm going to give it to them, control them as Chancer would have."

Ben drew his gun. "I can't let you do it, Yallahs."

The Mexican lifted his rifle. "I am not an evil man—this you must believe. I am only a man with a dream. If a few pounds of cocaine will bring back an empire, I am willing to use it. Now I must kill you, not because I hate you, but only because of my dream. I am sorry, deeply sorry."

His finger was tightening on the trigger when Ben shot him through the forehead . . .

Ten minutes later, Ben was splashing through the surf to the waiting boat. Irreel and the girl pulled him aboard, where he stretched on the deck in utter exhaustion. "How did you get away?" Marge Fisher asked.

Ben coughed and sat up, his soaking clothes clinging to his chilled body. "It wasn't easy. The Indians must have had a taboo about going up the pyramid. They were waiting at the bottom of the steps, so I went down the back of it. The levels are about eight feet apart, but I managed somehow."

"Yallahs?"

"Yallahs is dead. And the cocaine he was going to give the Indians is at the bottom of the sea. I saw to that on my way down here."

"Cocaine!" Irreel muttered. "That's how he was doing it!"

"I almost suspected it at times," Marge Fisher said. "But I had no proof."

The wind caught at their sails and pulled them out toward the open sea. With luck they would be beyond the Yucatan in a few hours. Beyond the Yucatan and back, back someday even to Texas. "There's a man I should look up," Ben said, almost to himself. "A man named Ventnor. He was willing to pay two thousand dollars for Wade Chancer's death."

"Will you collect it?" Professor Irreel asked.

"No," Ben answered, looking to see that the girl was out of earshot, busily adjusting the sails. "No, I won't collect it, Professor. Because it was you who murdered Wade Chancer."

"What do you mean? He died a natural death."

"I know next to nothing about it, Professor, so your secret is safe with me. I only knew a few paragraphs I was able to translate from a book on radium in your room. Radium is a new chemical element, just discovered in 1898, by some people named Curie with whom Wade said you worked. Not too much is known about its powers, but it could prove to be quite deadly. I think it did in the case of Wade Chancer."

Professor Irreel's face was impassive in the sea spray. Finally, after a few moments of silence, he said, "I had no knowledge that the radium would prove to be fatal. My own experiments with animals were inconclusive on that score. I only knew it would make him ill enough to remove the threat he posed."

"You acted as an agent of the French government in this?"

Irreel shrugged. "I am not free to say. I acted, shall we say, as an agent of men who feared Wade Chancer's dreams of power."

Ben nodded. "That's good enough for me, I suppose. I don't claim the power to punish you, or even to judge you." And then he said, "You might be interested in one effect of your radium. I think it fogged the girl's film when she tried to take a picture of Chancer. That was another thing to make me suspicious."

"You know where the radium was hidden?" Irreel asked, and there was a certain sense of pride in his voice as he spoke the words. "It was only a tiny sliver, of course, but it was enough to kill him in a month's time."

Ben gazed up at the sky, feeling suddenly sad, wondering what the future could hold for a world where rays of death could now kill invisibly. "I think I know," he answered. "I think it was in the medal you pinned on Wade Chancer's chest . . ."

THE VANISHED STEAMBOAT

The business that brought Ben Snow downriver to New Orleans during the early months of 1902 had been successfully concluded, but he found himself reluctant to return West. The weather was pleasant and he'd made some good friends, including a riverboat gambler named Eddie Abilene who had a way with a deck of cards and a good story. It was Eddie who coaxed him upriver to Vicksburg in the spring when the threat of the annual flooding had finally subsided.

"Tell me about yourself for a change, Ben," Eddie suggested one evening over drinks at a pleasant little café on the Vicksburg riverfront. "I'm always telling stories and all you do is sit there and listen."

Ben Snow merely smiled. "I've gotten through forty-two years without talking about myself, Eddie. No reason to change now."

But that wasn't good enough for Eddie Abilene. "Fellow told me yesterday you've got quite a reputation with a gun. I never even knew you to carry one."

"That's just talk. A story got started in my younger days that I was Billy the Kid. It's a tough reputation to live down—or live up to, for that matter."

Eddie's eyes narrowed. "Billy the Kid's been dead for twenty years."

"You know it and I know it, but there's a lot of folks who haven't gotten the word. And he'd be just about my age if he was still alive."

"But you are fast with a gun?"

"I used to be, when I carried one. But that was in Texas, and Mexico, and the Indian territories. I don't need one on the Mississippi."

Eddie Abilene let his blue-velvet coat fall open to reveal the little Derringer under his arm. "I'm never without one on the river. Sometimes the cards don't turn out right for some people and it makes them mad. You know the steamboat *River Ridge*? It's docked a few miles downriver now."

"I've seen it."

"I was on her last year on the run up to St. Louis, having a friendly game of poker with three strangers. One of them was losing pretty heavy and when I beat out his full house with four jacks, he went for his gun. His name was Jericho Jones and he was fast. Put a bullet through my coat before I even had my gun out. Then I missed him on the first shot and hit a big mirror behind him. The glass broke and came down on top of him. If that hadn't put him out of action, I don't know what would have happened."

Ben tried to backtrack on the conversation to remember how the subject of riverboat gun battles had come up, but he finally decided Eddie was just talking. "When are you shipping out again?" he asked.

"I don't know. When I need money, I guess. Vicksburg's a good little town but there's not much happening here."

As if to prove him false, a fight erupted on the dock at that moment. Three or four men were involved, and Ben could hear shouts and see them moving in the darkness. There was a sudden cry for help from one man and a scream cut off in the middle. "Let's go see what the trouble is," Ben said.

Before they reached the dock, the figures separated and two men took off in opposite directions. One man remained sprawled at the edge of the dock. "He's been stabbed," Ben said. "Get some help, Eddie. I'll stay with him."

While Eddie ran off, Ben tried to stop the flow of blood from a wound in the man's side. "Can you hear me?" he asked him. "Who stabbed you?"

But the man was beyond answering. There was blood in his mouth and a moment later he died. When Eddie arrived with help, it was too late. A crowd had gathered by that time, drawn from the bars along the riverfront. "I know him," one man said. "It's Frank Beecher, a gambler—he traveled on the *River Ridge*.

"That's him, all right," Eddie confirmed. "I met him once or twice in New Orleans."

No one shed many tears over dead gamblers, and even Eddie didn't seem sorry to see him gone. "Aren't you ever afraid you might end up like that?" Ben asked him later.

"Ben, if one thing don't get you, something else will. But this just might be an opportunity for me. I might take the *River Ridge* up to St. Louis again and see if I can make a little money along the way."

"Why would you do that?"

"There's an opening for a gambling man and those are hard to come by these days. All them railroads going into St. Louis—I'm afraid steamboats are a dying breed. A lot of them have stopped running already. They say in June they'll start running a train called the *Twentieth Century Limited* from New York to Chicago. It'll make the run in twenty hours. And automobiles! Last month something called the American Automobile Association started up, to encourage people to drive themselves. Trains and automobiles—that's the future, Ben, not steamboats. But some like the *River Ridge* got a few good years left in them, and I might as well keep riding them. Come along with me?"

Ben shook his head. "I'm not ready to head north yet."

He did, however, accompany Eddie Abilene to the dock in the morning and watch him walk up one of the familiar twin gangplanks as the steamboat tooted its whistle and prepared to shove off. Like most such boats, it was a stern-wheeler, able to push its bow into shallow river shores and dock almost anywhere. Some 180 feet in length, with tall twin stacks belching black smoke, the *River Ridge* was a majestic sight as Ben watched her pull out from shore and turn north on the river. She was carrying a cargo of molasses and cotton, with fifty-five passengers and crew. She rounded a bend of the Mississippi and passed out of sight.

Then all Ben could see was the wisp of smoke above the trees to mark her passage, and soon that, too, faded away in the morning sunshine.

B en was seated at a table in front of the Vicksburg café, watching dock-hands unload a southbound steamboat named the *Carrollton Belle* when a tall slim woman wearing boots and a fringed buckskin skirt approached him the following morning. "You're Ben Snow," she said.

"That's right. What can I do for you?"

She pulled out the other chair and sat down without invitation. "I'm Stella Daren. I want to hire you."

He'd heard the name before. "You own the *River Ridge*."

"That's right, along with some smaller riverboats and barges, and a couple of New Orleans warehouses. They all belonged to my father until he died last year." He guessed her age at around thirty and suspected she'd be a lovely woman if she ever smiled. Right now she was looking grim. "I want to hire you to find the *River Ridge*."

"That would be a simple task. She left here around eight yesterday morning. By now I'd estimate she's as far north as Helena, in Arkansas."

"You'd be wrong. The *River Ridge* never reached Greenville."

"What?"

"She disappeared on the river. Vanished. I want you to find her."

"A boat that big doesn't just vanish," Ben argued. "She must have hit something and sunk."

"In broad daylight? With fifty-five people on board?" She shook her head, dismissing the notion. "I talked to the captain and pilot of the *Carrollton Belle*. They just came downriver from Memphis and they didn't see a trace of my steamboat."

Ben shrugged. "They probably passed in the night. It's a wide river."

"The *River Ridge* would have been past Greenville before dark. And the *Belle* was below Greenville before dark. Besides, there's no way they could have missed each other's lights. It was a clear night without any fog."

"What do they say in Greenville?"

"That the *River Ridge* never arrived there. They telegraphed me in New Orleans last night and I made the trip up here overnight. The captain of the *Belle* confirms it's not on the river."

"I've been up and down the Mississippi a few times," Ben told her. "North of here's mostly dense forest on either bank, with only an occasional farm. No place to hide a steamboat. If she's not there, she sank."

"I think she was stolen," Stella Daren said firmly, "by someone who's out to ruin me."

"Any ideas who?"

"A great many people were unhappy when I inherited my father's shipping business, including my half brother. If anything's happened to the *River Ridge*, I think he'd be behind it. That's why I need a man who's fast with a gun."

He started to protest. "I'm not—"

"I'll pay you one thousand dollars in gold to locate the *River Ridge*."

It was a great deal of money, and in Ben's precarious financial position it was an offer he could hardly refuse. For that much money he could even strap on the gun he kept in his suitcase. And if the *River Ridge* was indeed missing, then his friend Eddie Abilene was missing, too. He wanted to find Eddie.

"I'll look around, but I'm promising nothing. You need the police, not someone like me."

"The Vicksburg police aren't too interested, but the River Commission has crews out dragging for wreckage."

"I can't believe she could have sunk without survivors or witnesses," Ben said. "The river's been fairly calm these past few days."

"I can't believe it, either. That's why I think someone stole her. I've sent telegrams to all the ports up the river, asking for information. If I'm right about river pirates, there could be danger."

"I can take care of myself. Tell me about this half brother of yours."

"Roddy—Roderick Daren. He was my father's son by a previous marriage, and he felt he should have inherited the steamboat and all the rest of it. He's five years older than me but he still looks and acts like a child. Father disowned him, and left him nothing in the will. Roddy was very unhappy and made a few veiled threats to me. And there were accidents."

"Accidents?" Ben asked.

"Starting about a month ago, seven members of the *River Ridge* crew have been killed or injured. One apparently fell off the dock in New Orleans and drowned. Another was killed by a falling bale of cotton. One was badly injured by a runaway carriage. Two more were beaten in a barroom brawl."

"I get the picture," Ben said. "You may not know it, but two nights ago a gambler named Beecher was stabbed to death right down there on the dock."

"Another one? He worked on the *River Ridge!*"

"That's what I heard. It seems as if someone has a grudge against the boat and everyone connected with it."

"I want to do some research of my own," she said, "with old river charts. Suppose you meet me at the office of the River Commission this afternoon at four."

"Good. That'll give me time to look around on my own."

She smiled for the first time as she left the table and Ben was right about what it would do for her face. He watched her walk across the plank flooring and up the narrow street that led into town. Then he decided he should speak with the skipper of the *Carrollton Belle*, but first he stopped by the room for his gun.

Docked in the shadow of the high railway bridge that spanned the river at this point, the *Belle* looked much like any other Mississippi steamboat except for twin red stripes that ran around its hull and superstructure. Ben went up one of the twin gangplanks and took the nearest stairs to the pilot house above. One or two crew members glanced up casually but no one questioned him.

The captain of the *Carrollton Belle* was a white-haired man with a Mark Twainlike mustache. His name was Thomas Botts and Ben found him hunched over his logbook.

"What can I do for you, sir?" he asked Ben, straightening up and closing the book. "If you're booking passage to New Orleans, you should see the—"

"It's not about passage. I'm looking into the disappearance of the *River Ridge*."

"A boat can't just disappear on this river," Captain Botts said, and then immediately corrected himself. "Though one did, thirty years ago—the *Iron Mountain*. But that was before my time."

"Tell me about it."

"Are you from the River Commission?"

"I'm working for the owner, Stella Daren. My name's Ben Snow. Tell me about the *Iron Mountain*."

"It started upriver out of this very port in June of '72, towing barges of cotton. Two hours later, another riverboat found the floating barges, but there was never a trace of the *Iron Mountain*. It looked as if the rope connecting the barges to the riverboat had been deliberately cut. Other boats searched the river, but there wasn't a trace of debris or survivors."

"A legend of the river," Ben said.

"No legend, mister. It really happened."

"How well do you know the *River Ridge?*"

Captain Botts held out his calloused hand. "Like the palm of my hand. She and the *Belle* were sister ships, both owned by a St. Louis company until they sold the *Ridge* to Daren and the *Belle* to my boss, a St. Louis businessman named Maxwell Greer."

"So the two were in competition."

"No, no—we mainly operate out of St. Louis and the *Ridge* is based in New Orleans. We pass on the river occasionally but that's about all."

Ben thought for a moment. "If I could rent a small boat for a few hours, would you go upriver with me while I look around?"

"The River Commission already has a search party out."

"I know, but I'd like to take a personal look and I need a guide. I'll pay you for your time."

Captain Botts studied Ben for a moment through half closed eyes. "I'll send my first mate. He knows the river as well as I do. You can wait outside for him."

"Thank you. I appreciate it."

Ben lounged against the pilot-house wall until he was joined by a burly man with a day's growth of beard. "I'm Roy Fox. Captain says you want a guide up the river."

"That's right. I'm looking for the *River Ridge.*"

"Come along. I know a place where we can charter a launch to take us up to Milliken's Bend. That's about a two-hour trip each way."

Once he was out on the wide Mississippi, Ben wondered what it was he expected to find. Steamboats left no trails like horses in the sand, and the area of their search was only a small portion of the river below St. Louis. Still, he had to start somewhere. As the launch chugged past the wall of trees that lined the banks on either side, he listened to Roy Fox's stories of the river, riverboat pilots, and unscrupulous land speculators.

"I know a fellow owned a plantation back in the country, miles from the river. The land's so flat here that one night he cut a gutter across a narrow strip of riverbank and changed the flow of the whole damn Mississippi! The river shifted a few miles to the west and came right up to his plantation, more than tripling its value."

"Is that possible?" Ben asked.

"Sure is. This river's constantly shifting its banks, especially in the southern portion below Cairo. Look at a map sometime and you'll see how it plays hob with state boundaries. When it shifts several miles to the east or west, seeking a lower route, it often forms deep horseshoe curves. Some of these horseshoes are later cut off when the river is shifted back and you get a whole series of crescent-shaped lakes. Some are even named Old River Lake."

"You know a lot about this area."

"I guess so. Been working it all my life."

Near Milliken's Bend, they came upon other search boats, some of which were dragging the river with long grappling hooks. Perhaps they hoped to snag one of the *River Ridge*'s twin smokestacks, but while Ben watched they came up with nothing more than the trunk of a dead tree.

"Sighted any debris?" Ben called out to men in the nearest boat.

"Not a trace," was the reply. "We don't think she went down around here."

"Then what happened to her?"

The man on the search boat shrugged. "Maybe she sailed south instead of north."

Ben and Roy Fox turned their own launch back soon afterward. The trip downstream was faster, and they were back at the Vicksburg dock by midafternoon. "Thanks for the tour," Ben told Fox, handing him a few dollars for his time. "Tell your captain I appreciated it."

"It didn't seem to help in finding the *River Ridge*."

"I think it'll turn up," Ben said, though he didn't fully feel the confidence of his words.

He found Stella Daren at the River Commission office at four o'clock as arranged. She was studying a large wall chart of the lower Mississippi and talking to a well-dressed man in a gray suit. "Oh, Ben—this is Ulysses Harris of the River Commission. We've been discussing the problem. Ben Snow, Mr. Harris."

Harris had a firm handshake and he came right to the point. "We have all our boats out searching, but there's no word yet. We have to accept the possibility that the *River Ridge* may never be found." He was a tall man and Ben guessed he'd been born during the Civil War and named after General Grant. That would make his age near forty.

"I have an idea," Stella Daren said, running her slender hand over the wall chart. "I read a great deal and I remember a story by that British writer, Conan Doyle. I think it appeared in the *Strand Magazine* a few years ago."

"What's that?" Ben asked.

"A British magazine. You must have heard of the Sherlock Holmes stories!"

"I don't get time for much reading. But tell me about it."

"This story, 'The Lost Special,' wasn't about Holmes, but it did involve a train that vanished between two stations. Just as the *River Ridge* vanished between two ports."

"What happened to the train in the story?" Harris asked.

"It was driven onto a siding and into a deep, disused mine."

Harris merely smiled. "There aren't any mines along the river."

"No, but there are sidings of a sort. Look at this map. See these arcs of water where the Mississippi used to flow?"

"A fellow was just telling me about those," Ben said. "He says they're now little lakes, without access to the river."

"It would be simple enough to cut a ditch and float the *River Ridge* into one of these lakes," Stella said, "then cover up the passage with tree limbs."

"That's a possibility," Ulysses Harris admitted. "I'll get some horsemen to search both banks."

"Do it now—today," Stella insisted. "I want the *River Ridge* back!"

Ben left the River Commission office with her and suggested they dine at one of the waterfront cafes. She was beginning to fascinate him in a way women rarely did and he found himself wanting to remain in her company as something other than a hired hand.

Over dinner he told her about his river cruise, but she wasn't impressed. "You spent the day at that and found nothing?"

"I wanted to get the feel of the river and check on the dragging operations."

"They won't find it. My enemies didn't sink the *River Ridge*."

"You still believe your half brother is behind this?"

"No one else."

His attention was attracted to the bar, where a slender man in black seemed to be watching them. "Do you know him?" Ben asked her.

"I never saw him before."

"Maybe he just likes to look at pretty women."

She chose to ignore his compliment and asked instead, "Did I show you the telegraph messages from the various points upriver?"

"No. I'd like to see them."

She passed the forms across the table and he read automatically: *No steamboats passed north or south in last 24 hours. No sign here of River Ridge.* It was signed *Jenkins, Greenville*, dated that morning.

"He's our freight agent there," Stella explained.

"Can you trust him?" Ben asked, his eyes straying to the bar once more. The slender man was still watching them.

"He could hardly lie about something like that. Fifty or a hundred people would have seen it pass, even at night."

"Excuse me a moment, will you?" Ben said. "I want to see what that man's up to."

He rose and strode quickly across the plank floor to the bar. The man in black tried to avert his gaze. "I don't want trouble, mister."

"Then what are you watching us for? Who are you?"

"Name's Jericho Jones."

"Jericho—You're the fellow took a shot at a friend of mine on the *River Ridge* last year."

He didn't deny it. "Eddie Abilene. I should have finished him that day, but I guess it don't matter now. He's feeding the fishes."

"You know that for a fact?"

"The boat's at the bottom, and Abilene along with it. Don't take her money for a job you can't do."

"You work for her half brother, don't you?"

"What if I do?"

"Did he sink the *River Ridge*?"

"No, but none of us are sorry it's gone. And Abilene along with it."

Ben gave the man a shove and turned away. That was his mistake. "He's got a gun!" Stella shouted from across the room.

Ben whirled, his own weapon already in his hand, and fired at the flash of Jones's Derringer, throwing himself to one side as he did so. The slender man screamed in pain as Ben, off balance, hit the floor. He was starting to rise when the bartender said, "You're hit, mister. There's blood on your back."

Ben hesitated. He felt no pain, but gunshot wounds are like that at first. Stella Daren was bending over him now, and she said, "No, it's only paint. He's all right. The bullet missed him."

"Glad to hear that," Ben commented, getting to his feet. The bartender joined the others in ministering to Jones's bleeding hand.

"How did you do that?" she asked, as Ben led her away. "I'd heard you were good with a gun, but you shot that Derringer right out of his hand without even aiming."

"It's not as hard as it looks," he explained. "When there's no time to aim properly, you fire at what your eyes are focused on. When I turned I was looking at his gun hand, and that's what I hit."

They were out on the street now. "Amazing. Why did he try to shoot you?"

"Because your half brother Roddy wants me off the investigation—that's the most likely reason."

"Should we have stayed there until the police arrived? You did shoot the man, after all."

"I'm not used to your Eastern customs," Ben admitted. "Out West, after you've shot a man you walk away fast. He might have friends who want to pursue the quarrel."

The sun had begun to sink beyond the row of trees in the western sky, and as they walked Ben felt the tension of the gun battle start to leave him. His months in New Orleans, away from the frontier life further west, had dulled his reaction time, tensed his muscles. Perhaps, past forty, he was only beginning to feel his age.

Suddenly, in the twilight, a tall figure stepped out from a little alleyway and loomed before them. His sudden appearance made Ben reach for his gun. Stella gasped in recognition.

"Roddy! What are you doing here?"

Seen all at once in the fading light, Roddy Daren was an angular man with a smooth face like a boy's, the picture of innocence. "I came to see you," he explained, "as soon as I heard the *River Ridge* had disappeared. I thought you might need help. I didn't expect one of my men to be shot up by your hired gun."

"This is Ben Snow," Stella said. "Ben is helping me find the *River Ridge*, he's not a hired gun!"

"Helping you find her? Here? Why isn't he out on the river?"

"I've been on the river, Mr. Daren, but I think the place to find the *River Ridge* may be right back here. When we know who's behind this plot, we'll know what happened to her."

"Why'd you shoot my man?"

"Jericho Jones? He drew on me. Men don't do that around here. He's lucky I hit his hand."

They were interrupted by the sound of a steamboat whistle from the dock area. "It's the *River Ridge*!" Stella said.

Her half brother shook his head. "Only the *Carrollton Belle*, getting ready to move south. They want to make New Orleans by tomorrow noon."

"That'll take some traveling," Ben said. "It was a twenty-four-hour trip upstream."

"The current will help."

Something was bothering Ben. "Would Ulysses Harris still be at the River Commission office?" he asked Stella.

"I don't know. It's getting late."

"I'll be back," he promised, and set off at a fast pace.

The River Commission office was locked, as he'd feared, and he hurried to the nearby telegraph office.

"What can I do for you?" the clerk asked.

"I want to send a telegram to St. Louis and wait for a reply."

"Sure thing. It'll take a while though. Someday maybe we'll get one of them fancy long-distance telephone cables like they have back East. Then you can *talk* to St. Louis."

Ben quickly wrote his message. "Send this to the River Commission or the dockmaster or whoever's likely to be working at this time of night."

The man read Ben's brief written question. "*I* can answer this for you."

"Never mind—just send it."

"It's your money." The clerk shook his head and turned to the teletype.

Ben went outside just as the *Carrollton Belle* gave a final blast of her whistle and edged away from the dock.

He stood looking at his reflection in the glass window of the telegraph office.

South instead of north, the searcher had said. Maybe she sailed south instead of north.

South instead of north. Paint instead of blood.

He was running down toward the dock, toward the river launch they'd rented earlier in the day. Ulysses Harris was standing near the dock with a man wearing a sheriff's badge. "Come with me!" Ben shouted. "We have to overtake the *Carrollton Belle!*"

Harris frowned. "Are you saying you think the *Belle* sank the--"

"No," Ben said, hurrying them toward the launch, "the *Belle* didn't sink the *River Ridge*—she *is* the *River Ridge!*"

When Roy Fox appeared at the *Belle*'s railing with a shotgun, Ben shot him once in the shoulder. That was the only shot fired as they climbed aboard and took command of the vessel. Captain Botts stood sadly in the pilot house, offering no resistance.

Ben found Eddie Abilene playing solitaire in the ship's lounge. Eddie smiled a greeting. "Hello, Ben," he said. "You've come to rescue me."

"What made you think you could get away with such a crazy scheme?" Ben said.

"It wasn't crazy at all. Even with the steamboat trade falling off, this boat is still worth a small fortune. If we'd gotten as far as New Orleans, we could have outfitted her so no one would recognize her. I've got papers to prove she's the stern-wheeler *Oklawawa*, out of Silver Springs, Florida. Easy profit, with a steamboat of my own and nobody hurt."

"Nobody hurt? What about the string of accidents to remove key crew members so you could substitute your own people? What about the killing of Frank Beecher so you could take his place on board at the last minute?"

Eddie Abilene shrugged. "He wasn't supposed to get killed, Ben. That was an accident. What more can I say?" He lifted his head and glanced out the windows. "We're changing direction."

"Going back to Vicksburg under the authority of the Mississippi River Commission. You'll all face charges there, and in New Orleans."

Eddie looked unhappy. "Too late for a deal, Ben?"

"Too late, Eddie."

"How'd you catch on? What did we do wrong?"

"The *River Ridge* might have sunk, or it might have lost its way up some hidden tributary, but there was no evidence of either. There was no evidence of *anything*, and that was your first mistake. The telegram from Greenville said no steamboats had passed there in twenty-four hours, north *or* southbound. But the *Carrollton Belle* supposedly was heading south from St. Louis. The mystery of why the *River Ridge* never passed Greenville from the south was compounded by the mystery of why the *Belle* never passed from the north. Was there an explanation? I knew there was when I remembered a few things.

"The boats were sister ships, meaning they were about the same size and appearance. Stella Daren heard the *Belle*'s whistle and thought it was the *River Ridge*. And when I was in a fight earlier, someone thought there was blood on my back—but it was only paint. Later, I stared at my reflection in a window and tried to figure out how I could have gotten red paint on my back. Then I remembered the twin red stripes around the *Belle*'s hull and superstructure. I remembered leaning against the pilot-house wall. Those stripes were freshly painted, along with the name, to change the appearance of the *River Ridge*. You couldn't paint the whole hull while it was in the water, but you could manage it when it turned around upstream. You already had a different captain, mate, and other crewmen on board disguised as passengers, and they took over when the boat sailed back downstream as the *Carrollton Belle*. Tell me, what happened to the rest of the crew and passengers—the ones who weren't part of your gang?"

It took Eddie a long while to answer. Then he said, "They're locked up, tied and gagged, below. We figured they'd come around after a while. If they didn't—" he hesitated "—we planned to dump them in the swamp outside New Orleans."

"Dead or alive?"

He lifted his eyes to Ben. "Does it matter now?"

"I suppose not. You hid below deck all day yourself so you wouldn't be recognized. But I wonder why you stopped here at all—it was taking a chance."

"The boats always stop at Vicksburg. It would have been suspicious if we didn't. Fox was supposed to throw debris overboard upriver so it would look like we sank, but he forgot. He's a dreamer." He paused again and then asked, "How did you know I was involved, Ben?"

"I knew when I figured those accidents and beatings were caused to remove crew members and replace them with other men—when I remembered *you* were one of the replacements, for a gambler who rode the *River Ridge*."

"You should have come along, Ben. I'd have cut you in."

Moments later, as they neared the dock, Ben saw Stella Daren waiting. He was first down the gangplank and she greeted him with a yellow telegraph form. "What does this mean? It's for you and it says, *Carrollton Belle undergoing repairs at St. Louis dock.* Isn't this the—?"

"This is your *River Ridge*, Stella—seized by a clever gang of pirates and given a fresh painting of red stripes so it could pass for the *Belle*. I wired St. Louis when I became suspicious, but I couldn't wait for the reply. They were going to overhaul it in New Orleans and sail it under another name."

"My captain—"

"He was held prisoner below decks, with a few dozen other passengers and crew. They've been freed, and the sheriff has the pirates under arrest."

"I owe you my thanks in addition to your fee, Ben. You found the *River Ridge* for me!"

And I lost a friend, Ben thought. He glanced up at the gangplank as Eddie Abilene and the others were being led down. He started to wave but changed his mind.

BROTHERS ON THE BEACH

The temperature was in the mid-forties on the December day when Ben Snow stepped off the train at Elizabeth City and went about the business of renting a horse and buggy for the remainder of his journey to the shores of the Atlantic.

He often felt there was something contrary about his gradual journey east at a time when the nation had just about completed its western expansion. There were forty-five states now, stretching from coast to coast, and already there was talk that the territories of Oklahoma, New Mexico, and Arizona would soon be admitted to the Union. He'd fought Indians in the West in his younger days, and even journeyed to Mexico on occasion, but now it was the East that drew him. Cities like Buffalo and Savannah and New Orleans.

Rivers like the Mississippi and the Delaware had only been names on a rarely studied map when he was young. Now that he was past forty and the nation had entered the twentieth century, things were different. The West didn't need Indian fighters anymore, or hired guns whose draw was as fast as Billy the Kid's.

Ben Snow had never been a man to settle down as a ranch hand. He'd considered working for Pinkerton's, putting his crime-solving abilities to some use, but the detective agency's deep involvement in strike-breaking wasn't to his liking. So he drifted, taking jobs where he found them, helping out old friends when he could.

He'd never been as far east as North Carolina before, and he quickly noted that back here men didn't wear gun belts on the street in 1903. He left his in his suitcase while he dickered for the horse and buggy. "Kitty Hawk," he said to the man at the stable. "How far is it?"

"About thirty-five miles," the man answered. "You take the road east to Barco and then turn south along the coast. It's on a narrow cape that runs all the way down to Hatteras and beyond, but you can get a ferry to take you across. Why'd anyone want to go to Kitty Hawk in December, though? There's nothing there but a beach, and it's too damn cold for swimming. The wind beats across there like a gale most of the time."

"I have to see a man," Ben answered. "How much for the horse and buggy?"

They dickered a bit before Ben finally drove off in the buggy. He'd noticed a few automobiles—as people were starting to call them—on the streets of the city, but he hadn't felt brave enough to try one. Besides, he didn't know what sort of roads awaited him along the coastal sand spit.

It was shortly after he'd passed through Barco and headed south along the coast, getting his first view of the turbulent Atlantic, when a lone horseman overtook him. The man was young and handsome, with curly blond hair, and he sat well in the saddle. "Would you be Ben Snow?" he asked, drawing abreast of the buggy.

"That's me."

He leaned over to offer his hand. "Roderick Claymore. My brother Rudolph hired you, but he had to go to the state capital on business and he asked that I meet you."

They pulled up and Ben swung down from the buggy. "I'm a lot more comfortable on a horse," he admitted, "but with my suitcase, the buggy seemed best."

Claymore took out a cigar and offered Ben one. "How much did my brother tell you?"

"Only that he was hiring me to guard a section of beach at Kitty Hawk for the next week or so. He wanted someone from far away, and that's what he got. He hired me last week in St. Louis."

Roderick Claymore nodded, puffing on the thin cigar. "About three years ago, a pair of brothers from Dayton, the Wrights, started coming here and flying gliders off the dunes at Kitty Hawk. Seems they wrote the Weather Bureau and were told this was the best testing area for gliders because the winds off the ocean blow at a fairly constant twenty miles an hour or better."

"Does this glider testing bother you?"

"It didn't at first. No one paid much attention to them. But now things are changing. We own some land nearby and it's important that we don't have a lot of trespassers. They're planning something for Monday that could bring the whole country to our door."

"What would that be?"

"Last summer they started shipping in parts for a powered craft they've been constructing there on the beach. They built their own lightweight gasoline engine—four cylinders, watercooled."

"I don't know much about engines," Ben admitted.

"It's to drive two eight-foot wooden propellers mounted to the rear of the wings. This craft won't be a glider. It'll take off and fly by itself, with one of the Wrights aboard. That's why we need you."

Ben Snow smiled slightly. "To shoot it down?"

"Hardly."

"Back in '96, out West, there was a fellow billed himself as The Flying Man. He strapped wings to his arms and tried to glide off hilltops. Somebody killed him one day during an exhibition, and I helped solve the murder. I'm just telling you so you'll know which side of the fence I'm on. I've killed plenty of men in my day, but never one who didn't deserve it. I'm not a hired gun, despite what you and your brother might have heard."

"Look here, Snow, we don't want any hired guns. But if those crazy Wrights bring a thousand people to that beach to see their flight on Monday, we want them kept off our property any way that's necessary."

"All right," Ben agreed. "Where am I staying?"

"There's a lady teacher has a house in Kill Devil Hills, just a few miles from Kitty Hawk. We rented a room there for you."

"That'll be just fine."

It seemed ironic to Ben that he'd had to travel east to North Carolina to find the legendary pretty schoolmarm who was supposed to inhabit every Western town. Elizabeth Boyers was a dark-haired beauty, probably past thirty but with a fine girlish figure and a smile that could melt the coldest heart. She lived alone in the house across the street from the one-room school building where she taught.

"There aren't many children here," she admitted. "They're mostly from older families who've lived here all their lives. But someone has to teach them. If I left, they'd have to take the ferry to the mainland."

It was Sunday and they were strolling on the beach together, looking over the site where the Wrights would attempt their flight the following day.

"Do you think they'll make it?" he asked.

"Frankly, no. Not after what happened to Langley last Wednesday."

"Who's Langley?"

She laughed. "You don't keep up with the newspapers, Mr. Snow. Samuel Langley, the inventor, had a $50,000 grant from the War Department to develop a flying machine. He spent five years on it, and last Wednesday he tried to launch it from the roof of a houseboat on the Potomac River with boatloads of Washington reporters and government officials looking on. But a wing tip caught on its catapult and the craft broke apart in the air. Langley is secretary of the Smithsonian Institution. If he can't build a proper flying machine, these brothers from a bicycle shop in Dayton can hardly be expected to do it."

"Will there be reporters here tomorrow?"

"Not if the Wrights can help it. They're trying to keep it secret until the flight is successful. Then they'll send a telegram to their father asking that the press be notified."

"Then why is Claymore so worried?"

She hesitated before answering. "Who hired you—Roderick or Rudolph?"

"Rudolph. He's the older one, isn't he? He came to me in St. Louis and offered to pay my expenses and a week's salary if I'd come here to guard his beach. It seemed to me he could have hired someone from here in town for half the money."

"They do own some land down the beach. I've seen them digging there. I kidded them about looking for pirate treasure. These islands along the Atlantic coast have always had pirate legends connected with them."

"Why did you ask which one hired me?"

"Oh," she answered casually, "I've had a little trouble with the younger one, Roderick—the one who brought you here yesterday. I went out with him a few times last year and he asked me to marry him. I said no, but he won't accept that. Now I'm engaged to someone else and he's bothering me. I wouldn't have taken their money for the room if I didn't need it."

"What do they do for a living when they're not digging for buried treasure?"

"They have an ice business. They deliver blocks of ice to homes and businesses in all the towns around here."

"Never had anything like that out where I come from."

She smiled at him. "This is civilization. This is the twentieth century."

When they returned to the house after inspecting—at a distance—the Wright brothers' flying machine, Ben found Rudolph Claymore waiting for him. Rudolph was larger and tougher than his younger brother, and while Roderick sat well on a horse Ben couldn't imagine this man ever riding one. In St. Louis, where he'd hired Ben, Rudolph had seemed like a successful businessman. Here, in his home territory, there was something vaguely sinister about him.

"You saw that flying contraption of theirs?" he asked Ben.

Ben nodded. "Looks backwards to me. The tail seems to be in the front. But flying isn't my line."

"If we're in luck, they'll crash tomorrow like that fellow Langley did. But if it's successful and people start pouring in here, I'll need you to guard our beach property for the next week or so."

"Couldn't you have hired someone from one of the towns around here for that purpose?" Elizabeth said. "Why bring Mr. Snow all the way from St. Louis?"

"I want someone who'll be here today and gone tomorrow, not one of the town boys who'll have a few drinks at the bar and get to talking too much. Mr.

Snow's got a good reputation out West. When I asked around for someone to hire, he was the one everyone mentioned."

Claymore took Ben aside and gave him a down payment on his fee, along with the travel expenses. "You brought your gun, didn't you?"

"I have it," Ben assured him.

"Wear it tomorrow, but keep it under your coat."

When he'd gone, Ben asked Elizabeth, "What do you think is so valuable about that strip of sand?"

"Besides the pirate treasure?" she answered with a smile. "I have no idea."

Ben slept restlessly that night, wondering what the morning would bring. What it brought was more of the same as far as the weather was concerned. A cool breeze was blowing off the ocean and he found he needed the wool jacket he'd brought with him from the Midwest. He buckled his gun belt under it, making certain all chambers of the Colt six-shooter were loaded. He wondered vaguely if there were laws back East against carrying concealed weapons. Maybe that's why the Claymore brothers had wanted someone from far away.

"Are you up, Mr. Snow?" Elizabeth called to him through the bedroom door.

"Sure am. I'll be right down."

"Breakfast is ready. My fiancé, Mark Freen, is joining us."

Freen was an agreeable chap with brown hair and a ready smile. Like Elizabeth, he was a teacher, though his school was on the mainland. "I'm playing hooky today," he explained. "We both are. This might be an historic occasion—right here at Kitty Hawk."

Ben was surprised to see that a fair crowd of local residents had gathered along the beach. "Those are the Wright brothers," Elizabeth said, pointing out two men in caps and jackets. They seemed to be in their thirties. "Orville and Wilbur."

"Do you know them personally?"

"I've spoken with them. They've been here since September assembling the *Flyer*. That's the name of it. And last year they made over a thousand controlled glider flights here. Everyone knows them by now."

They were interrupted by the arrival of an older man with thick glasses and a beard. "Oh, Professor—I want you to meet Ben Snow!" Elizabeth Boyers performed the introductions as if they were both her oldest friends. "Ben, this is Professor Minder from the university at Raleigh."

Ben shook hands and asked, "Did you come all this distance for today's flight?"

"Not exactly," the professor replied. "I'm doing research just south of here, on Roanoke Island. You may remember it was the site of Sir Walter Raleigh's Lost Colony."

Ben nodded and turned up his collar against the chill wind. "I hope they get started soon. It's cold out here."

The *Flyer* had been pulled from its storage shed by the Wrights and five assistants. Ben heard someone in the crowd comment that it weighed over six hundred pounds. They positioned it on a level stretch of sand at the base of a hundred-foot-high dune named Kill Devil Hill. Then the brothers flipped a coin and Wilbur won the toss. After the *Flyer* had been placed aboard a low trolley on the single sixty-foot rail of a greased launching track, he climbed aboard and lay face down in a cradlelike harness across the lower wing, working the wing and rudder controls with his body in a final check before takeoff.

The crowd tensed and Ben glanced around for some sign of the Claymores. There were figures farther down the beach, but he couldn't tell who they were. His attention returned to the *Flyer* as the gasoline engine sputtered into life. The twin propellers started to turn and the machine glided down its greased track. There was the beginning of a roar from the crowd and cameras poised to capture the moment of flight.

Then, unaccountably, the engine stalled at takeoff. The *Flyer* dropped to the sand with a soft thud.

As the crowd groaned, Orville rushed forward to pull his brother from the craft. "It's over," Elizabeth said sadly. "It'll never fly."

"Another Langley," Mark Freen said, summing it all up.

Wilbur stood up, free of the craft, and the brothers began inspecting the damage. Ben turned and noticed Professor Minder sitting on the sand. "Excitement too much for you?" he asked in fun, bending down to offer his hand.

That was when he saw the knife protruding from Minder's back and realized the man he'd just met had been murdered.

The investigation of a murder case was far different in the East than anything Ben had known out West. There, a sheriff bothered little with clues or suspects. There he looked for eyewitnesses or the person with the likeliest motive, and if justice came at all it was usually swift and deadly. On that windswept beach in North Carolina, while the Wrights worked to repair their damaged aircraft, justice was slow and plodding. Justice was a pair of State Police officers with notebooks, taking down names and addresses and setting up a camera to take a photograph of the murder scene.

There was general agreement among all witnesses that the brothers Wright couldn't have had a hand in the killing, since all eyes were on them during the entire period. But that did little to narrow the field of suspects. Any one of the dozens of spectators could have been the guilty party, and in the eyes of the State Police that included Ben Snow.

"Private citizens don't wear gun belts in North Carolina," one of them told him pointedly. "This isn't the wild West."

"Tell that to the dead man," Ben replied.

The officer's name was Rellens, and he eyed Ben as if he'd like to lock him away in a cell. "What are you doing here, anyway?"

"I was hired by the Claymore brothers to guard their strip of beach land. They feared some of the crowd might wander down that way."

"So you're guarding it from up here?"

"I can see it from here. I can see no one's on it."

"Were the Claymores here today?"

"I didn't see them."

"Pretty strange if they missed something like this," Rellens said.

Ben had been thinking the same thing as his eyes traveled over the spectators. Some had started to drift away, but the majority had stayed after giving their names, drawn by the twin spectacles of the murder investigation and the Wrights' efforts to repair their flying machine.

Then he saw Rudolph Claymore striding over the dunes in their direction. He left Rellens and went to meet his employer. "What happened here?" Rudolph demanded. "I just got word there's been a killing—"

"That's right," Ben said. "A professor named Minder."

"Minder! I know the man! He's been working on an island nearby!"

"Someone stabbed him."

"Is my brother here?"

"I haven't seen him all morning."

"He didn't come to work today and I assumed he was down here. I had to cover the entire ice route myself." Rudolph Claymore glanced along the windswept beach. "What about our property?"

"No one's gone near it," Ben assured him.

"Not Minder, before he was killed?"

"Not unless it was early this morning before I got here. You didn't say anything about guarding it day and night."

"No, no. I just thought you might have noticed him wandering down that way."

"I think it's about time you tell me what this is all about," Ben said. "I might be able to help the investigation if I knew all the facts."

"All right," Claymore agreed. "Come to my house tonight. I'll have my brother there, too, if I can find him. Here's the address. It's in the village of Kitty Hawk."

Elizabeth and Freen had been over by the damaged aircraft and were hurrying back. "Orville says the repairs will take a few days, but they hope to try again on Thursday," she said. "Will you be staying that long, Mr. Snow?"

"I expect so. The Claymores hired me for the week."

"I saw that policeman, Rellens, talking to you. Did he ask for your help?"

"Not exactly."

"Does he have any suspects?"

"Right now I may be his prime suspect. He noticed I was wearing a gun belt."

"That's absurd! We were all standing together."

"But Professor Minder was right behind us. With all eyes on the Wrights and their machine, I suppose I could have reached around and stabbed him. Someone did."

"But why? He was a sweet old man. Why would anyone kill him?"

"What do you know about him? What was he doing here?"

"Mark knows more about him than I do. He went over to see him on Roanoke Island a few weeks ago."

"He was studying evidence of the so-called Lost Colony," Freen explained. "You know, the colony founded by Sir Walter Raleigh that vanished from that island between 1587 and 1590."

Ben's knowledge of early colonial history was vague at best, but he nodded and urged Freen to continue.

"Well, a colony of some eighty-five men and women remained on the island in 1587 while a ship returned to England for supplies. The war between England and Spain prevented the supplies from reaching Roanoke until 1590, and by that time all that could be found was a deserted, ransacked fortress. None of the settlers was ever found. The name *Croatoan* was carved into a post—apparently the name of an island to the south. They may have gone there, or they may have been killed by Indians. It's one of the mysteries of history."

"And Professor Minder thought he'd found new evidence of what happened," Elizabeth Boyers interjected. "He was over here a few times pursuing his studies."

"Interesting," Ben admitted. "But why should anyone kill him? Why would something that happened over three hundred years ago cost a man his life?"

They returned to the house without an answer. Later that afternoon, while Elizabeth and Freen were alone, Ben walked back up the beach. From a distance he watched the Wright brothers and their helpers working on the flying machine. He saw that Rellens was still there, too, pacing back and forth as he examined the trampled sand.

That evening Ben Snow rode over to the address Claymore had given him It was one of a handful of houses in the tiny village of Kitty Hawk, and Rudolph came out onto the porch to greet him as he parked his buggy. "Come in, Snow. My brother's already here."

Ben entered and took a chair in the sparsely furnished parlor. A woman's touch was obviously lacking and it occurred to him for the first time that the elder Claymore was probably not married. He shook hands with Roderick and said, "I didn't see you this morning."

"I had business," Roderick answered. "I hear the flying machine never got off the ground."

"They're repairing it. They plan to try again on Thursday."

Rudolph came in and sat down. "Some of the folks around here are helping them. We got more important things on our minds."

"Tell me about it," Ben suggested. "Tell me why that property of yours is so valuable. Is there really pirate treasure buried there?"

The older brother smiled slightly. "Next best thing, according to Professor Minder. You know about the Lost Colony and that business on Roanoke Island?"

"A little."

"Well, historians have always speculated that the colonists went south to another island, if they weren't killed by Indians. Minder went there and nosed around. He decided they came north instead, right here to the beach at Kitty Hawk. Look at this here map. You can see that the abandoned Fort Raleigh was at the very northern tip of Roanoke, not ten miles across the water from where we are now."

"Minder told you this?"

"Damned right!" Roderick said. "He did a little digging by our property there and came up with evidence of settlement!"

Rudolph showed Ben a bowl with a piece missing from it. "See this? It's not Indian. It's the sort the colonists brought with them from England."

"But you were keeping this a secret?" Ben asked.

"Had to! Other people own some of that beach land, especially near the village here. We started buying it up. An old settlement like that could mean a spot people would pay to see. It could make us rich."

"Who knew about this?" Ben asked.

"Only the two of us and Minder. That's why I went so far away to hire a guard. I didn't want any of the locals getting wind of what we were trying to hide."

"How much land have you bought?"

"Around twenty thousand dollars' worth so far. Minder agreed to act as a middleman so the people wouldn't know we were the buyers."

"And that's what you've been digging for?" Ben asked.

Rudolph nodded. "We uncovered some more things on our own, too—a few trinkets and a sword."

Roderick scratched at his cheek. "We'd better check on those land deeds in the morning. With Minder dead, we could be out twenty grand."

"I've already thought of that," his brother answered sourly.

Ben left them going over their records, trying to establish the extent of their possible losses.

On Tuesday afternoon, the State Police officer, Rellens, showed up at the Boyers house to see Ben. He sat down heavily and flipped open his notebook. "This case has taken a couple of surprising turns," he said. "I need to interview witnesses again, especially those who were standing closest to the victim."

"Miss Boyers is teaching today," Ben told him.

"You'll do for a beginning. It seems one of the men in that crowd of spectators gave a false name and address. Dick Roer, of Kill Devil Hills. No such person."

"You think you let the murderer walk away?"

"Looks like it," he said glumly. "I seem to remember him vaguely. Had a Teddy Roosevelt mustache and was wearing a wool cap. Of course, the mustache could have been a fake. Do you remember anyone looking like that near you?"

"No," Ben answered honestly. "But I wasn't concentrating on the crowd."

"All right." Rellens closed his notebook, preparing to leave.

"You said the case had taken a couple of surprising turns. What else?"

"The dead man—Minder. It turns out he was a fake, too. There's no Professor Minder connected with any of the universities in Raleigh."

"Interesting," Ben admitted. "Two men with false identities on the beach yesterday—one a murderer and one a victim."

"It looks that way," Rellens nodded.

"But why was Minder using a false name? Who was he?"

"We'll find out," Rellens promised. "You'll be here for the next few days, Mr. Snow?"

"At least till after Thursday's flight."

"That's good," Rellens said and was gone.

On Wednesday Ben Snow sought out Rudolph Claymore on his ice route. He found him lugging fifty-pound blocks into a little cafe in Kill Devil Hills. "I wanted to ask you about your brother," he said

"He's back at the ice house. You can find him there."

"He was in love with Elizabeth Boyers, wasn't he?"

"Still is, far as I know. But she's sappy over that teacher, Mark Freen. It hit my brother hard."

"Ever hear of someone named Dick Roer around here?"

"Can't say that I have."

"Rellens thinks that was the name the killer used on Monday."

"Never heard of him." Claymore climbed into the back of his wagon and used an ice pick to loosen another fifty-pound block.

"That looks like hard work."

Rudolph shrugged. "It's a living." He flipped the pick into the next block in line. "It pays the bills till something big like that Lost Colony comes along."

"What if the Lost Colony never happens? What if Professor Minder was a fraud?"

Rudolph Claymore blinked and stared at Ben. "What are you saying?"

"Have you and your brother checked on that property yet?"

"He's doing it today."

"I wish you luck," Ben said and started to walk away.

"Wait a minute!" Claymore said, hurrying after him. "What are you trying to tell me?"

"That Minder was a fraud. That wasn't his real name, and chances are those trinkets in the sand were put there by him so you'd find them. Out West we call it salting a mine—putting a few gold nuggets near the surface for the suckers to find."

"But the property—"

"If he was trying to swindle someone, it must have been you. He probably took your twenty thousand and faked some papers, without ever buying the land."

"That—"

Ben left him standing by his ice wagon, still swearing.

The younger Claymore was a bit more difficult to track down. He was gone from the ice house by the time Ben reached it and he had to stop at a couple of nearby bars before he spotted Roderick's horse tethered outside the village stable. He found the young man inside, seeing to the repair of one of his saddle stirrups.

"I had a talk with your brother this morning," Ben told him. "Could I have a few words with you outside?"

Roderick shrugged. "I suppose so. You going to be on guard at the beach again tomorrow?"

"I'll be there. But when you hear what I have to say, you may decide you don't need me." Ben told him quickly what he'd told his brother, about Professor Minder's false identity and the probable swindle. Roderick's reaction wasn't quite as violent as his brother's, but it was obvious he was upset.

"I always wondered about that guy. He didn't seem right for a professor."

"Have you checked on the deeds yet?"

"I was on my way there now."

"There's something else," Ben said.

"What's that?"

"The police think Minder's killer is a man named Dick Roer."

The color drained from Roderick's face.

"That's you, isn't it? Dick Roer is a simple anagram for Roderick."

"I don't know what you mean."

"You were on the beach Monday morning, wearing a wool cap and a false mustache. You killed Professor Minder."

"I didn't! That's not true!"

"Why else would you be there in disguise?"

"That's none of your business. We hired you to guard our property, not to snoop around."

"If you don't answer me, you'll have to answer to the police."

He glowered and started to walk away, then thought better of it. "All right —if you must know. I wanted to see Elizabeth!"

"See her?"

"With him. With that Freen fellow. I wanted to hear what they were talking about."

"You disguised yourself to spy on Elizabeth Boyers?"

"Yes." His voice had dropped and he wouldn't meet Ben's eyes. "I love her."

"You can't accept the fact that she might find pleasure with another man?"

"I just wanted to hear what they talked about, to see for myself if she really cared for him. That's all. I barely realized Minder was there."

"All right," Ben said, not knowing whether he believed him or not. "Will you be there in the morning?"

"Yes," Roderick answered.

"In disguise?"

"There's no point in it now, is there?"

Thursday morning dawned clear but freezing cold. When Ben reached the beach at Kitty Hawk in the company of Mark Freen and Elizabeth, they were saying the wind off the ocean was blowing at twenty-seven miles an hour. The few spectators were bundled against the cold and some were doubting the Wright brothers would attempt the flight.

But shortly after nine a.m., Wilbur and Orville gathered up their five assistants and once more hauled the machine from its shed. It was lifted onto the trolley at the base of Kill Devil Hill.

In addition to Elizabeth and Freen, who'd taken off another day from their teaching, both Claymore brothers were in attendance. And Ben saw Rellens pacing nearby. The cast was assembled.

Rudolph came up to stand next to Ben. "What did you say to my brother yesterday? Whatever it was, he's been pretty upset by it. He didn't even want to come out here today."

"I notice he's staying clear of Elizabeth Boyers."

"Well, they used to go together. I suppose he's jealous of her friend."

It seemed to take the Wrights forever to make their adjustments to the *Flyer*, and the cold wind drove a few of the less hardy souls away. Orville was busy setting up the tripod for his camera, then aiming it at the end of the launching track. If the plane became airborne, he wanted a picture for the ages.

Finally, at 10:30, they were ready.

It was young Orville's turn to be at the controls this time and he glanced around for someone to snap the shutter of his camera. He called to one of the townspeople who'd been helping out and asked him to take the picture if the plane became airborne. Then he climbed aboard the *Flyer* and strapped himself down. Wilbur pulled the cap down more snugly on his head and gripped the lower right wing tip of the biplane.

The engine started and the propellers began to turn. The *Flyer* moved on its track. Wilbur began trotting alongside, holding the wing tip steady.

"He didn't do that on Monday," Rudolph Claymore remarked.

And then Orville opened the throttle more, bringing the engine to full power. The time was 10:35.

"No, he didn't," Ben Snow agreed. "But how did you know if you weren't here?"

The *Flyer* lifted from its track, airborne. Wilbur released the wing as the camera shutter clicked. A cheer went up from the small group of spectators.

The machine wobbled and swooped down, its runner hitting the sand. The flight had lasted only twelve seconds, never more than ten feet off the ground, but it had covered 120 feet.

People were running forward. Rudolph Claymore started to move, but Ben restrained him. "You knew what happened on Monday because you were here. Because you came to murder the man who'd swindled you."

"You think I was this Dick Roer?"

"No, that was your brother, spying on Elizabeth."

"But everyone else in the crowd was accounted for!"

"You never joined the crowd, Rudolph. You hid behind a sand dune, and while all eyes were on the Wrights at the crucial moment, you sneaked up just close enough to *throw* that knife into Minder's back, just like you flipped that ice pick into the cake of ice yesterday. You never came closer than fifteen or twenty feet, and the sand was too trampled to show footprints. No one saw you because we were all looking in the opposite direction."

"But I didn't know he was a swindler until you told me yesterday!" Rudolph argued.

"You put on a very good act, but I think you knew. When your brother met me, he said you'd gone to the state capital on business. That's Raleigh, where Minder claimed to teach. You checked on him while you were there and discovered he was a fake. You came back here and killed him the first chance you had."

Rellens had been overhearing the conversation and now he stepped forward. "Do you have anything to say, Mr. Claymore?"

The fight had gone out of Rudolph. "Only that he deserved to die for swindling us. No jury will convict me."

B en Snow left town the following morning. The Claymores' land didn't need protection any longer and he never heard what the jury decided. For that matter, it was a few years before he heard the Wright brothers mentioned again. They made four successful flights that December 17th at Kitty Hawk, and their father spread the news, but only two newspapers in the country carried a report the following day.

No crowds came to Kitty Hawk. The Claymores hadn't needed Ben Snow after all.

THE 500 HOURS OF DR. WISDOM

The business at Waycliff Station came very early in Ben Snow's career, at a time when his reputation as a fast draw with a gun often led people to confuse him with that other boyish gunman, Billy the Kid. Billy had been dead two years by the time Ben rode into Waycliff Station on that November afternoon in 1883, but news traveled slowly in the western territories in those days. After all, it had taken more than a week for the news of Custer's massacre at the Little Big Horn to reach Washington in '76, and that was a far bigger story than the shooting of Billy the Kid.

So perhaps it was not surprising in those days that people confused the 24-year-old Ben Snow with Billy—though in a place like Waycliff Station it hardly mattered, because the five hundred residents led a life almost completely cut off from the outside world. Even the train that came through at noon every day, prepared to stop if it was flagged down, brought little contact with Eastern civilization.

It was the sort of sleepy Western town that Ben Snow liked, one where his growing reputation as a gunfighter wouldn't matter, where perhaps he could find a few weeks of peace before moving on.

The few score houses and stores were clustered around the railroad tracks, and when Ben rode into town on his horse, Oats, there were some children playing in the streets. "Which way's the boarding house?" he asked one—a sandy-haired boy, who eyed his pistols and asked, "You a gunfighter, mister?"

"No, just a traveler."

"Seen any Injuns?"

"Nary a one."

"You can stay at Mrs. Jester's place," one of the older boys volunteered. "The white house at the end of the street."

"Thanks."

Ben rode on, taking note of the saloon and the blacksmith's shop, the only establishments he was likely to need during his stay at Waycliff Station. Mrs. Jester's house proved to be a neat-looking place with a fenced-in front yard. There was a small sign in one window: *Rooms by day or week.* He tied Oats to the hitching post out front and went inside.

Mrs. Jester was a slim, middle-aged lady with a ready smile. "We don't get many strangers in Waycliff Station," she told Ben. "How long you fixin' to stay?"

"A week or two maybe. I been drivin' cattle up from Texas and I need a bit of a rest."

"You won't find no wild goings-on around here, if that's what you're hankerin' for."

"Nothing wild," he assured her. "Just some peace and quiet."

"All right, you can bed down in the room at the top of the stairs. Here's the key. It'll be five dollars a week, meals included."

"Seems fair enough." He hefted his saddlebags and started up the stairs.

"Cash in advance. Since my husband died, I gotta be a business-woman."

"Sure." Ben handed over some silver dollars, smiling, finding her attractive for a woman probably in her forties.

"Dr. Wisdom's in town tonight, so we'll be eating early."

Ben paused on the bottom step. "Dr. Wisdom?"

"He comes through with his medicine show about once a month—does a little magic and then sells his tonics and stuff. He's got a girl named Katie traveling with him now."

"I'd like to see it," Ben said, deciding it was probably the most he could expect in terms of local entertainment.

The upstairs room was pleasant and flowery, with a fancy spread on the bed. He hung his duster in the wardrobe and glanced out the window. There was a good view looking down the town's main street toward the railroad tracks at the far end. A pleasant little place, he decided. A good place to relax.

It was starting to get dark as the townsfolk gathered around the wagon just down the street from Mrs. Jester's boarding house. Ben stood at the edge of the crowd, marveling at the cheers that greeted the appearance of a slender, bearded man with deep dark eyes.

"Good evening, folks," he began. "It's always a pleasure for me and Katie to visit in Waycliff Station. I've brought you some new wonders this month— and one of them is the biggest wonder you're ever likely to see. I'm selling you something better than all the patent medicines ever made, something more valuable than money. But first let me introduce my gorgeous assistant, Katie!"

Katie stepped from the back of the wagon and stood at his side. She was a pretty redhead dressed in spangled tights that seemed somehow shocking on the dusty street. One of the men standing nearest her immediately made a grab for her leg, but she fended him off with a smile and a firm hand. Then, while Dr. Wisdom continued his patter, she moved from one corner of the wagon to another, lighting torches with magical ease until the area was bathed in firelight. The spectators moved in a bit closer, as if the flames offered protection from the night.

Dr. Wisdom and Katie put on a little show for the next fifteen minutes, running through a series of simple magic tricks with cards and silver dollars. Ben had seen better in the cities, but this wasn't bad for a town out in the middle of nowhere. When they'd finished, he figured a sales pitch for Wisdom's tonics and nostrums would come next, but Dr. Wisdom was selling something quite a bit different.

"This month, my good friends, I'm selling *time*—the most important commodity in the world! Out here you might wonder what's so important or valuable about it, when one day's pretty much the same as another. But let me tell you, time is the greatest tonic of them all. And I assure you this is no trick. I'm prepared to sell you extra time, by the hour or by the day—time that will not be part of the calendar or the clock. If you buy a day or a week or a month from me, it will not count toward your lifetime. You may do with it what you will, and at the end of the period the time outside Waycliff Station will resume as if nothing had happened. Time—and life—in the rest of the world will have remained frozen while you do what you will with those extra hours."

A stout man in the front row of spectators spoke up. "Come on now, Doc, you're kidding us! You expect us to swallow that hogwash?"

"Not without proof, Sheriff Spofford. I sure don't want to get run in for false advertising. That's why I've prepared a little demonstration. I have five hundred hours for sale tonight, enough to sell one hour each to every resident of Waycliff Station. You'll experience it for yourselves. I will sell these individual hours for the modest sum on one dollar each, as a demonstration."

There was a stirring in the crowd, and Mrs. Jester spoke up. "If we buy one, when do we get our hour?"

"November eighteenth, at noon. That's the day after tomorrow."

"It's Sunday!" someone said. "Nothing ever happens on Sundays anyhow."

Dr. Wisdom smiled. "Something will happen this Sunday. There'll be twenty-five hours in the day for them that buys an extra one."

"What'll we do with an extra hour on a Sunday?" Mrs. Jester wondered.

"Have a picnic," the sheriff suggested. "We'll shut down the town and have ourselves a picnic."

"Too cold for a picnic," another voice chimed in.

And then a tall man in a top hat stepped forward. Ben hadn't noticed him before. His clothes seemed completely out of place for the little town, as if he'd gotten off the train at the wrong station. Ben edged through the crowd to Mrs. Jester's side and asked, "Who's that?"

"Felix Bowles, the town banker. Got more money than he knows what to do with."

Bowles had taken center stage in the little torchlit drama, holding up his hands for silence. "If this man can do what he says, it will be truly amazing. I, for one, am willing to pay for an extra hour on Sunday. And I'll put up the money for everyone in Waycliff Station—all five hundred dollars!"

A cheer went up from the crowd, and Wisdom and the banker shook hands. Ben decided his stay in the town might turn out to be more interesting than he'd expected.

That night in the saloon there was much conversation about Dr. Wisdom and his bizarre offer. Some thought he was downright crazy, but the barkeeper, a muscular young man named Matt Audrey, figured it wasn't costing them anything to find out.

"If old Bowles wants to waste five hundred bucks, I figure we should let him," he said.

"Has Wisdom ever proposed anything like this before?" Ben wondered.

"No, he's been content to sell his snake oil till now."

"That's a cute little gal he travels with. They married?"

Matt Audrey shrugged. "They're gettin' to it. She turned up a few months back and has been with him ever since. I guess he hits all the small towns in this part of the territory. Everything west of Dodge City."

"What are you going to do Sunday during your extra hour?"

"I'd like to open up the bar and give everybody a free drink, but the minister would never stand for that."

Ben paid for his drink and wandered outside. There was an autumn chill in the air, with a breeze sweeping down from the distant mountains. But the sky was clear and he could see stars everywhere. On the way back to Mrs. Jester's, he passed Dr. Wisdom's wagon. There were voices inside, but they were too faint for him to understand the words.

In the morning, he and Oats took a ride around town, stopping at the blacksmith's to have a shoe repaired. It was just before noon when they reached the railroad tracks and Ben saw Dr. Wisdom's woman Katie standing there as if waiting for the train. "Going somewhere?" he asked.

She smiled at him and tugged the Mexican shawl around her shoulders. "No, just out for a stroll."

"Do you get an extra hour tomorrow, too, or just the townsfolk?"

She studied him before she replied, perhaps weighing the amount of sarcasm in his question. Finally she decided to ignore it completely and ask one of her own. "You're new here, aren't you? I don't remember seeing you before."

"I'm just a cowhand resting between cattle drives. Name's Ben Snow."

"Funny thing—you wear those pistols like a gunfighter."

"I've been told that before."

In the distance they could see the approaching train. It slowed when the engineer saw them, but Katie shook her head and waved it on. "Right on time," she observed. "High noon."

"Don't they even have a station here?"

"Just this little shed for waiting. You flag down the train if you want it and buy your ticket on board. They can't afford to pay a stationmaster in a town this small."

"Do you and Doc Wisdom ever go anywhere on a train?"

"No, it's just the wagon for us. Someday, though—someday he's goin' to hit it big."

"Maybe tomorrow."

She glanced at him. "Maybe."

That evening Sheriff Spofford came to visit Ben at the boarding house. It was just after dinner and Ben was relaxing on the front porch before the night air turned cool. "Mr. Ben Snow," the sheriff greeted him. "That right?"

"That's me."

"Glad to have you stayin' here for a few weeks. Anything special bring you to this part of the territory?"

"Just seemed like a peaceful place," Ben told him.

"See, we aim to keep it that way." Spofford hitched up his gun belt. "We gotta be extra careful because there's no telegraph line through here yet. If we had a decent train station, the railroad would have supplied one, but we ain't. So we don't hear about all the crime and bank robberies and such. Unless the train stops to let someone off, we don't hear much of anything."

"Sometimes that's best."

"Sure, sometimes. But I got me to thinkin' about that extra hour tomorrow noon. Maybe some stranger might use it to try robbin' Mr. Bowles's bank."

Ben merely smiled at him. "I didn't notice any strangers around today."

The sheriff's hand brushed lightly against the butt of his gun. "Well, you keep your eyes open, Mr. Snow. If you see anything suspicious, you just let me know. And I'll sure as hell keep my eyes open, too."

On Sunday morning after breakfast, Mrs. Jester asked, "You goin' over to church?" She was dressed surprisingly flashy in a bright red dress.

Ben hadn't thought about it, but he could see it was the thing to do. "I guess I will," he decided.

"Then take off your guns. No one wears guns to church."

He grinned at her. "You remind me of my mother."

The minister was a dour-looking man around fifty, with eyes that were cold as gun metal. Mrs. Jester introduced him to Ben as the Reverend Dixon. He was new to the town, Ben gathered, but his sermon left no doubt as to his willingness to speak out on issues.

"You foolish people—you are children of God but you allow yourselves to be seduced by a serpent. And what does he promise you? Eternal life? Freedom from disease? Worldly wealth? No, he promises you nothing but an extra hour in the day, as if he could stop the sun and moon! And for that you would sell your souls. Beware—beware my children of God! Satan does not come amongst us with horns or hoofs! No, he comes today in a wagonload of promises!"

Neither Dr. Wisdom nor Katie was in the church, and when the services were over there was no sign of them on the street outside. It was nearly noon already and the townspeople were more interested in them than in what Reverend Dixon had said.

"How will we know?" one woman asked. "Will the clocks all stop?"

Felix Bowles, the banker, was leaving church and he answered her. "The train, dear lady. The noon train is due in seven minutes and it's never late unless the weather is bad."

And so they waited. Everyone waited. Even Reverend Dixon came out to wait with them.

"It's noon," Matt Audrey, the barkeep, said at last.

No train came.

"Your watch is fast," someone said.

But they waited another five minutes and still no train came.

Finally people began drifting home. Some of them commented on how still the air was. Ben Snow walked up to Reverend Dixon and asked, "What do you think? Is it a miracle?"

"More likely the devil's work."

As Ben walked away, he noticed the sheriff standing in the shadow of the blacksmith's shop, watching him.

By some unspoken agreement, the people of Waycliff Station began gathering near the railroad tracks as the next hour approached. Ben lingered a bit behind them, like the outsider he was. He glanced at the sunlit front of the blacksmith's shop but Sheriff Spofford was now nowhere to be seen.

"Here she comes!" Felix Bowles shouted as a little puff of smoke appeared on the horizon. It was indeed the noon train, running exactly one hour late by every clock in Waycliff Station.

As the train slowed and the engineer waved, several people shouted, "What time is it?"

"Twelve o'clock!" he yelled back. "We're right on schedule."

"He did it," Mrs. Jester said, a touch of awe in her voice. "He really did it. We had a whole extra hour and nobody did anything with it."

Ben smiled to himself as he walked back down the dusty street. The saloon was open now and business was brisk. People wanted to talk about what had happened, to analyze and explain it. But he had other things on his mind. When he reached Dr. Wisdom's wagon he glanced about to make sure no one was watching, then lifted the back flap and ducked inside. He had only the vaguest notion of what he was searching for, but within five minutes he'd found it. Hidden away under the bedding was a week-old Dodge City newspaper with the banner headline: RAILROAD TYRANNY!

He skimmed quickly through the article and stuffed the paper under his shirt. Then he slipped out of the wagon and headed back toward the boarding house. He was almost there when he saw Dr. Wisdom walking down the center of the street toward him. Wisdom must have seen him come out of the wagon.

Ben continued on, walking slowly. The scene reminded him of countless gunfights he'd seen on the streets of Western towns, except that he wasn't armed and he certainly hoped Wisdom wasn't. When they were about twenty feet apart, Wisdom said, "What were you doin' in my wagon, mister?"

"Catching up on my newspaper reading," Ben replied, watching the man's hands for any sudden movement.

Wisdom started to respond, his face flushed with anger, when the sound of a single shot cut the afternoon air. Ben crouched defensively as Wisdom grabbed at his chest and went down.

No second shot followed. The street was empty. Ben ran to the man and turned him over. He was dead. The bullet had gone through his heart.

"Stay right there, Snow!" a voice shouted. "Move and you're a dead man!"

He looked up to see Sheriff Spofford coming out of the alley by the blacksmith's shop. He had a six-gun aimed at Ben's head.

"You can *see* I didn't kill him," Ben protested. "I don't have a gun on me!"

Spofford had taken him to the sheriff's office next to the church, marching him down the dusty street at gunpoint while others came to remove the body. The only visible grief at Dr. Wisdom's death came from Katie, who ran out of the saloon to sob over his fallen body. Others came to stare, but they said nothing. Instead they eyed Ben as if already certain of his guilt.

"I know all about gunfighters," the sheriff told him. "You carry those little Derringers up your sleeve or in your boot."

"Go ahead, search me."

"Don't worry, I will."

But when the search yielded no gun, Spofford wasn't ready to give up. "You might have dropped it someplace, or passed it to that gal when she came running out of the saloon."

"Sheriff, I heard the shot that killed him. It sounded like the crack of a carbine to me."

"I don't know about that. You were standin' there in the street with him, and it sure looked to me like you shot him."

"Why? Because I'm a stranger?"

The sheriff squinted through half-closed eyes. "I got an old Wanted poster for Billy the Kid. Looks something like you."

"News travels slow to Waycliff Station. Billy the Kid is dead."

"So they say." Spofford thought about it another minute and then shifted tactics. "What's this newspaper I found inside your shirt? Where'd it come from?"

"Dodge City, originally. I'd just found it in Wisdom's wagon. If you read it, you'll find out what happened with that extra hour."

"This is about the railroads," the sheriff said, picking up the newspaper.

"Exactly. Today at noon, New York time, the American railroads created four new time zones, replacing the fifty regional time zones that covered the states and territories. Some places gained time, other places lost it—anywhere from a few seconds to an hour or more. There's a great debate about whether or not people should allow the railroads to dictate their time, but apparently most places plan to go along with it. You can see from the map they printed that Waycliff Station gained an hour's time."

Spofford squinted at Ben. "What could Wisdom hope to gain by making us think it was part of his magic? We'd have learned the truth before long. It's a wonder someone didn't know it already."

"The town has no telegraph, Sheriff, it has a reputation for being cut off from everything. But Wisdom wasn't taking any chances. He had Katie down at the tracks yesterday noon, just in case the train dropped off an announcement of some sort."

"Got any ideas who killed him?"

"You know *I* didn't, so turn me loose."

Spofford thought about it. "The slug that killed Wisdom came out his back, at a lower position than the entrance wound. So he was probably shot from above, and probably with something more powerful than a Derringer or even a six-shooter. I guess I could take a chance that you're innocent. But if you try anything funny, remember I'll be watchin'."

W hen Ben walked into the saloon a few minutes later, Matt Audrey set up drinks on the bar. "Good work, Snow! We all heard how you got the best of that swindler!"

"I didn't kill him."

"No matter. You exposed him and now he's dead. The town thinks you're a hero."

Ben shook his head. "I'm no hero."

Audrey started to say more, but Ben caught a glimpse of Wisdom's girl Katie slipping out the back door. He decided any investigation had to start with her. He found her with one of the wagon horses, unhitched and saddled. "Going somewhere?" he asked.

She turned cold eyes on him. "You're the one who killed Artie."

"Was that his name?"

"Artie Wilcox. The Dr. Wisdom was just for show."

"I guess most people figured as much. But I didn't kill him."

"I don't care. I loved him—he was going to marry me. I suppose I knew he'd end up dead in the street somewhere. Men like Artie don't die in bed."

"He was a swindler, wasn't he? A con man?"

"Sure. But he put together a pretty fair act. All that magic stuff with the torches, and the card tricks. He taught me a lot. But I begged him to forget that damned wagon and just put together an act for dance halls." She tightened a strap on the saddle angrily. "But he had to be on the move. I don't think he was happy unless he was out in the open air, giving his pitch and talking as many townsfolk as he could out of their money."

"What about this railroad business with the time zones?"

"It was another one of his schemes. We were in Dodge City a week ago when he saw the newspaper story about what the railroads planned to do. He figured it would be a great trick to find a little place that didn't know about the time change and con the people into believing he could sell them extra hours. We'd both been here to Waycliff Station before and we agreed it was the perfect place. Sometimes I think the folks around here don't even know Garfield was assassinated two years ago!"

"But Wisdom didn't sell those five hundred hours—he gave them away. Or at least the banker was going to pay the whole thing."

"That was just to convince the folks he could do it. He was working his con on one person—I don't know who—and there was a lot of money involved. He was supposed to collect the money this afternoon and we'd be gone before anyone realized about the new time zones."

"You're heading out now?" he asked as she climbed into the saddle. The wagon horse seemed uncomfortable with the bit in its mouth.

"I sure am. I don't want that narrow-eyed sheriff deciding I was an accomplice to any swindle and slappin' me in jail." She paused with her hand on the reins. "How come *you* knew about the railroads changing the time? Did you read it somewhere?"

"Not until I found that Dodge City newspaper in your wagon. But if Wisdom really was doing something supernatural, making time stand still for an hour, you'd expect the sun would stand still, too. When I passed the blacksmith's shop shortly after Wisdom's magic hour began, I saw Sheriff Spofford standing in its shadow. Later in the hour, the sun was hitting the front of the same shop. I figured if the sun's position was different, that meant time hadn't stopped at all. That's when I decided to take a look in your wagon."

She nodded. "Congratulations. I'll be on my way."

But before she could spur the horse on, Sheriff Spofford appeared again, blocking the mouth of the alley. "You ain't goin' anywhere just yet, Miss."

"Out of my way!" she shouted, and guided the horse as if she meant to run him down. Spofford's arm shot up and grabbed the reins with one hand, pulling her from the saddle with the other. She fought him, but he was much too strong for her. Ben could have gone to her aid, though he knew the sheriff wouldn't hesitate to use his gun if pressed. He decided to do nothing for the moment.

"Sorry, little lady, but no one leaves town till we get to the bottom of this shootin'."

"I didn't kill him!"

"I just heard you tellin' Snow about a plot to swindle someone."

"But I don't know who!"

"Maybe the swindle worked and you're lightin' out with the money."

"You can search me if you think that!"

"Maybe I will."

"Sheriff—"

"Stay outta this, Snow! I'll get Mrs. Jester to help me."

They trooped down to the boarding house and Mrs. Jester was given the task of searching Katie while the sheriff went through her saddlebags. They found nothing except clothing and a few small possessions. The only money was a little more than five dollars in her pocket.

"I didn't want anything of Artie's," she told them. "I'm not a thief. The only thing I was taking was the horse. I figured I could get to another town and sell it for some extra money."

"You'd better just stay around here another day," the sheriff told her.

She was wrapped in one of Mrs. Jester's robes while the landlady finished inspecting her clothing, finally reporting, "There's no money except that five dollars. I guess she's telling the truth." She dumped Katie's clothes unceremoniously at her feet. It was then Ben's eye caught something amidst the small pile of her possessions. She had a few items of makeup, probably for her part in Wisdom's act, that she carried in a cloth bag. The rough bleached cloth reminded Ben of the sort of bag banks used to store and ship silver dollars and other coins. He picked it up and turned it over. On the other side was printed WAYCLIFF STATION BANK.

"What's that?" the sheriff asked.

"My makeup," Katie replied.

Ben looked at her. "Where'd you get the bag?"

"From the bank, one time when I was here before."

"Felix Bowles gave it to you?"

"The banker, yes, I guess that's his name."

Ben nodded. "The banker's the only one in this town with enough money to interest a con man. And we already know Bowles was gullible where Dr. Wisdom was concerned."

"You're right," Spofford agreed. "Let's go talk with Mr. Bowles."

The banker was at his home on the edge of town when Ben and the sheriff reached it. He greeted them in a parlor more suited to a home back East, where muddy boots were not likely to track across the oriental rugs. "What can I do for you fellows?" he asked, eyeing Ben with some distaste.

Before the sheriff could speak, Ben said quickly, "We understand you gave Dr. Wisdom a large sum of money."

The banker flushed slightly. "I didn't *give* him the money. It was more of an investment. He had a couple of ideas that interested me."

"Like selling you extra time?" Ben speculated. "Enabling you to make a killing on the stock exchange?"

Felix Bowles seemed to sag visibly. "I suppose there's no harm in telling it now that he's dead. He explained it all in great detail, how the new time zones imposed by the railroads had so confused the nation that it might be possible to make a profit on the New York Stock Exchange. A mining company was about to announce a large gold strike near Salt Lake City. Once the strike was confirmed, Wisdom thought he could use the extra hour to telegraph an order to a New York broker to buy shares in the stock before the market closed that day."

"There's no telegraph in Waycliff Station," the sheriff pointed out.

"That's why he needed my money to take back to Dodge City. He did this business with the extra hour as a demonstration, to prove that a whole town could be fooled by the time change."

"How much did you give him?"

"Ten thousand dollars," the banker croaked. "Did you find it on him?"

"No," Sheriff Spofford replied.

"It must be in his wagon."

"I've already searched the wagon."

"That girl—"

"I had her searched, too." The sheriff paused and asked, "Mr. Bowles, why didn't you come forward and report this matter as soon as you learned of Wisdom's shooting?"

"I didn't want my wife to know. She's upstairs, ill. She's always said I was foolish with money—"

"You'd simply abandon that much money?"

"I planned to come see you about it later."

Unless he was just a gullible fool, Ben could see that his story didn't hold water. Deceiving five hundred people in a town cut off from civilization as to the time of day was a great deal different from fooling people in cities like Salt Lake or Dodge, linked by telegraph with the East Coast. Maybe he hadn't worried about the ten thousand dollars because he'd already retrieved it after he shot Wisdom for swindling him.

But Ben kept his thoughts to himself. When they left the banker's home, Spofford said only, "It looks like whoever shot Wisdom might have done us all a favor."

"Maybe," Ben agreed.

When the sheriff returned to his office, Ben went back to the boarding house. He unlocked the door to his room and went inside with a feeling of dissatisfaction. Trouble seemed to follow him like a restless hawk waiting to pounce, and he knew he should be moving on before something else happened. Waycliff Station hadn't been quite as peaceful as he'd hoped.

He buckled on his gunbelt and got his long lightweight duster out of the wardrobe. A breeze was coming up and he'd need it riding across the arid plains. Then he picked up his saddlebags and was packing the rest of his gear when he felt something small and hard in the duster pocket.

It was a cartridge case, too small for his Colt .45s—more the size for rifle or carbine bullets.

A noise from the street attracted him to the window. Nearly at the spot where Wisdom had died, the Reverend Dixon had intercepted Katie leading her horse. He was shouting something at her and she looked as if she needed help. Ben left his duster and the saddlebags on the bed and ran downstairs.

As he reached them, Katie was shouting, "That's not true! He was going to marry me next week in Dodge City! You worry so much about sin and your town's full of it! What about the person who murdered Artie?"

The minister, red-faced and fuming, told her, "Get out of my town, you sinful woman!"

"That's just what I'm trying to do—the sheriff won't let me!"

Dixon was pulling her by one arm when Ben grabbed him. "Let her go, Reverend. Spofford's given her enough trouble already."

"Who told you to interfere? You're a stranger here."

"I'm only trying to—" Ben's words were cut off by a sudden glint of sunlight on metal, glimpsed from the corner of his right eye. His reflexes took over and he whirled, pulling the .45 from his holster as he thumbed the hammer and fired up at the window of his own room.

Katie screamed and then he was running back toward the boarding house, through the front door, and up the stairs.

She was lying there by the window, wearing his duster that was now soaked with her blood. The carbine was beside her on the floor.

"Mrs. Jester," he said, trying to lift her.

"Never mind." There was blood in her mouth. "I killed him. And I wanted to kill her, too. I wasn't after you. He was goin' to marry her. After all his promises, he was goin' to marry her."

"I'll get help," he told her, turning to see Sheriff Spofford enter the room.

"Don't bother. It'll save the cost of a trial," Spofford said.

Ben stared at him. They managed to get her on the bed, but she died five minutes later.

It was the saloon keeper, Matt Audrey, who expressed the town's opinion to Ben Snow after the sheriff had refused to press charges in the shooting. "You killed Mrs. Jester," he said. "There never was a more popular woman in Waycliff Station than Mrs. Jester."

"I know," Ben said, "and I'm sorry she's dead. If I'd have known it was her in that window, maybe I wouldn't have fired so quickly."

"Who'd you think it was?"

"I didn't think. I only say the glint of sunlight on that rifle barrel sticking out my window. Of course I noticed the good view of the street the first day I was up there, and again just before the shooting today. The sheriff told me Wisdom was shot from above, but I didn't connect it with my room till I found a cartridge case in the pocket of my duster. She wore that both times over her red dress so she wouldn't be spotted in the window. Then she dropped the ejected cartridge into the pocket and forgot about it. Once I realized the killer had used my room, I should have known it had to be Mrs. Jester. I kept my door locked and she was the only one likely to have a duplicate key."

"Don't matter what she did," Audrey told him. "You shouldn't have shot her. If she killed Wisdom, she was a hero—like I thought you were, earlier."

"Her motive was more down-to-earth. Wisdom had been romancing her on his previous monthly visits. He even convinced her that Katie was only part of the act and meant nothing to him. Then he told her on Saturday that he was getting married. She went up to my room after church this noon and shot him in the street, just at his moment of triumph when you all thought he'd succeeded in stopping time. She was trying to kill Katie, too, when I shot her."

But Matt Audrey and the others didn't want to hear it. They only wanted him gone.

H e rode out of town with Katie. When they had gone for perhaps two miles, he told her, "Your horse is still having trouble with that bit. Maybe I should take a look at it."

"You don't have to," she said quickly, but Ben was already out of the saddle, prying open the horse's mouth. There was a small package wrapped in oilskin and attached to the bit.

"Well, what's this?"

"Damn you!" she shouted. "That's mine!"

"More likely it's Felix Bowles's missing money. That was quite a trick, getting the horse to keep it in its mouth while you were searched. I figured if you had the empty sack, you had the money too, somewhere."

"What are you going to do?" she asked.

"Let's talk about it while we ride," said Ben as he climbed back in his saddle.

THE TRAIL OF THE BELLS

Ben Snow had been on the trail for two days before he found the dying man by the water hole. He drew his horse Oats up slowly, right hand resting on the butt of his pistol, aware that he might be riding into a trap. But then he saw the bloody bandage across the man's chest and recognized him as Tommy Gonzolas, the half-Mexican gunman who'd ridden with Poder since the beginning. His horse grazed on the sparse grass nearby.

Ben still approached slowly, even after he knew Gonzolas was dying. Although the desert terrain allowed little cover for a rifleman, he knew that Poder wouldn't be above the ruthlessness of baiting a trap with a dying man. "Are you armed?" he asked Gonzolas. "Throw me your gun."

The man barely lifted his head, and the hands that clutched at his chest made no movement toward the pistol that lay on the sand a foot away. Ben stepped quickly forward and kicked the weapon out of reach. Then he stooped to examine the wound.

"I'm dying," Gonzolas said quite clearly. He'd been wounded during the bank robbery back in Tosco, and the only reason Ben Snow had taken on the job of tracking Poder through the desert was the belief that the serious wound might slow down the fugitives. But Poder had left the man to die beside a water hole with his gun and ridden on without him.

"Tell me about Poder," Ben asked the man. "Where's he headed? What does he look like without his mask?"

Gonzolas tried to laugh, but his mouth was filling with blood. "You'll never get Poder," he managed to gasp. "Nobody will."

"Come on, Gonzolas, he left you to die. You owe him nothing."

But it was too late. The Mexican's head lolled to one side and his eyes closed. For an instant it seemed he was dead. Then, as Ben started to straighten up, Gonzolas uttered his last words. "The bells," he said. "Listen for the bells and you will find Poder. Or Poder will find you."

Whether the words were meant to help or to lead Ben to his death, Ben didn't know. But the bells were the only lead he had, and after pausing long enough to bury Tommy Gonzolas at the water hole and unsaddle and set free his horse, he rode on in search of them.

It was the following day that he came upon the girl with the dead horse. She was dressed in denim pants and a man's shirt, but even from a distance there was no doubt about her sex. She held her head high and proud, with long dark hair hanging halfway down her back, and the rifle in her hands was warning enough that she was not to be tampered with. Still, with no towns or trails in sight, Ben felt an obligation to offer assistance. As he drew nearer, he was glad he had. The dead horse on the ground at her feet fitted closely the description of the pinto that Poder had ridden out of Tosco.

She lowered her rifle as he approached on horseback. "I thought at first it was him coming back," she said.

"Who? What happened here?"

"Masked man stole my horse."

Ben dismounted and went over to inspect the dead horse. It had been killed by a shot through the head at close range. "What did he look like?"

"I told you he was wearing a mask—a cloth bag that covered his head, with holes for his eyes. He was short, about my height, and he knew how to handle a gun."

"What are you doing out here alone?"

She started to raise the rifle again. "Who wants to know?"

Ben smiled, stepped up to the weapon, and pushed the barrel gently aside. "The man who stole your horse is known as Poder, and Poder never would have left you with a loaded rifle to shoot him in the back as he rode away. He took the bullets, didn't he?"

"You seem to know everything, Mr. —"

"Snow. Ben Snow."

She seemed to relax a little, as if knowing his name made him more acceptable. "I'm Amy Forrest. My brother and I have a small ranch in the valley about forty miles from here. I was looking for strays—"

"In the desert?"

"Sometimes they come this far, especially the young ones that don't know any better. There are some water holes nearby."

"I saw one yesterday."

"Anyway, I heard a shot and rode over this way. When the man saw me coming, he pulled that hood over his head and drew a gun on me. Said his horse twisted a leg and he had to shoot it, and he was taking mine. He emptied the bullets out of my rifle, just as you guessed, and left me here. I wish I'd seen his face."

"If you had, you'd have been a dead woman. That masked man who calls himself Poder has never been seen by anyone. He's robbed banks and stage-coaches all over the New Mexico territory. Generally he doesn't even speak.

A sidekick named Tommy Gonzolas did the talking for him. But Gonzolas is dead now."

"How come you know so much about him?"

"He killed a banker in Tosco a few days ago. I happened to be in town and they hired me to go after him—sort of a one-man posse."

"What makes you so good?"

He smiled at her. "They got some crazy notion I'm Billy the Kid."

"He's dead."

"Don't tell them. They're paying me well to bring back Poder, dead or alive."

"Does he have a first name?"

"He doesn't have any name, far as I know. *Poder* means 'power' in Spanish. It's just an alias he started using. Nobody knows a thing about him. Nobody but Gonzolas ever saw his face, and now he's dead.

"I guess I'm lucky to be alive. Can you get me back to my ranch? It's due north of here."

He stared out at the stark landscape, searching for a clue as to the direction Poder might have taken. "I don't know. I was figuring more on heading west. If you plot the locations of Poder's robberies on a map, they seem to be centered west of here. But my horse could carry us both as far as the next settlement and I could drop you there."

"Well, that's something."

He climbed into the saddle and helped her up behind him, surprised at her quick agility.

They'd barely started their trek when he thought he heard something far in the distance. Something that sounded like bells. "What's that?" he asked her.

She listened, cocking her head to the left. "You mean the bells? That's the mission at San Bernardino. It's only a few miles from here. Is that where you'll take me?"

"I think so," Ben decided. "Yes."

The mission came into view at the top of the next rise, and Ben judged it to be about five or six miles from the spot where Poder had stolen Amy Forrest's horse. He rode down the last dune slowly until he reached firmer ground, then urged his horse forward through the scattering of cactus and sagebrush. The mission itself sat in a small oasis and consisted of a white adobe church with a long, low building at the back. Amy explained that this was a monastery of the religious order that staffed the mission and raised what crops they could. "There are only a few priests. The rest are lay brothers who work in the fields. And there are Indians and Mexicans who have a sort of trading post outside the mission."

"You sound as if you know the place well," Ben said.

"I usually stop whenever I ride this way. Women aren't allowed into the monastery, of course, but I like the peacefulness of the church. It always seems cool there, even on a hot day."

He watched several dozen people emerging from the church. "What's going on?"

"It's a Sunday morning. They've been to Mass."

"I forgot. Out here the days get to be the same."

"They have just the one Mass at ten o'clock, and that's the only time the bells ring all week. It's a wonder we heard them at all."

"Perhaps we were being called here," Ben murmured . . .

They dismounted near a paddock where the horses were kept and Amy ran to the railing. "That's King!" she pointed. "That's my horse!"

"The big brown one?"

"I'm certain of it!"

Ben spoke to an Indian standing nearby who seemed to be in charge of the paddock area.

"You there—what's your name?"

"Standing Elk. I am a Pueblo."

"All right, Standing Elk. Did you see who brought that big brown stallion in?"

"No, I do not know him." The Indian wore a suit of fringed buckskin, with a headband but no feathers. He was shorter than Ben and seemed younger.

"You saw no one ride in here about—how long ago, Amy?"

"An hour or so. He stole my horse an hour before you came along. Of course, he might have ridden faster than we did."

"I see no one," Standing Elk insisted.

"All right," Ben said. "Come on, Amy. We'll worry about your horse later."

A priest in Sunday vestments was standing outside the mission church, keeping carefully within the shadow cast by the mission's bell tower. He was young and fair-haired and Ben imagined his skin would burn quickly in the heat of the New Mexico desert.

"Good morning," he greeted Ben. "Welcome to the Mission of San Bernardino. And how are you today, Amy?"

"I'm fine now, Father. This is Ben Snow, Father Angeles."

The priest bowed his head in greeting and Ben noticed for the first time the cowl protruding from the back of his vestments. "I'm sorry you're late for

Mass, Ben. We have only the one service here, at ten o'clock. There is also a weekday Mass every morning."

"Ben rescued me from the desert, Father. A gunman stole my horse."

"A gunman? Near here?"

"We think he rode this way, Father," Ben told him. "He's a killer and bank robber known as Poder."

"Power," the priest translated automatically. "I have not heard of him." He turned to Amy. "But, my dear child, you must be exhausted after such an experience—come inside and let Mrs. Rodriguez tend to you."

Amy started to protest but Father Angeles insisted. Ben followed along until Amy had been delivered into the hands of a fat Mexican woman with a motherly look. Then he waited while the priest reverently shed his vestments and put them away.

"This is a lovely place to find in the middle of the desert," Ben said. "I don't know these parts as well as I should."

"Where are you from?" Father Angeles asked, brushing the sandy hair back from his forehead.

"The Midwest, originally. But I've been roaming for years now. I guess I don't really have a home." As they passed along a cloistered walkway leading to the monastery, he asked, "How many of you live here?"

"Father Reynolds, Father Canzas, and I. There are only five lay brothers at present, along with a few people to help us out. Mrs. Rodriguez cooks the meals, Luis rings the bells on Sunday, Standing Elk tends to the horses, and Pedro Valdez runs the trading post. The others are passers-by who stop to see us when they're in the neighborhood. Like Amy."

A monk with a boyish face came through the monastery door and Father Angeles stopped to introduce him. "Brother Abraham, this is Ben Snow, a traveler who has paused to rest with us."

Brother Abraham bowed slightly as the priest had done. "A pleasure to have you here. I hope your stay will be a pleasant one."

"I'm sure it will be," Ben told him and the monk continued on his way.

"Abraham," Ben said. "An Old Testament name."

"A presidential name," Father Angeles corrected. "The babies named after Lincoln have come of age now."

"Do you have any trouble with the Indians around here?"

"Nothing since Geronimo surrendered last September. The Apaches were a bother at times, but they seem at peace now. The Pueblos have always been our friends. Large numbers have converted to Christianity, though they cling tenaciously to their ancient rites."

He showed Ben through the monastery with its stark cell-like rooms. "It's almost like a prison," Ben observed.

"In a way, although the spirit is free. The lay brothers like Abraham toil in the fields, and often we're at their sides. One of us says Mass each morning, and generally all of the Indians and Mexicans at the trading post attend."

"A great many Mexicans," Ben observed.

"The border isn't that far from here."

"Do you know a man named Tommy Gonzolas? He would be half Mexican."

"I believe he's been here from time to time. Why do you ask? Are you searching for him?"

"I've already found him."

As they returned to the mission church, they passed beneath a large crucifix and Father Angeles crossed himself. "You wear your pistol like a gunfighter, Mr. Snow. I hope no harm has come to Tommy Gonzolas."

"The harm had already been done when I found him, Father. I buried him out on the desert."

"May God have mercy on his soul."

"He was a bank robber and murderer, Father. He rode with the man called Poder, whom I've come to find."

"The person who stole Amy Forrest's horse."

"The same one."

"I know nothing of him."

"Was anyone away from the mission this week?"

"There is no way to tell. As I have said, they come and go. Standing Elk might know better than I do—he tends to the horses."

"Yes. I'll have to talk with him again."

The mission food was slight but tasty, and Mrs. Rodriguez seemed to take special pride in cooking for them. Ben was only sorry Amy couldn't join them at the table, but the woman served her a special lunch in the kitchen. Only one of the five lay brothers was Mexican, and since he spoke no English Father Canzas conversed with him in Spanish. The third priest, Father Reynolds, had been a Civil War cavalry officer who'd come west to fight Indians and found God instead.

"I decided it was more important to save their souls than kill their bodies," he said. "But you would have been too young to remember the war."

"I was six when it ended," Ben said. "I'm twenty-eight now."

"You look older—or more mature, I should say. And riding in the sun has weathered your face."

Brother Abraham sat across the table from him, between Brother Franklin and Brother Rudolph. None of them were especially talkative but Abraham seemed the quietest. Ben wondered what his story was.

After lunch Father Canzas walked out to the trading post with Ben and introduced him to Pedro Valdez, a handsome moustached man who ran the place with a group of half-breed assistants. He joked with Father Canzas, and the fat priest seemed to enjoy what had obviously become a friendly ritual between them. "You are a friend of the Father's?" he asked Ben. "A new friend, surely, or he would have fattened you up to his size by now."

After more casual conversation, Ben asked, "Do you know a half breed named Tommy Gonzolas who often comes here?"

"I know him, yes. I know many people."

"He died recently and I'm trying to get word to his close friends. He told me he had a friend at the mission here."

Valdez lit a thin Mexican cigarillo. "You were with him when he died?"

"I was, yes."

"I know nothing about it. He talked with the others, but had no special friends."

Ben remembered the dead horse. "Who around here might ride a pinto?"

"Mottled or spotted horses are common out here, where wild herds still roam and interbreed. Standing Elk must have a half dozen pintos in his corral right now."

Ben sighed. "I only want to give a message to the friend of Tommy Gonzolas. You're not much help."

Father Canzas had drifted away, looking over some of the blankets and trinkets offered for sale by the Indians. It was a meager trade at best, Ben decided, with only a handful of people even knowing of the place's existence—the mission of San Bernardino was not exactly on the regular wagon routes. He wondered if its very remoteness was the reason Poder came here.

"I'm looking for a man named Poder," Ben said finally. "Do you know him?"

Valdez smiled and his eyes seemed to twinkle. "The people of Tosco have hired you to capture him. Yes, Mr. Snow, the word has reached here already. An Indian told me just this morning that Billy the Kid was riding to capture Poder, or to kill him. But you're much too tall for Billy. He was short like me. And besides, he's dead. He's buried over in Fort Sumner, not far from here, where Pat Garrett dropped him with two bullets at his girlfriend's house." Valdez studied the burning tip of his cigarillo. "Billy should have taken General Lew Wallace's offer of amnesty if he left the New Mexico territory. He met with Wallace, you know, but he refused the offer."

"Is there a message here for me?" Ben wondered. "Should I get out while I can, too?"

The Mexican shrugged. "Where do you think you might find Poder? Do you think it is fat Father Canzas who rides with the mask over his face? Or one of those Indian children playing in the dust? Do you really care?"

"I've come a long way."

"We have all come a long way, Mr. Snow." Valdez turned away as a loud dispute erupted among the children. He shouted something at them in Spanish and they fell silent. Ben turned and headed toward the corral.

There were over twenty horses penned up, but no sign of Standing Elk. Perhaps he, too, had gone to lunch. Ben wandered back toward the mission and noticed one of the monks hurrying along the cloister. His hood was up and there was no way of identifying him, but there was something about his movements that attracted Ben's attention. He was moving too fast, almost running.

Ben boosted himself over the low cloister wall and followed in the direction the monk had taken. He knew it led to the monastery itself, and as he stepped through the doorway he was aware he was entering forbidden territory. There was no Father Angeles with him now, giving him a tour.

The shadows were deep here, with only an occasional hint of the afternoon sun outside. He moved along the passageway, past the empty rooms where the lay brothers slept. Once he thought he heard a footstep behind him and whirled, his hand on his gun, but there was no one. He seemed to be alone in the building.

Then he rounded a corner and froze.

Straight ahead was a wooden partition, with spiraling bars like a grillwork. A man's arms extended between the bars and then hung down, as if he had been caught in the instant of escape.

It was the Indian, Standing Elk, and he was dead.

Father Reynolds was the first to arrive on the scene in response to Ben's shouts, and he administered the last rites to the dead man. "There's blood," he said as he finished.

"He's been stabbed."

Father Angeles arrived then, with Brother Franklin. "What's happened here?"

"Standing Elk has been murdered," Ben said. "I should have guessed it would happen."

"You can't blame yourself," Father Angeles said.

"My coming here was the cause of it. Poder killed him before he could tell me who rode here on Amy Forrest's horse."

"I cannot believe this person you seek is hiding here," Father Reynolds said.

"There's the evidence of it," Ben said, pointing to the body.

"If the body is here," Brother Franklin said, "does that mean one of us killed him?"

Ben shook his head. "If Standing Elk could enter this building, so could any other Indian or Mexican. Dressed in one of your robes with the hood up, who would know the difference?"

"There is no sheriff within a hundred miles," Father Angeles said. "What shall we do?"

"Bury him. I'll report it when I return to Tosco. You certainly can't leave the body above ground in this heat."

"We must have a Funeral Mass," the priest said, rubbing his sandy hair. "But we have no method of embalming here. He must be buried soon."

The Funeral Mass was held late that afternoon, with Father Angeles officiating. While the mission bells tolled mournfully, the people of the oasis filed into the church for the second time that day. Ben sat near the rear of the church with Amy Forrest, watching the ancient rituals. When the priest had finished, another Pueblo, Running Fox, came forward to add some beads and bracelets to the plain wooden coffin Pedro Valdez and his assistants had fashioned.

After it was over, after Ben and Amy had stood with the others in the little graveyard behind the mission, he studied the faces of the departing mourners. But if one was the face of Poder, there was no sign of it. Ben asked Father Canzas if he had a map of the territory. "There's one in our library," the fat priest answered.

He showed Ben and Amy to a book-filled room near the cloister and left them. On a map Ben measured the distance from the mission to the sites of Poder's crimes as well as he could remember them. As he worked, Brother Abraham came in to watch over his shoulder. "What are you doing?"

Ben glanced up from his task. "The man I seek, who probably murdered Standing Elk, committed a crime at each of these sites. All are within three days' ride of this mission."

The monk nodded silently, and after a time he left. Ben asked Amy, "Do you know anything about him? He seems a bit strange."

"Just that they say his parents were killed by Apaches when he was ten and he's been here ever since."

Ben returned to the map and she wandered over to the bookcases. "They have quite a library here. Melville, Victor Hugo, Dickens, Hawthorne. There's even a copy of *Ben Hur*, the novel by our territorial governor."

"I'm surprised they'd have Hugo. I heard once that the Church doesn't approve of his novels."

"I don't suppose anyone sees it but the priests and brothers. Most of the Indians and Mexicans probably don't read English."

"Do you think that's why Poder rarely speaks?" Ben asked. "Because his English is limited?"

"I had the same idea when you said this Gonzolas person usually did the talking. I wondered if it was because Poder's English was poor."

"But he talked to you when he stole your horse."

"Just a few words, and they were muffled by his mask."

"There is one other explanation of why he rarely spoke," Ben said quietly. It was something that had been hovering at the back of his mind all day. "Do you have your rifle handy?"

"I brought it into the kitchen when we arrived. It's probably still there."

"Let's go get it."

She seemed puzzled by his request but she went along with it. They found the rifle standing in a corner while Mrs. Rodriguez worked on the evening meal. "We eat soon," she said. "Do not go far away."

"Just outside," Ben assured her.

They walked into the courtyard by the cloister and Ben pointed the weapon toward the sky. "I was saying there was one other explanation of why he rarely spoke. Poder could be a woman."

"I—"

"You might have been riding toward the mission when your horse twisted its leg. You had to shoot him, and when I happened along you feared I might recognize that pinto as Poder's. So you made up the story of his stealing your horse."

"Do you really believe that?"

"There's one way of testing it. If your story was false, then he didn't empty your rifle at all. It should still be loaded now." He squeezed the trigger.

There was a loud crack as the weapon fired toward the sky.

A my Forrest stood her ground, staring at him. Neither of them moved for a full minute. Then she said, "I bought some cartridges from Valdez this afternoon and reloaded it. You can ask him if you don't believe me."

He lowered the rifle. "I believe you."

"Poder isn't a woman. It was a man's voice that spoke to me." She turned and went into the house.

Ben stood there for a moment, looking after her. Then he turned and walked out toward the trading post. There were few people around and he went to sit by himself in the shade of a large cactus, drawing letters in the sand.

Presently Father Angeles joined him. "I heard a shot," the priest said. "And I saw Amy. She's very upset."

"It's logical," Ben told him. "She killed Standing Elk not because he saw who rode into the corral this morning, but because he knew no one rode into the corral. He would know she lied."

"Logic is not always the same as truth," the priest said. "If Poder is really here, it is not that young woman."

Ben raised his eyes to stare at him. "You know the truth, don't you, Father? Poder had confessed to you."

"He had not, but of course I could not tell you even if he had." His eyes strayed to the letters Ben had traced in the sand. "What is this?"

"*Poder* and *Pedro* have the same letters. One is an anagram of the other."

"So you have a new suspect in place of Amy."

"Is Valdez the only Pedro here?"

"Yes. But go slowly this time, Ben."

The priest left him as Mrs. Rodriguez summoned them to dinner. But as Ben got to his feet and smoothed over the sand in front of him, he remembered one of the books in the mission library. His education was far from complete, but he had read the classics as a boy in the Midwest. Perhaps part of the answer was in that book.

A sudden movement among the cloisters caught his eye and he saw again the hurrying monk he'd been pursuing when he came upon Standing Elk's body. He broke into a run, intent on catching him this time. The man had been spying on him, and that could mean it was the one he sought.

"Stop!" Ben shouted as the cowled figure pulled open the door of the monastery. His fingers reached out, grasping the back of the hood and pulling it off just as the monk was about to disappear through the entrance. And as the figure turned around toward him, he saw what he'd hoped and feared.

There was no face. There was only a cloth mask with holes cut in it for the eyes.

"Poder! We meet at last!"

From beneath the folds of the cloak a pistol appeared. Ben grabbed it, wrestling at close quarters to keep it from pointing at him. There was a shot as a bullet tore past his head, and he relaxed his grip for just an instant. Too close to aim again, Poder swung the gun hard against Ben's temple.

Dazzling lights and a searing pain cut across his head and he felt himself falling. He clawed at the hooded face before him, managing to catch a finger in one of the eyeholes. As he went down, he pulled the mask with him, praying that with his dying breath he would at least see the face of his killer.

And then he saw it—the face of Poder.

It was the face of a man he had never seen before.

As his vision cleared and he returned to consciousness, Ben recognized Amy and Father Angeles kneeling by him. "Who was it?" Amy asked. "Who hit you?"

"Poder."

"Did you see his face?"

"Yes." He tried to stand up. His head hurt, but otherwise he seemed all right. His pistol was still in its holster. "I have to go after him."

"He'll kill you," Amy said.

"He didn't just now."

"We came running and frightened him away."

Ben leaned against the wall to steady himself and then took a few steps. He was all right. He could do it now. "You two stay here," he said.

"Do you know where he is?" Father Angeles asked.

"I know."

He left them and went to the church. Once inside, he found a ladder leading the way up and began climbing. He kept climbing until he reached the top of the bell tower, some fifty feet above the ground.

Poder was waiting for him, standing behind the two mission bells with his back to the sky.

"I knew you'd come up here," Ben said. "Luis is your name, isn't it? I remember Father Angeles telling me this morning, 'Luis rings the bells on Sunday.' I thought I saw everyone at Standing Elk's funeral, but of course I didn't see you because you were ringing the bells then, too."

"You should have stayed away," Poder said. "You shouldn't have come up here."

"I was hired to bring you back."

"Gonzolas told you, didn't he? I was afraid someone might find him before he died, but I couldn't bring myself to kill him."

"He said to listen for the bells and I would find you. I didn't take it quite as literally as I should have. I thought he only meant you were here at the mission. But your mistake was in stealing Amy Forrest's horse."

"I had to take it."

"I know. Your time was running out. You must have had a moment of panic when your pinto twisted his leg and came up lame. But then you saw her, and took her horse. When I thought about it, I asked myself why. You were only five miles from the mission—certainly not a long walk for a man capable of robbing stagecoaches and banks. Why risk showing yourself, even masked, and then leaving the witness alive?"

"I have never killed a woman."

"But why risk it all when you could have walked the distance in eighty or ninety minutes? Why—unless you had to be back at the mission for some Sunday morning duty? I asked myself what that duty might be. There was the Mass at ten o'clock, of course. Could Poder be one of the mission's three priests? No, because they said Mass daily and Poder had been gone all week, riding three days to Tosco and three days back. He'd been away that long, or nearly that long, before. So he couldn't be a priest, nor one of the lay brothers who worked daily in the fields. Nor Mrs. Rodriguez, who prepared all their meals. But the Indians and Mexicans came and went at will, and certainly wouldn't be missed at Sunday Mass. Only one person was free the rest of the week, to the best of my knowledge, but had Sunday morning duties—Luis, who rang the bells on Sunday. If those bells didn't ring at ten o'clock, people would ask where Luis was."

Poder shifted slightly and Ben saw the pistol in his hand. He stepped a bit to his right, putting the bells between them. "Draw!" Poder said. "The time for talking is over."

But Ben kept on talking. "I suppose it was the view from up here that did it to you. Looking down on all those little people can give a sense of power. Hugo's Hunchback of Notre Dame was a poor deformed creature until he looked down from his bell tower on the streets of Paris far below. It can make one feel like God up here—invincible, with the power to rob and kill. The mask and the silence were part of the image, adding to your legend."

"Draw, damn you!" Poder shouted, and fired his six-shooter. The bullet clanged off the bell, sending tremors through the air.

Ben drew his gun.

He stared down from the tower for a long time, watching the tiny figure on the ground, seeing Father Angeles and Amy running out to where it had landed. The priest knelt in the dust and prayed over Luis's body while Ben watched.

He could feel the power from up here, the power that Luis had felt, and finally he had to look away, toward the vastness of the desert horizon, until he felt small again.

THE PHANTOM STALLION

Because no one had need of his gun or his wits, Ben Snow had hired on as a temporary ranch hand one summer, working at the sprawling Six-Bar spread of Horace Grant in west Texas. Grant himself was a broken man in his seventies by this time, confined to bed in his room following a fall from a horse that had left him paralyzed. But he still approved all the hiring, and on Ben's first morning at the Six-Bar Ranch he was ushered into the old man's bedroom by Grant's eldest son Terry.

"Don't worry, it's just a formality," Terry Grant assured Ben. Terry was a husky man of around forty. Ben guessed he left most of the hard work to his younger brother. "This is probably the only time you'll see Dad all summer."

"Can't you take him out in a wheelchair?"

Terry Grant shook his head. "Not in the hot weather. In his condition, he can't stand it. Breathing is an effort for him. That's why we rigged up this air-cooling device you'll see in his room. It's like the one they used in the White House after President Garfield was shot back in '81."

Ben entered the sickroom, not knowing what to expect. The dull clatter of machinery, which he'd heard from outside, became more pronounced, and as the first cool air hit his face he saw a large cast-iron box about the shape of a coffin that almost filled one end of the bedroom. This was the source of both the sound and the air, and he'd never seen anything like it before.

But his attention was immediately distracted by the figure in the bed—a gruff, white-haired old man who asked, "You come to see me or that gadget?"

"Dad, this here's Ben Snow, a new temporary hand I'd like to take on for a few weeks. Claims he's good with horses."

Horace Grant eyed Ben from beneath drooping lids. "Worked at any other ranches around here, Snow?"

"Not around here," Ben answered. "But you won't be disappointed in me." His attention wandered to the sunlit window that looked out across the valley. About a mile away an impressive structure that looked like an Italian villa was rising toward the sky. "Looks as if you're building a new ranch house over there. Don't see many houses that expensive around here."

"My sons are buildin' it for me," the old man answered proudly. "It's the one thing I want before I die. I always promised their mother I'd own a place like that. She didn't live to see it, but there it is, by God!"

Terry Grant cleared his throat. "What about it, Dad? Is it all right if we take Snow on for a few weeks?"

"Sure, sure—looks like a good man to me."

"Thank you, sir," Ben answered respectfully. "You won't be sorry."

They left the bedroom and Terry said, "I told you it was just a formality. He never turns anyone down, but we like him to feel he still has a say in the way things are run."

"It must be a terrible thing to be bedridden after such an active life."

"We try to keep him as comfortable as we can. My wife Lorrie brings all his meals to him, and my brother Silas and I rigged up that air-cooling gadget. It costs a fortune to operate, but it's worth it to keep him comfortable."

"How does it work?" Ben asked.

"We have blocks of ice brought out from town by the wagonload. That's the most expensive part. The ice is shaved and mixed with salt to form a sort of briny slush in the top of that iron tank. It trickles down onto terrycloth screens. A steam-driven electric generator powers a fan in the lower part of the tank. Warm air is sucked in from outside and cooled as it passes across the screens."

"There must be some way to muffle the noise of the fan. I'm sure President Garfield's machine didn't clatter like that."

"I believe it was in an adjoining room with a duct through the wall," Terry admitted. "But we couldn't do that because of the kitchen next door. My father insisted on a ground-floor room so he could oversee things, and that parlor was the only room we could convert to a bedroom."

Ben was studying the heavy drapes that hung on either side of the windows in the main living room. "If you don't mind a suggestion, some drapes like those, hung from ceiling to floor between the cooling machine and the bed, would muffle the sound and also cut down the size of the area to be cooled. You could run a duct through a hole in the drapes."

"What an excellent suggestion!" a voice behind Ben said. He turned to see a handsome woman in a fringed riding costume standing near the front door. "Who is this wise young man, Terry?"

"Ben Snow, a new temporary hand. Ben, I'd like you to meet my wife Lorrie. She runs the house, and anything she says here goes, just as if it came from me."

Lorrie Grant seemed a bit younger than her husband, probably in her mid-thirties. She had pale blue eyes and when she removed her hat he saw she had blonde hair gathered into a bun at the back. "Pleased to be working here," he told her.

She eyed him for a moment and then addressed her husband. "Terry, if you'll loan me Mr. Snow for the remainder of the afternoon I think we could have that drape in place by suppertime."

"Go ahead," her husband said with a wave of his hand. "I have to ride out to the north pasture to see about the branding. You help my wife, Ben, and I'll show you around the place tomorrow."

When they were alone, Lorrie Grant bustled about, fetching a curtain rod from one room and some thick brown drapes from another.

"You from Texas, Mr. Snow?"

"Please call me Ben. I'm only an employee."

She laughed. "Sometimes I think that's all I am, too . . ."

Horace Grant was dozing when they started their task, but he came awake as Ben gently hammered the nails holding the curtain rod in place. "What—?" he mumbled. "It's that damned horse again!"

Lorrie Grant hurried to soothe him. "No, no—we're only putting up some drapes to make it quieter in here. Ranger is dead. He won't be coming here any more."

"What was that?" Ben asked when they'd finished putting up the drapes and returned to the living room.

"He dreams about Ranger, the stallion that threw him and caused his injury. Terry's brother Silas shot Ranger after the accident, but Horace still dreams about him, imagines him right in that room sometimes, rearing up and pounding the bed with his hoofs."

"I imagine he was a vigorous man in his younger days."

"He was."

"I see the new house they're building across the valley. At least he has that to think about."

Lorrie Grant looked away. "Yes, well, it's a long way from being finished. I think he wanted it mainly to have as big a place as Nathan Lee, who owns the Running-W Ranch in the next town. They've been feuding and trying to top one another for as long as I've been in the family. Grant and Lee—it's like the Civil War all over again."

She walked around outside with Ben, pointing out some of the buildings around the main house.

"Where do I sleep?" he asked.

Lorrie glanced up at him. "In the bunkhouse. It's that long building over by the corral. Take it easy and you'll get along fine here. Don't try to rush things."

"I just do what I'm told," he said, reacting to her sudden coolness.

She took a step back. "Oh, and Ben—next time you're in the house, leave your gun belt outside. I don't like weapons in my home."

He tipped his hat politely and left her in silence,

For the rest of that first week, Ben worked mainly with Silas Grant, Terry's younger brother. He was a man in his early thirties, about Ben's age, and he handled himself well on a horse. If he lacked his brother's authoritative manner, he made up for it with a toughness that seemed to come naturally to him.

They spent their days riding the range, engaged in routine ranch chores like stringing barbed wire and rounding up strays. By the end of the week Silas had become more talkative and a bit more friendly. "I still remember everything about that day Ranger threw my father," he said, getting out a chew of tobacco. "Terrible thing, terrible! Reared up and tried to trample him. I didn't think twice. Drew my Colt and blasted that beast right between the eyes. It was too late for my father, though."

"It saved his life."

"If you call that living—confined to a bed with only the view from a window to keep him company."

"You've made it comfortable for him, cooling the air—"

"That was a damned-fool idea of Terry's. Costs us a fortune, lugging that ice out from town."

Their conversation was interrupted by the sight of a lone horseman heading toward them across the range. "That one of our men?" Ben asked.

Silas dropped a hand to his pistol butt as if checking to see that it was in place. "Damned if it's not Nathan Lee! Come on!"

They spurred their horses to a gallop, with Ben falling back a little on his mount, Oats, to let Silas overtake the intruder first. When he rode up, Silas was sitting with his right hand on his gun. "A bit away from home, aren't you, Mr. Lee?"

Nathan Lee was a white-haired man in his sixties. His face had the weathered look of someone who'd spent his life on the range. "Looking for strays, like yourself. You know my brand, Silas. Seen any of the critters?"

"Not likely. Let us ride you back to the boundary line."

"I can find my own way."

Silas motioned to Ben. "See that Mr. Lee gets back to his own property, Ben. By the shortest route."

Ben did as he was ordered, riding silently at Nathan Lee's side for about a mile before the older man broke the silence. "You're new here, aren't you? I haven't seen you in town."

"Just temporary," Ben explained. "Earning a little money to tide me over."

"You wear your pistol like a gunfighter."

"No, not me," Ben assured him.

"I just wondered if old man Grant was bringing in hired guns to use against me."

"I wouldn't know about that. I'm just passing through."

They rode on a little farther. Far off to his left Ben could see the walls of the new villa. No one seemed to be working there today, but when he thought about it he realized he hadn't seen any workers there all week. "What do you think of Grant's Folly?" Nathan Lee asked, motioning across the valley toward the villa.

"Horace Grant seems pleased with the way it's progressing," Ben answered cautiously.

"The fool would be," Lee replied with a chuckle. "He doesn't know what's going on right under his nose."

Ben left him at the boundary line, a meandering creek with a string of barbed wire along one bank. On the way back to the ranch house, he decided to detour for a closer look at the villa that was nearing completion. As he neared it, slowing Oats to a trot, he realized something was wrong. Coming at it from this angle, the fancy stone front of the place looked one-dimensional, like a stage setting.

And, once up to it, he saw it *was* a stage setting!

The stonework of the supposed villa had been painted on canvas, stretched upon a wooden frame that was held upright by wooden supports anchored to the ground. The whole thing was a fake, an illusion that appeared real from the one vantage point that mattered—the bedroom window that was Horace Grant's only view of the world.

Ben was still puzzling over his discovery when another rider approached. He saw that it was Paul Wooster, foreman of the ranch, a beady-eyed man with a knife scar on his left cheek. Ben hadn't yet worked with him, but they'd gotten to know each other during the long evenings in the bunkhouse.

"What you doin' over here, Snow? Snoopin' around?"

"I was riding with Silas Grant and we came upon Mr. Lee looking for strays. I escorted him off our land."

"I asked what you were doin' *here*."

"Thought I'd ride over and take a look. It's all painted canvas. It's a fake."

"And it's also none of your damned business! If you want to keep your job, keep your nose clean. Don't stick it where it don't belong. This here's a family matter."

"But Mr. Grant thinks—"

"Don't matter what he thinks. He can't live much longer and they're just makin' his final days more pleasant. They put up that air-coolin' machine in his room and they put up this nice scene for him to look at. You forget you ever saw it close up. If Mr. Grant ever asks you, just say the place is almost finished. Understand?"

"Sure," Ben agreed. "I'm not here to make trouble . . ."

A s the days passed, the summer heat increased. Ben found himself working on the range more often with Paul Wooster and the others. He saw little of the Grant brothers and nothing at all of Lorrie Grant. Sometimes at night in the crowded bunkhouse, he thought of her while Wooster told stories of knife fights with Mexicans along the Rio Grande.

Ben had worked at the Six-Bar for two weeks when Lorrie Grant summoned him to the main house one morning. A new wagonload of ice had arrived from town and she needed someone to shave and shovel it into the machine in Horace's bedroom. "Do you like it here?" she asked him as he went about the task.

"It's a good job."

"Silas thinks you're a gunfighter hiding out from something. He even thinks you might be Billy the Kid."

"Billy the Kid's been dead over ten years."

"Still, people hear stories."

She helped him refill the machine. She was wearing workpants, with a shirt tucked in at the waist. Horace Grant was asleep in his bed, snoring gently as they worked.

"How's he been?" Ben asked.

Lorrie shrugged. "Not so good. He dreamed about his horse again last night, woke up screaming that Ranger was in the room with him, trampling him."

Ben glanced out at the distant villa. "How's the new house coming?"

She shot him a look. "You know better than I do. I heard you were over there last week."

"I was riding by."

When they'd finished loading the ice in the top of the machine, she said, "That duct through the curtain is coming loose. Could you tighten the supporting arm?"

"Sure."

It was easy to fix and took only a few minutes. He joined her in the living room. "All fixed now. Anything else you want me to do around here?"

She seemed to weigh his words and her reply before she answered. "You've been very helpful. I may call upon you again soon."

"Any time."

He went out to the corral where Terry Grant was breaking in a new horse. Until now, Ben hadn't seen the older brother do much in the way of physical labor, but he showed his strength in keeping the big stallion under control. Finally, Terry climbed down and turned the horse over to one of the cowhands. He came over to the fence and asked Ben, "Did you help Lorrie out?"

"All finished. We loaded the cooler with more shaved ice."

Later in the day, when Ben and Terry returned from checking fences, Lorrie told them, "Horace says he's feeling better. He'd like to come out in the wheelchair."

"It's too hot for that," Terry replied abruptly. "It would kill him."

"That's what I said, but he's serious. And he wants us to take him in the buggy to see the villa tomorrow."

Terry cursed under his breath. "We'll talk about it tonight."

It was past midnight when Ben was awakened by an unaccustomed sound. As his eyes became adjusted to the dark, he saw Paul Wooster slip out of the bunkhouse door and walk quickly across the yard to the barn. Ben was almost back asleep when he heard him return about an hour later and wondered what he'd been up to.

The following morning Ben helped Lorrie fill the machine with shaved ice again. About an hour later, as he was working by the stable, he saw Nathan Lee ride up the road. Neither of the brothers was in sight, so Ben strolled over to intercept him. "Can I help you, Mr. Lee?"

"I came to see Horace. I think you men are stealing my calves!"

"We're not—"

"Take me to Horace Grant!" His friendliness of their previous encounter had vanished.

"I can't do that, sir."

Lee dismounted his horse and headed on foot toward the stable. Ben flipped the horse's reins around a fencepost and ran toward the house.

"What is it?" Lorrie asked, seeing him appear in the doorway.

"Nathan Lee rode over here to see Horace—Mr. Grant. He's out at the stable."

"He can't see him. It's out of the question. He's resting now. If I wake him up he'll want to go outside."

"All right. I'll tell him."

But Lee wasn't in the stable. Nobody was. Ben circled the corral and saw that his horse was still there, but there was no sign of its rider. Then he saw Lorrie in the doorway of the ranch house, motioning to him.

"What's the matter?" he asked, running toward her.

"There was a noise in his room and he called out. He may have been dreaming again, but I can't get the door open. It's stuck or something."

Ben went to the door and tried the knob. It turned but the door wouldn't open. "It seems to be locked," Ben said.

"Now I'm worried. Do you think we should break in?"

Ben hesitated. "Where are Silas and your husband?"

"Heaven knows—they could be at the other end of the range!"

"Stay here," he decided. "I'll go around and look in the window."

The earth around the back of the house was soft and sandy, and Ben found himself unconsciously checking it for footprints. There were none—only the tracks of a small prairie dog had disturbed the earth. He boosted himself up to the window, saw it was latched from the inside, and stared at the bed in which Horace Grant lay. He was half uncovered and his head rested at an odd angle. Beyond the bed, Ben could see that the only door was latched on the inside.

He smashed the window with the butt of his gun, unlatched it, and raised it high enough to crawl through. One look at Horace Grant's face told him he was dead. The side of his head had been crushed and the imprint of a bloody horseshoe was clearly visible.

B en drew his .45 again and looked around, stepping quickly to the drapery that hid the air-cooling machine from view. He pulled it aside, but there was no one behind it. The room was empty except for Ben and the dead man. He went to the door and examined the latch without touching it. A little lip ran down along the frame—it was impossible that it could have been locked from outside. He opened it carefully and faced Lorrie, blocking her view of the bed.

"What is it?" she asked, the terror plain on her face.

"He's dead. Someone or something crushed his skull."

"My God!"

Ben rubbed his slightly damp fingers together. "It might have been a horseshoe, from the look of the wound."

"The phantom stallion that haunted his dream? It couldn't have been Ranger!"

"You'd better go find your husband and Silas."

She noticed the gun in his hand for the first time. "What's that for?"

"Nathan Lee is still prowling around somewhere and I want to find him."

"Do you think *he* killed Horace?"

"Someone did."

She looked beyond him, seeing the bed and the broken pane. "Ranger—"

"Forget the horse. This door was latched on the inside. Horace was paralyzed and it certainly wasn't latched by a dead horse from his dreams."

"Then how was it latched? And if the window was locked, too, how did the killer get out?"

"I don't know," Ben admitted, "but I'm going to find out."

He located Lee near the holding corral out behind the big barn, deep in conversation with Paul Wooster. "You'd both better get up to the main house," he told them. "Horace Grant's been killed."

"Killed?" For a moment Lee didn't seem to comprehend. "What do you mean?"

"It looks like murder."

Wooster turned on Lee. "You're the only enemy he had around these parts, Mr. Lee. I'd hate to think you'd gun down a paralyzed old man."

"I didn't."

"He wasn't gunned down," Ben explained. "His skull was crushed by a blow from a horseshoe. An easy enough weapon to find around here. Who does your blacksmithing, Paul?"

Wooster scratched his head. "We generally take the horses into town when they need work, but some of the boys can drive a nail if we have to. I've done it myself."

On the way back to the ranch house, Ben fell into step beside the foreman and asked him quietly, "How long were you with Lee?"

"Only a few minutes. I saw him nosin' around and asked what he was doing."

"What was he doing?"

"Seeing who he could hire away from us to work the Running-W. Hell, I think he was even making me an offer, but he didn't come right out and say it."

Ben nodded. "Almost as if he knew Horace Grant was dead."

Terry and Silas Grant had both reached the house by the time Ben and the others arrived. A few of the cowhands were there, too, and the cook. Terry had taken charge, ordering someone to ride into town for the sheriff. Silas stood to one side. Ben was surprised to see he'd been crying.

"I guess we can tear down our canvas villa now," he said with a trace of bitterness. "There's no one left to fool."

Terry looked at him. "Was that meant for me?"

"It was your idea, wasn't it?"

"Only to keep him happy in his last months, to make him think we were building the house he always wanted."

"How could you know they were his last months? Maybe you helped him along with that talk of phantom stallions!"

Terry looked as if he might hit his younger brother. "The horse was in his dreams! I had nothing to do with it!" He saw that Nathan Lee was anxious to leave and turned his attention to him. "You were trespassing on our land," he pointed out, "and while you were here my father was killed. Now you'll just have to wait and answer some questions when the sheriff gets here."

Lee shoved his restraining hand away. "If I wanted to kill your father I had plenty of opportunities—and with a six-gun out on the range, not sneaking around here and beating him to death on his sick-bed. Who'd want to murder a dying man, anyway?"

Ben thought it was a good question. He remembered the old man's desire to go outside in his wheelchair. Had someone feared he'd discover the distant villa was only a stage set?

Sheriff Long, when he arrived, proved to be an aging man with a tired expression. "I knew old Horace like my own kin," he said sadly. "Sorry to see him go this way."

He listened to the details of the scene, and to Ben's account of breaking into the room.

"What do you think, Sheriff?" Terry Grant asked him.

"Death by misadventure, I guess. Hell, maybe that damned horse did kill him."

Terry appeared dumbfounded. "In a locked room?"

"I was thinkin' maybe that blow to his head happened when the horse threw him, and the wound just now appeared when he died."

Even Silas wouldn't accept that. "I'd believe in a ghost horse before I'd believe that."

"What about Nathan Lee?" Terry argued. "He hated my father, and everyone in the county knows it. He was on our land today without permission and—"

"I'll question him," the sheriff agreed. He took Lee into the dining room and sat down with him. They were out of earshot, but Ben had already guessed from his manner that he had no intention of antagonizing another big landowner in his district.

Terry and Lorrie went about making funeral arrangements and Ben drifted out to the corral. No one had asked him to help with the case. They didn't need him. Maybe it was time to think about moving on.

There was grumbling in the bunkhouse that night. The men were worried about getting paid. They feared a power struggle between Terry and Silas, and they talked about the offers Nathan Lee had made to some of them. A few were tempted to bolt to the Running-W, but that sort of talk ceased quickly when Paul Wooster walked in. The foreman looked troubled by the day's events and said little, though when Ben approached him with a routine question about the following morning's work he answered readily enough.

"Everything will go on as usual, Ben, you can count on it. The funeral's in two days and we'll all be there, of course, but otherwise we'll be out on the range doing our job."

"What about Lee's offer?"

"To hell with Lee!"

That night, after twelve, Wooster left the bunkhouse again. This time Ben slipped into his pants and boots and followed the foreman through the starry darkness across the corral area to the barn. He hadn't brought a gun, and he hoped he wouldn't regret it. But as soon as he slipped into the barn behind Wooster he knew he wouldn't need a weapon. He heard Lorrie's soft voice saying, "I didn't know if you'd come tonight."

"Why? Because the old man got himself killed? The shape he was in, it was more like a mercy killing. Nothin' to grieve over."

"Terry and Silas were fighting again after the sheriff left."

"Don't worry, your husband knows how to handle baby brother."

"My husband—"

"That's what he is. You ain't about to leave him."

"No," she admitted.

"Come here."

Ben saw their figures merge in the darkness. Then he slipped back outside through the partly open door, thankful for the brightness of the sky that guided him to the bunkhouse.

In the morning, Silas Grant came out to the bunkhouse during breakfast to tell Wooster that the canvas villa should be taken down. "Get rid of it today," he ordered. "I don't want to look at it any more."

"All right," the foreman said.

Ben caught up with Silas as he walked toward his horse. "Will you still be needing me?" he asked.

"Sure. Why not? My brother hired you, not my father." He lifted himself into the saddle and headed toward a work party of cowhands who were awaiting him.

Ben stayed around the bunkhouse, figuring that Wooster would need help taking down the painted canvas, but it was Lorrie who finally came looking for him. "We don't need the cooling machine anymore," she said. "Would you help me empty it?"

The fan had been shut off and the big machine was silent for the first time since Ben's arrival. He lifted the lid of the coffinlike compartment where the shaved ice was loaded and found something unexpected.

It was a length of wood with a bloody horseshoe loosely nailed to one end. "What's that?" Lorrie asked.

"The murder weapon, unless I'm mistaken."

Lorrie gasped, putting her hand to her mouth.

Ben lifted it out carefully. "There's your phantom stallion, about as I'd expected."

"Of course," Lorrie said. "After he killed Horace, the murderer hid in the top of the tank, in the ice compartment. There's room enough for a body. When we went for help, he slipped out, either through the front door or the window you'd raised."

Ben glanced out the broken window at the soft earth below, but Sheriff Long and the brothers had all been back there and the ground had been trampled now by too many footprints to yield any clues. "He was right here in the room with us all the time," Ben grumbled, "and we let him escape."

"But who?"

"Wooster told me he occasionally does some shoeing. I found him with Lee, but he said they'd only been together a few minutes. That leaves both of them without alibis." He watched her face for a reaction to the mention of the foreman's name, but there was none.

"What will you do?" she asked. "Tell the sheriff?"

"First I'd like to have another talk with Wooster." Ben knew that whatever he found out, it might endanger his job at the ranch, but he left the house and mounted Oats, riding off across the valley in the direction of the canvas villa. He could see men working there and assumed the foreman was one of them. As he neared the spot, he left his horse and approached on foot, keeping one hand near his gun. Up close, the painted villa had a dead, unreal look that would have fooled no one. But the sons had always known their father wouldn't see it up close.

"Wooster!" he called out. "Are you here?"

Suddenly a large piece of canvas seemed to come loose in the breeze, as if freed by some unseen hand, and Paul Wooster's large grey stallion appeared, running directly toward Ben. He had to throw himself out of the way to avoid being trampled.

"You all right?" Wooster called out, seeing what had happened.

Ben picked himself up, brushing the dirt from his clothes. "I'll live."

Wooster gave a whistle to summon his horse back. "Sorry. We were unhitching the canvas from those wooden supporting poles and the space was too confined. There wasn't enough room. When that canvas came loose, Runner just broke away from me. I was usin' him to help me reach the high places, to pull the nails out."

"Not enough room," Ben repeated.

"Yeah. You sure you're all right, Snow?"

"I'm all right."

"Then give me a hand here. I need your help."

But Ben ignored him and went back to his horse. There was something he had to do. With Wooster shouting after him, he headed Oats back toward the ranch house.

As he entered, Lorrie came out of the kitchen. There may have been something about his expression that told her he knew the truth before he asked, "Why did you kill that old man, Mrs. Grant?"

S he stared at him, her hands working nervously. "I couldn't have killed him. The door was latched from the inside. And the killer was hiding in the air-cooling machine."

"No, I'd filled that compartment with shaved ice only an hour or so earlier. There wouldn't have been room for anyone to hide in there."

"The door was latched from the inside," she repeated.

"Easiest thing in the world to arrange. After you beat him to death with that horseshoe, you hid the club in the air-cooler and took out a tiny piece of the shaved ice. You used it to prop up the latch as you closed the door. After a minute or two the ice melted and the latch dropped into place, locking the door from the inside."

Her face had gone deathly pale. "Even if that's what happened, anyone could have done it. Why me?"

"Because it didn't make sense for anyone but the killer to lock that door in the first place. The whole idea of the horseshoe must have been to give the crime a supernatural air, to tie in with Horace's dreams everyone had heard about. But latching the door defeated the whole purpose. Neither a paralyzed man nor a ghost horse could have locked it, so why was it locked? Who benefited by its being locked like that? Only you, Mrs. Grant, because you were the one on the other side of that door. You would have had the best opportunity to kill Horace Grant if that door was unlatched. Anyone else—

your husband, your brother-in-law, your foreman, or even Nathan Lee—would have left it open."

"Suppose the killer heard me coming after he'd struck the blow and latched the door so I wouldn't walk in on the murder scene? Have you thought of that?"

"Yes," Ben answered with a touch of sadness. "If that was the case, the killer would have fled when you left the house to summon me. He wouldn't have stayed trapped in there with his victim."

"I—" Her voice faltered and broke. She'd run out of arguments.

"Why did you kill him?" he asked again. "It was because of Paul Wooster, wasn't it?"

"You know about that?"

Ben nodded.

She sighed. "I spoke to Paul the other day in Horace's room, like I did with you. I thought the old man was asleep. But he heard us and he threatened to tell Terry. It would have ruined our marriage. I couldn't risk that for a few hours with a sweaty ranch foreman. I think I did the old man a favor, anyway. He wanted to die."

"Not like that, he didn't," Ben assured her. "A pillow over his face might have been merciful, but not a horseshoe nailed to a piece of wood."

A sly look came into the pale-blue eyes. "Maybe I thought that would point to one of the cowhands."

"Like your lover, Paul Wooster? He'd have gotten that horseshoe nailed on more firmly. The job you did showed inexperience in nailing horseshoes."

Neither of them had been aware of Terry Grant, who'd entered the house as they talked. He stepped forward then, and the sight of him was the final blow to his wife. She collapsed, sobbing, against his shoulder.

"I'll handle things now," he told Ben. "Gather your gear together and get a move on. I'll pay you through the end of next week."

"Shouldn't the sheriff be told?"

"I'll handle that."

Ben left the ranch within the hour with his wages and headed north.

He never saw any of them again, and it was only the following spring, at a bar in Durango, that someone told him of the shooting at the Six-Bar Ranch and how Terry Grant had gunned down his wife and his foreman before taking his own life.

THE SACRAMENTO WAXWORKS

Sacramento was on the main line of the transcontinental railroad in 1885, and it was by railroad that Ben Snow arrived there in the company of Seymour Dodge. He'd never been to California before and never visited a city as large as Sacramento. He was only twenty-six that year, still pursued by the bizarre rumor that he might be Billy the Kid.

He knew Billy was dead, shot by Sheriff Pat Garrett back in '81, but news traveled slowly in the West if it traveled at all. It had taken Washington eleven days to learn of Custer's defeat at the Little Big Horn and wanted posters for Billy the Kid were still being printed in Las Vegas a year after his death in New Mexico. The frequent gunfights between outlaws and sheriffs became almost mythic, with the myth often traveling faster than the actual news.

Seymour Dodge was a man who fostered myths. A slender gentleman whose wisp of a beard made him appear older than he was, he'd approached Ben at a Carson City café with an unusual proposition. "Come to Sacramento with me," he'd offered. "I'll pay for your train fare and hotel room and give you one hundred dollars besides—all for a couple of days' work."

"I'm not a gunfighter," Ben told him, feeling uncomfortable under the man's steady gaze.

"Didn't say you were. But you *know* gunfighters—you've traveled among them. I can tell by the way you wear that holster. It's low, for a fast draw."

"I'm fast," Ben conceded. "And I hit what I aim at."

Seymour Dodge bit off the end of a cigar and struck a match to light it. "Ever meet Billy the Kid?" he asked casually. "You'd be about his age."

"Never met him."

"How about Pat Garrett or Wyatt Earp? The James boys?"

"Nope."

"Still," Dodge said, a bit disappointed, "you've known others like them, and that's what I need. I bought myself a waxworks in Sacramento—Turner's Waxwork Theater—and I'm adding a section of famous Western sheriffs and outlaws. I need advice on the costumes, on the way a man wears his gun or his hat, on the look of his boots."

"I suppose I could tell you that much," Ben agreed.

"Fine. You can stable your horse here and come back for him. The train trip is only a hundred and thirty-five miles. Won't take us any time at all."

The journey and his first view of Sacramento were wonders enough for Ben Snow, especially the impressive State Capitol building in its spacious park. "Took 'em fourteen years to get that built," Dodge remarked as they rode past in a hired carriage, bound for the waxworks. "This is all gold-rush country, you know. If it hadn't been for Sutter's Mill nearby, this would still be a tiny settlement instead of the capital of the state."

"How long has the waxworks been here?"

"Richard Turner opened it in 1857 after a visit to Madame Tussaud's in London. He figured the newcomers pouring into Sacramento after the gold rush would really go for it, and he was right. It was an instant success—especially the main exhibit of a guillotine scene from the French Revolution. It was so realistic there was talk of ghosts haunting the place in its early days. Old Turner finally died and his heirs were going to close the place, but I bought it."

From the outside, Turner's Waxwork Theater was a garish melange of signs and lights, but once Ben followed Dodge through the front door the place took on an atmosphere of slumbering menace. The lights were dim, barely illuminating the dozens of wax figures that stood poised for action. "This way," Seymour Dodge said, leading Ben down a narrow aisle past a display of the state's history.

They passed the guillotine display Dodge had mentioned, with one victim kneeling to lose his head while several others stood by—all dressed in the faded finery of the French aristocracy. "They look real enough to be alive," Ben commented.

"Turner claimed some of the costumes were the actual ones worn by victims at the time. But this is what I hired you for."

They passed beyond the guillotine to the rear of the building. A large sheet of canvas hung from the ceiling, blocking the newest exhibits from the public's view. Dodge lifted one end of the flap and Ben ducked beneath it. "Here, let me turn on a light," he said. The sudden bright illumination fell upon more than a half-dozen figures in Western garb, many with their pistols drawn. They were so realistic Ben almost went for his own weapon before he remembered he'd packed the gun belt in the saddlebags he'd left at the door.

"Quite impressive," he admitted. "They look almost alive."

"Here's Wyatt Earp, with Doc Holliday at the O.K. Corral. And this is Jesse James. This one's Bat Masterson from Dodge City. Judge Roy Bean from Texas." He paused dramatically. "And here's Billy the Kid with Pat Garrett."

Ben drew a breath, facing the lifelike re-creation of this man who had become his nemesis even after death. In truth he looked nothing like Billy, except for the accident of their births which had made them the same age. Even then, Billy Bonney had been born in New York, half a continent away from Ben Snow. He'd been a slight young man, barely five feet seven inches tall, with blue eyes and light brown hair. That much the model maker had gotten reasonably correct. And he'd even captured the touch of cruelty in the boyish face. But there was something wrong.

"This isn't right," Ben said suddenly, motioning toward the gun belt. "Billy wasn't left-handed."

"I thought—"

"He wore only one pistol, on his right hip, and often carried a rifle as well. Everything else seems about right, except for the hat. Billy didn't wear a traditional western hat. It had a narrower brim than that."

Seymour Dodge seemed pleased. "That's exactly the sort of information I need. But I thought you said you never met Billy."

"I've seen pictures of him."

Dodge took out a big gold watch and opened the lid. "Getting on toward dinnertime. I should get you settled at the hotel. Then tomorrow morning we can really work at this."

"Are there any other exhibits planned, or just these?"

"I've got Black Bart and some others in the basement, if we can get the right costumes for them. I might do something with Indians, too, and maybe Custer."

The hotel where Ben was staying proved to be in the next block, a recently built place that seemed like a palace to him. And it wasn't only the hotel that was luxurious by frontier standards. He ate in the fancy dining room with linen tablecloths on the tables and then strolled out to the lobby, where he was approached by a stunning young woman in a long silk dress. "You new in town, mister? Want to have some fun?"

"What kind of fun?" Ben asked innocently.

"How about a drink and we can talk it over."

"All right," Ben decided. "I like that dress. What's your name?"

"Molly." She led the way into a bar off the dining room. "The dress is Chinese. A sailor gave it to me. What's *your* name?"

"Ben. I'm in town on business."

"You look like a cowboy," she said, draping herself in a chair.

Ben sat down across the table from her. "Why do you say that?"

"Your boots. And you walk with your right hand sort of open and tense at your side, as if you're used to wearing a gun belt and you're always ready to draw. Am I right?"

"Close enough, Molly," he admitted. "This is my first time in California."

"Well, folks don't wear gun belts in Sacramento. It's the state capital. We're very law-abiding here."

"I was down at the waxworks today. I'm doing some work there."

She waited while the bartender took their order and then said, "You must know Seymour Dodge."

"I met him in Carson City. I'm working for him while I'm here, advising him on a new exhibit."

"He bought the waxworks earlier this year. The family was going to shut it down after Mr. Turner died."

"Is it a popular attraction?"

She smoothed the front of her dress provocatively. "Oh, sure—especially with visitors. Sacramento gets lots of visitors from all over the state, people who come here to get land bills passed by the legislature."

"You do a big business with the visitors, I'll bet. You're a fine-looking girl."

"I do all right."

"Do you have a last name, Molly?"

She shrugged. "What's yours?"

"Snow. Ben Snow."

"Molly Harper," she relented.

"You in show business?"

"I was. They've got a theater here and—" She spied someone across the room. "Excuse me a minute. There's Senator Watkins. I have to see him."

She hurried over to a white-haired man wearing eyeglasses who looked vaguely familiar to Ben. They conversed for a few minutes, with the senator chuckling at something Molly said before they parted at the door and she returned to the table. "You certainly travel in the right circles," Ben remarked.

"He's the majority leader of the state senate—a very important man in this town."

"I'll bet he likes to party."

"Once in a while," she admitted. Finishing her drink, she asked, "Do you want to come up to my room?"

"You got a room at this hotel?"

"I know the room clerk. He lets me use one of the empty ones, as long as I don't stay too long."

Ben squeezed her hand across the table. "Maybe another night. I'll be here a few days."

H e strolled around the city for a while alone, getting the feel of the place. It was a political town, at least with the legislature in session, and it seemed like a foreign country to him. He missed the sound of horses' hoofs on dirt streets. Somehow, carriages on cobblestones weren't the same thing.

He slept well, and in the morning found the Sacramento morning newspaper outside his door. There was an artist's sketch of Senator Josh Watkins on the front page, looking exactly as Ben remembered him from the night before, under the headline SENATE LEADER NAMED IN LAND SCANDAL. The accompanying article was filled with innuendos, hinting bribery and malfeasance without ever becoming too specific. The details of the land scandal were too complex for Ben to understand, and with no knowledge of California politics he wasn't particularly interested. Still, he wondered what Molly Harper would think about it.

Seymour Dodge was already at the waxworks by the time Ben finished breakfast and strolled down the block. It was a warm spring day and the street was crowded with carriages. Occasionally a single horseman rode by, but dressed so formally he would never be mistaken for a working cowhand or a roaming gunfighter. Some horsemen even tipped their hats as they passed ladies in carriages. This, Ben decided, was civilization.

"Enjoying the city?" Dodge asked as he entered the wax museum.

"It's certainly different from my usual territory. Sometimes I don't see a tree for months at a time."

"Travel a lot, do you?"

"Always. I don't remember ever having a home for more than a year at a time, even when I was a boy."

Dodge showed Ben around the waxworks, taking more time than he had the previous afternoon. There were four main exhibit areas—the French Revolution with its guillotine, a Gallery of Horrors in which famous murderers were depicted, the California History section with explorers and political figures of the past and present, and the Wild West section which he was in the process of expanding. As Dodge was showing him the California History exhibit, including an imposing waxwork of the governor, Ben spotted something out of place. "This fellow doesn't belong in California. He's General Lew Wallace —he was governor of the New Mexico territory a few years back. He wrote a novel called *Ben Hur*."

Dodge seemed puzzled. "You're right, of course, but how did he get moved over? I had him in the Wild West exhibit across the room over there."

"These governors like to stick together," Ben said, making a joke of it.

"No—this could be serious. I believe I mentioned that the waxworks had a reputation for being haunted in its early days. The haunting took this exact form—statues moving or changing position overnight."

"I don't believe in ghosts," Ben told him. "If the statue moved, somebody moved it."

He carried it back to where Dodge indicated, surprised that it didn't weigh more. It left an obvious gap in the California display, but Dodge rearranged some of the other figures to compensate for it.

"They're not as heavy as they look," Dodge agreed. "We use beeswax. It melts at a low heat and mixes well with coloring. Wax figures of deities and even wax fruits were used by the ancient Egyptians, and the art survived through Roman and medieval times. The first exhibition of wax figures was shown in Germany in the early eighteenth century, though of course the most famous is Madame Tussaud's, which she opened in London a few years after her imprisonment during the French Revolution. It's from her that the tableau of the guillotine is almost a tradition of every wax museum today."

Ben, whose knowledge of French history was limited, inspected the Revolution section with interest. "Who's the man being stabbed in the bathtub?"

"Marat. He's being murdered by Charlotte Corday."

"What was he doing in the bathtub with a book?"

"He had a skin disease. He spent much of his time in warm baths."

Ben spent most of the day helping Dodge with details of the Western costumes. When they'd finished with the wax figures in the main exhibit area, they went to the basement workroom where the head of Black Bart was nearing completion. "I can't help you on this one," Ben said. "I never saw a picture of him. All I know is that he held up some Wells Fargo stagecoaches."

"I have a picture of him here. See—he usually dressed well, sometimes in a derby and a long coat. He wore a hood for the robberies, but I want to show his face. I have to age it a bit and add a moustache, though. They let him out of prison early because of his age, you know. He's around sixty-five, I think."

They were finishing up for the day when there was a loud knocking at the front door of the waxworks. Dodge answered it and admitted a rough-looking man with an untrimmed beard. "I gotta see you, Dodge," he insisted.

"The waxworks is closed for a few days, Tracy. We're preparing a new exhibit."

The man called Tracy spat on the floor. "I don't give a damn about your waxworks! I want my money!"

"You'll have it. I've just had a little setback is all."

"You're gonna have a big setback if I don't get my money. Them deeds are valuable."

"Give me another couple of days," Dodge pleaded, and finally the bearded man departed with a promise to return.

When the waxworks owner returned to Ben's side, he brooded, "Maybe I ought to hire you as a bodyguard instead of a consultant."

"You got trouble?"

Dodge shrugged. "Nothing I can't handle, I guess. Tracy is a loudmouth, but I don't really think he's dangerous. He let me use some deeds as collateral on a loan for this place when I bought it. Now he wants the deeds for some deal of his own and I'm having trouble repaying the loan as quickly as I'd hoped."

They closed the place and had a drink together, and Dodge paid Ben fifty dollars.

"One more day should do it. Maybe only half a day. I'll pay you the rest of the money and you can be on your way back to Carson City by nightfall."

"Fair enough," Ben agreed.

"What do you think of our city?"

"The people are certainly friendly," Ben remarked, thinking of Molly Harper.

After dining with Seymour Dodge at a seafood restaurant on the Sacramento River, Ben made his way back to the hotel. He sat for a time in the lobby and wasn't surprised when Molly reappeared from the direction of the bar.

"How'd it go today?" she asked.

"Pretty good. It's easy money."

"You get all those Wild West characters dressed in their costumes?"

"Most of them. I'll finish up tomorrow." He chuckled a bit. "I've been learning a lot about the business. Most of the figures only have wax heads and hands. The parts that don't show are often little more than dressmakers' dummies."

"How about a drink?" Molly suggested.

"In the bar?"

"I was thinking of my room."

"Upstairs?"

She shook her head. "Upstairs is for business. I want to take you back to my room. It's just in the next block, over the poultry market."

Ben hesitated for only an instant. Why not? It would probably be his last night in Sacramento and he didn't want to spend it alone. "Let's go," he said.

They left the hotel and crossed the narrow street, avoiding a stagecoach that was just starting its journey. "Until they finish the railroads, the stage is still the only way to reach some places," Molly said.

"Dodge was telling me about Black Bart today. He did pretty well robbing them."

"Until he got caught." She paused before the darkened windows of the market. "This shop opens at eight in the morning, just when I'm getting my best sleep. Come on—I'm right up these stairs."

Her apartment seemed to be the only residence in the building. A small kitchen and bathroom led off the main room, about half of which was occupied by a double bed.

"It's very nice," Ben said, admiring the draperies and the view of the street.

"I'd like it a little quieter, especially in the morning, but it's all right."

She opened a bottle of good whiskey, and over drinks he noticed the six-shooter on the stand next to her bed.

"Is this thing loaded?"

"Sure, it's loaded. Sometimes guys try to follow me home. I gotta have some protection here."

He opened the cylinder and spun it. "Nicely balanced weapon."

"I bought it at the hardware store."

"Ever use it?"

"I fired it over somebody's head one night." She giggled at the memory. "He sure took off after that!"

He returned the gun to the bedstand. "You got a lot of guys?"

"Off and on. You probably saw in the morning paper about Senator Watkins."

"I couldn't miss it. He one of them?"

"He's been up here once or twice. He thinks he's in love with me, but he gets so damned jealous! For a while I had to be careful he didn't see me with anyone else. He's better now, though. This trouble he's in will probably take his mind off me."

It was getting dark out and she started to switch on a light, then thought better of it. "Let's keep it romantic," she decided.

"I'll be leaving tomorrow," he reminded her.

"Hell, I'm not askin' you to marry me. I just like you, that's all."

"I'm glad you do." He sat down on the edge of the bed and kissed her.

Moments later, when darkness had fully settled over the room, Ben heard a noise at the door. Someone was fumbling with the lock. Molly Harper sat up, suddenly tense with panic. "Who's there?"

"You know damn well who it is!" a gruff male voice responded, and in the same instant the door swung open. "How many people got a key to your apartment?"

The light from the hallway silhouetted a white-haired man with glasses, his right arm half hidden by the doorframe. He stood stock-still as if trying to peer toward the bed. "My God!" Molly gasped to Ben. "It's Senator Watkins. If he sees you—"

"Who's that with you?"

"No one, Josh!"

"I'm sick of your lies, Molly."

Ben saw the right hand appear, holding a tiny derringer. Before he could move, Senator Watkins fired. He heard the bullet strike the wall a foot above his head.

Ben knew the double-barreled pistol held a second bullet. He didn't wait for Watkins to fire it. He ducked his head, grabbed the revolver on the bedstand, and fired a single shot at the man in the doorway. Watkins toppled stiffly backward and hit the floor with a thud.

Molly was out of the bed in a flash, running to his side. Ben followed more slowly, dropping the gun among the blankets. He stared down at the closed eyes of the senator and stared mesmerized at the blood on his chest.

"You've killed him!" Molly said. "You've got to get out of here!"

They were alone in the building and the shots had attracted no neighbors. Molly quickly threw a blanket over the body. "I'll do something," she said, "make up some story. Don't blame yourself, Ben. Hell, you saved my life!"

"I think I was trying to save my own life," he told her. "Why can't we call the police and tell them what happened?"

"He's majority leader of the senate, Ben! Next to the governor he's probably the most important man in this town! No one would believe our story. They'd have you swinging from the end of a noose before you knew what happened—and maybe me, too! Get to the station and hop a train out of here tonight!"

It seemed like sound advice at the moment. "What about my things back at the hotel?"

"You'd better leave them," she advised. "I'll have to report this to the police."

He started to reach for the derringer lying next to the body but thought better of it.

"It has to stay with the body," he decided, "whatever story you tell them." He kissed her lightly on the cheek. "I'm sorry it turned out this way."

She led him down the back stairs to the street and he hurried into the night.

He didn't go directly to the station, however. His gun was still in the saddlebags in his room and he wasn't leaving town without it. He reached the hotel without trouble and took the bags from his room. No one noticed as he left the lobby. When he passed the wax museum he saw it was in darkness. There was no sign of Seymour Dodge.

The next train east was in two hours and he hated to wait that long in the lonely station. "Train to San Francisco in thirty minutes," the ticket seller told him, "if you don't care which way you travel."

Did he care?

There was nothing waiting for him in Carson City except his horse Oats.

"Two hours, you say?"

"If it's on time."

He didn't buy a ticket yet. Instead, he strolled outside and stood looking at the distant dome of the State Capitol in the moonlight. He wanted to get out of Sacramento fast, before the police caught up with him. He wanted to run, and keep on running, back to the open range where the only thing he needed to trust was the six-shooter on his hip. But the more he thought about it, the more he realized he couldn't leave Sacramento quite yet.

He made his way back to the poultry market and waited in the darkness in sight of the door that led upstairs. If he was correct, he wouldn't have long to wait.

It was thirty-five minutes later when a familiar figure passed beneath the streetlight and went through the door that led up to Molly's rooms. Ben waited only a few seconds before following, moving as quietly as he could.

At the top of the stairs the man was knocking on Molly's door. "Molly," he whispered. "It's me. Open up."

As soon as the door began to open, Ben moved. He cleared the top two steps with a single bound and threw himself at the man, knocking him out of the way just as a shot sounded from within the room. Ben rolled over in the hallway, aiming his own gun, and ordered, "Drop it, Dodge! This isn't the waxworks anymore!"

He waited until Seymour Dodge dropped the pistol and joined Molly in raising his hands above his head. Then Ben got to his feet and helped Senator Josh Watkins up from the dusty floor.

It was the senator who demanded explanations. Seymour Dodge and Molly Harper didn't need any.

"It must have seemed like a perfect crime to them," Ben began, keeping his pistol steady on the couple. "Dodge traveled to Carson City and kept an eye out for someone who looked like a gunfighter, who wore his gun belt low for a fast draw. He needed a man who would shoot first and ask questions later. I looked like I filled the bill, so he hired me to come back here with him on the pretext of advising him about the costumes in his waxworks."

"But why did they need you?" Senator Watkins asked.

"The idea was that you would be murdered and I would be blamed for the shooting. Not only would I be blamed, but I would actually believe that I had committed the crime. The murder of the majority leader of the state senate would be avenged with a quick trial and I'd have ended up with a rope around my neck. You see, an hour or so ago, while I was in here with Molly, Dodge carried his wax dummy of you up here and stood it in front of the door. Then he opened the door and shouted something at me. I'd never heard your voice and in that instant, in the dim light, the whole thing had a terrible realism to it. The dummy's right hand was carefully hidden by the doorjamb and Dodge reached past it to fire a derringer at me. I already knew there was a loaded six-shooter by the bed, and they were certain I'd fire back. My bullet knocked the wax figure over, with a little help from Dodge. When Molly ran to the supposed body in the dark, she smeared some red liquid on the shirtfront—"

"Chicken blood," Molly said, her voice flat and resigned. "From the market downstairs."

"I can't believe any of this," the senator told her. "Why did you want to kill me? I thought you loved me, at least a little."

"It was Dodge who wanted you dead," Ben explained. "I don't know all the details, but I imagine it's something about the land scandal. A man named Tracy was demanding money from him today, threatening him over some deeds."

"Seymour found out about—"

"Shut up, Molly!" Dodge barked. He might have gone for her if Ben hadn't been holding the gun.

"Let her talk," Ben ordered. "Tell me, Molly."

She brushed the hair back from her forehead. "Seymour found out about the newspaper investigation last week. He was afraid it would spread to implicate him. With the senator dead, the investigation would have stopped and his own land dealings wouldn't be involved. He knew I was friendly with the senator, so he paid me to help him with the scheme. I'd entice you up here and help fake the shooting, using the waxworks dummy. Then after you fled the scene, and the dummy and the derringer were removed, I'd lure the senator up here for the real killing."

"How could you have done this to me, Molly?" Senator Watkins asked sadly. "After all I've given you—"

She could only shrug. He waited but there was no answer.

Watkins turned back to Ben.

"How'd you get wise to all this?"

"When I first saw you last night at the hotel I thought your face looked familiar," Ben explained. "I'd noticed your waxworks figure when Dodge first showed me his museum. It was gone from the California History section today —Dodge tried to fill the space with a misplaced figure from another exhibit. When yours turned up outside this door an hour ago I should have realized what it was by the stiffness when it fell, and by Molly's haste in covering it with a blanket—she couldn't have me examining it too closely. Dodge had made an important change in the face. The eyes behind the glasses were closed."

"You knew we were in it together?" Molly asked.

Ben nodded. "I'd only told you I was advising Dodge on a new exhibit, yet tonight you asked if I'd gotten all the Wild West figures dressed in their costumes. Only Dodge could have told you what I was doing there. Even after I realized that much, I still didn't catch on until it occurred to me that the scheme must involve the real murder of Watkins, along with framing me for it. The police would have telegraphed ahead to Carson City and I'd have been arrested when I left the train."

"What if something had gone wrong?" Watkins asked. "What if you hadn't shot at the dummy?"

"Then they would've lost nothing. That was why the real murder had to take place after the fake one, to make sure I performed as planned."

"I'll get the police," Watkins said, "if you'll keep these two covered here."

"Gladly," Ben told him.

"You have to admit it was a good try," Seymour Dodge said when the senator's footsteps had receded down the wooden stairs. "If it had worked, no one would have believed your story that the senator fired first."

"It wasn't such a good try," Ben told him. "There was one other thing I didn't mention. Molly had to spread the blood on the dummy's chest so it looked like a fatal wound. When I fired, I was aiming at the shoulder, not the chest. Even with a strange gun, I knew I couldn't have been that far off target."

THE ONLY TREE IN TASCO

On the afternoon Ben Snow rode into town, they were preparing the only tree in Tasco for a hanging. It was an old sturdy pine at one end of the main street, and Ben figured it had been put to such use many times in the past. He was on his way south, toward the Mexican border, and planned to pause in Tasco only long enough for a couple of drinks and a hot meal.

"When's the hanging?" he asked the bartender at the saloon.

"First thing in the mornin'. They got the rope up already."

"I saw it."

"Mexican fella. Used a knife on our town banker. Gouged out half his chest. A terrible bloody murder! You ask me, hanging's too good for him."

Ben finished his drink and asked directions to the town's eating place. The bartender directed him to a small house called Molly's Kitchen. "Best food between here and Santa Fe," he said. "Take my word for it."

The food at Molly's Kitchen was good, and Ben appreciated it after several days on the trail. He appreciated Molly Tyne even more. She was a handsome young woman from back East, full of energy and bustle, and as he finished the meal he couldn't help asking, "How did you happen to find your way to a place like Tasco?"

"I came West with the railroad," she explained while she wiped off a table just vacated by a middle-aged couple. "After working at a couple of Harvey restaurants, I decided to beat them to it and open a place of my own. I came to Tasco a year ago because I'd heard the railroad's southern route was coming through here. I'm still waiting for it."

"Not a pleasant place to wait," he observed, "what with stabbings and hangings."

"Pedro Mapimi—the Mexican they want to hang—is innocent. He was helping me clean the kitchen at the time of the murder. But no one will listen to me."

"They must have some reason for thinking he's guilty," Ben said, taking a sip of his coffee.

"Only because of the knife. They have this warped notion that if somebody uses a knife for murder, it must be a Mexican."

"Did they have a trial?"

"Sure." She tossed her brown hair angrily. "Or what passes for a trial in Tasco. It was held this morning, and the victim's son was the judge. Does that sound fair?"

Ben hated to become involved in local affairs, and he was anxious to be on the trail again. Still he wouldn't sleep well if he rode out of town knowing a possibly innocent man might be swinging from that tree limb in the morning. "What's the judge's name?" he asked. "And where can I find him?"

"His name is Earl Kaiser. His father Bert owned the bank."

"Was there evidence of robbery?"

"None. The murder wasn't at the bank, it was at his home. Bert Kaiser would never have let Pedro through his front door in the first place. That's why the whole thing is so unbelievable."

Ben didn't bother pointing out that Pedro might have entered through a rear door, uninvited.

"Did Earl live with his father?"

"No. He lives upstairs over his drygoods store. He's only judge part of the time."

"I think I'll go see him," Ben said.

"Why do you care whether Pedro lives or dies?" she asked.

"Maybe I don't. That's what I want to find out."

It was early evening when Ben climbed the stairs to the living quarters above the drygoods store, but the summer sun was still high in the western sky. Earl Kaiser wasn't alone, and for a moment Ben thought the young blonde woman with him was his wife. When she made a quick and embarrassed exit into the bedroom, he realized his mistake.

"What can I do for you?" Earl Kaiser asked, not yet ready to allow Ben past the doorway. "The store's closed till morning."

"It's not about the store. I'm interested in the murder trial."

"Pedro Mapimi got a fair trial, and he'll get a fair hangin' in the morning."

"I'd like to talk about it. Seems to me it can't be all that fair when the judge is the victim's own son."

Kaiser's eyes narrowed. He had an unpleasant look at best, and that only reinforced it. "You wouldn't be a U.S. marshal by any chance, would you?"

"Name's Ben Snow. I'd like to come in and ask you a few questions."

Kaiser stepped aside reluctantly. "I can give you five minutes. As you could see, I'm entertaining a young lady."

Ben sat down. "Tell me about your father's murder."

"He was done in two nights ago by that thieving Mexican. I'm the only judge outside the county seat, so I tried the case. We had a jury of six local men and the evidence was presented good and proper. Most towns around here, Pedro Mapimi would have been shot dead on the spot. We gave him a fair trial."

"I understand Pedro had an alibi."

"Worth nothing! He was helping Miss Molly for about a half hour, but the killing could have happened any time between eight and ten o'clock. I found my father's body at ten when I stopped at the house to see him."

"What was the condition of the body?"

"My father's chest had been gouged by repeated stab wounds. It was horrible! I thought at first someone had tried to cut out his heart."

"What made you think of Mapimi?"

"They'd argued recently. He wanted a loan from my father's bank to buy some cattle. Can you imagine that—a Mexican owning a cattle ranch up here?"

"But would he have killed your father over that?"

"He made threatening remarks at the saloon. People heard him."

"Still—"

"He's a vicious man. I saw him pull his knife one night at the bar just because someone made a remark about Mexicans."

"Surely a great many people in Tasco carry knives."

"No, they don't. We try for a bit of civilization here, Mr. Snow." He glanced pointedly at Ben's gun belt. "You'll notice the townsfolk don't generally carry weapons at all."

"I'd like to speak with Pedro before the hanging."

"That's up to Sheriff Scott. He's in charge of the prisoner."

Ben nodded. "Thank you for your help."

"Where you from, Marshal?"

"I didn't say I was a marshal," Ben told him as he went out the door.

The jail was a one-story building two blocks down from Molly's Kitchen. Sheriff Scott had just turned the night duty over to a deputy and was preparing to leave when Ben walked in. "What can I do for you, stranger?" he asked.

"I'm here to see Pedro Mapimi before the execution. Judge Kaiser said it would be all right."

"He did, did he? What do you want to see him for?"

"I'm looking into the trial. I want to make sure it was all honest and aboveboard."

"There was nothing wrong with the trial."

"It came quite soon after the murder."

"We'd have had it yesterday, but we had to bury Bert Kaiser first."

"And with his son being the judge and all—"

"It was a fair trial."

"You examined the murder scene?"

"I sure did. Earl came running for me as soon as he found the body. I never seen anything like it—only a Mexican could have cut him up like that."

"I understand there was no sign of a robbery."

"No, but Kaiser's six-shooter was near his body. Looked as if he took it out to protect himself, or to capture a thief."

"Could I see Pedro?"

The sheriff pointed at Ben's holster. "The gun belt stays out here."

"Of course." Ben unbuckled it and laid it on the desk.

Sheriff Scott roused himself from behind the desk, picked a ring of keys from a wall hook, and led the way through a barred door to the prison area. There were only three cells, and just one was occupied. "You get ten minutes," the sheriff said. "No more."

Pedro Mapimi glanced up as Ben entered the cell. "Who are you?" he said in fair English. "What do you want?"

"I'm a friend of Molly's. She asked me to help you if I could."

"No one can help me. They will hang me in the morning."

Ben sat down on the hard bunk next to him. "Did you kill Bert Kaiser?"

"No. I never even see the man except at his bank. I would never go to his house and threaten him. I am not a criminal."

"You have no alibi for the time of the killing," Ben said.

"I was with Miss Molly. She told them, but they would not listen."

"But Kaiser did turn you down for a cattle loan. You threatened him."

"I may have said something in the bar about not liking the man, but I never threatened to kill him. And I did not kill him—someone must believe me!"

"Is there anyone at all besides Miss Molly who might support what you say?"

He shook his head. "No one has come forward."

"What about your knife? Did they examine it for bloodstains?"

"They said I had washed it off. Even keeping a shiny knife is evidence of my guilt."

Ben wanted to believe the man, if only because he himself had once been falsely accused of murder. Some even accused him of being Billy the Kid long after the real Billy was dead and buried. "What about the money? After Kaiser turned you down, did you try anywhere else?"

The Mexican thought for a moment. "I asked Sam Easton. He was the one selling me the property and I thought some arrangement might be worked out. He offered me a generous mortgage, but I still had no money for the down payment."

"I might talk to him," Ben decided. "Where can I find him?"

"Maybe at his ranch just outside of town, on the north road." The Mexican stared into Ben Snow's eyes. "Do you really think there's any chance for me?"

"We'll see."

Ben took his horse Oats out of the stable and rode along the north road until he came to the Easton ranch. He'd once worked at a ranch in Texas that was huge by comparison, but in the fading light he could see this one had some good grazing land. As he dismounted there was a muffled explosion from across the field, and he watched a cloud of smoke and rock shoot into the air. A stocky white-haired man spotted his arrival and headed in his direction, calling out to some other ranch hands, "Getting too dark for any more blasting. Better start gathering up the equipment."

"You'd be Mr. Sam Easton?" Ben asked as the man drew closer.

"That's me, son. Lookin' for work?"

"No, just information." Ben nodded across the field where the blasting had been.

Easton motioned with his hand. "That south pasture's full of boulders. We been blasting for two days now and there's more to be done." He took off his wide-brimmed hat to beat the dust from it. "What sort of information you lookin' for?"

"I'm investigating the murder of Bert Kaiser the other night."

"Yeah. That poor Mexican kid got himself in a heap of trouble."

"Pedro says he was buying some ranch land from you."

"Fifty acres, if he could raise the money. That's the way I got started, and I wanted to help him out if I could. What'd you say your name was?"

"Ben Snow."

"Come along with me, Ben. I got to lock up the dynamite box." They started strolling back toward the field and Easton ran over the details of the land transaction. "I suppose I can't blame old man Kaiser for turning him down. He's done the same thing to me on occasion. But I still felt sorry for Pedro. It was a terrible disappointment for him."

"Enough of a disappointment that he'd kill Bert Kaiser?"

Easton shook his head. "I just don't think he did it. I wish to hell I'd been on that jury."

"His son doesn't seem too broken up about it."

"Why should he be? He inherits that nice big house and the banking business, too. It beats running a drygoods store." They'd reached a couple of wooden boxes and Easton picked one up. "Can you bring the other?" he asked Ben. "There are only a few sticks in it. Don't worry—it won't explode."

It was dark by the time they'd locked the dynamite in a wooden shed for the night. "How far is the Kaiser house from here?" Ben asked.

"About two miles across the pastureland. Farther by road. Come on in the house, Mr. Snow. I'll treat you to some good whiskey."

Easton's wife was a pretty, middle-aged woman named Julie who fussed around, making their guest comfortable. "It's a shame about Pedro," she agreed, bringing out some fancy glasses for their drinks. "I don't think I'll sleep a wink tonight, thinking about him hanging in the morning."

"You didn't happen to notice any strangers nearby the night of the killing?" Ben asked, savoring the whiskey.

Easton thought about it. "Can't say that I did. I was out hunting early that evening, but I didn't notice anyone else."

Ben walked to the stone fireplace and studied a rifle that hung there. "I never saw a gun like that. Could I examine it?"

Easton took it down. "It's my favorite hunting rifle—a .457 caliber Winchester, big enough to kill a buffalo, or an elephant if one was around. Look at the size of this cartridge! There isn't another weapon like this in the whole county."

"It's impressive," Ben admitted, fingering the long rifle cartridge. "But what do you hunt with it?"

"I was after deer the other night, but you never know when a stray bear might wander down this way."

"Did you see anything?"

Easton shook his head. "Didn't get a shot."

"Stop boring Mr. Snow with your hunting exploits, dear," his wife said. "Will you be in town long, Mr. Snow?"

"Probably just till tomorrow. I've been talking to people who might be able to help Pedro's case, but I'm running out of names."

"How about Mrs. Fernandez?" Julie Easton suggested. "She was Kaiser's nearest neighbor. She might have seen something."

"Thanks," Ben said. "And thanks for the drink. I'll be going now."

"Come again," Easton told him. "Visitors are always welcome here."

On the ride back to town, Ben wondered about this man with a charming wife who handled dynamite and a large-bore rifle with such ease. Perhaps he was the sort that was needed to tame the West.

Mrs. Fernandez lived in a small house down the road from the Kaiser place. She was reluctant to let a stranger in after dark and so Ben was forced to speak with her through the partly opened door. "I don't know anything," she informed him, speaking with a thick accent. "I see nothing, no one."

"It would have been about this time, shortly after dark—"

"I tell the sheriff everything I know. I hear one shot, nothing more, from the direction of the house."

"A shot?" Ben remembered Sheriff Scott saying Kaiser's pistol had been found near the body. "Do you remember the time?"

"Sure. I look at clock. It was nine-fifteen."

He tried to remember if Molly had pinpointed the time Pedro was with her. "Did you tell this to Sheriff Scott?"

"I tell. He say I am mistaken. Must be hunter in field if there was a shot."

"Thank you, Mrs. Fernandez." Ben left the house and headed back toward Molly's Kitchen. Sam Easton had seen no other hunters and had not taken a shot himself, so the sound Mrs. Fernandez heard had not been from a hunter.

The eating place was closed, but there was a light inside. Ben pounded on the door until Molly finally arrived to open it. She stared at him an instant before she remembered who he was. "Oh—Mr. Snow, isn't it? What brings you back? I'm afraid we're closed now."

"I spoke with Earl Kaiser, and also with Pedro. I've had a busy evening."

After staring at him several moments longer, she stepped aside to let him enter. "Come in, please." In the light from the lanterns, her skin had a soft angelic glow.

"I need to know one thing. Earl Kaiser says Pedro was only helping you for half an hour."

"A little longer than that. He was here from just before nine until nine-thirty. I know Earl says his father could have been killed any time between eight and ten, but I don't believe that. Earl found the body at ten, and the killer certainly needed more than a few minutes before and after the crime."

"If we could show that Kaiser was killed at nine-fifteen, could you swear that Pedro was with you?"

"Certainly!"

"Then I think we have a chance."

But she seemed more depressed than ever. "We're just too late. Everyone has gone to bed now, and Earl Kaiser is hardly going to order a stay of execution."

"An appeals court would never allow that verdict to stand, with the victim's son sitting as judge."

"Of course not. But by the time anyone hears about it, Pedro will be dead and buried."

"Maybe not," Ben told her. "Maybe there's a way to delay the execution."

"What do you mean?"

"It's better if you don't know," Ben said.

He headed back out toward the Easton ranch. It was nearly midnight now and there were no lights burning in the main house when it came into view. Ben dismounted, tied Oats to a bush, and went the final distance on foot. When he reached the locked shed where the dynamite was stored, he used the barrel of his revolver to pry the hasp from the old wood to which it was screwed. He'd been prepared to fire a bullet into the padlock, but happily that wasn't necessary.

He rode back toward Tasco with three sticks of dynamite in his saddlebag. His original plan was a simple one—to blast a hole in the wall of the jail and ride off with Pedro. But when he reached the sleeping town, he saw at once that there were at least two drawbacks to such action: two deputies had been stationed outside the jail with rifles and Ben wasn't prepared to risk innocent lives, and an explosion against the wall of Pedro's cell might well injure the man he was trying to rescue.

Ben's first reaction was one of frustration. Perhaps he should forget the whole thing, but Mrs. Fernandez's story about the gunshot, along with Molly's alibi for Pedro, had convinced him of Pedro's innocence. He turned Oats away from the jail and headed back to the edge of town, toward the only tree in Tasco.

A single stick of dynamite should be enough, he decided, tying it to the trunk of the tree near the ground and lighting the fuse.

It was shortly after one o'clock when the blast shattered the silence of the night. Watching from a distance, Ben saw the ancient pine tree shudder and begin to topple. It hit the ground with a sigh, its limbs cushioning the fall.

Molly Tyne had promised Ben a cot in the storeroom of the Kitchen and he caught a few hours' sleep there, trying to ignore the muffled shouts and commotion from the street. The explosion had roused the town.

Molly woke him just after dawn, shaking him gently. "Ben! Ben, wake up!"

"What is it?" he asked, catching the panic in her voice.

"Sheriff Scott has his deputies at work on a temporary scaffold outside the jail. He says Pedro will be hanged as soon as it's finished."

Ben drank a cup of Molly's coffee while he dressed, then strapped on his gun belt and headed for the jail. Sheriff Scott intercepted him on the way. "Been looking for you, Mr. Snow. We had a bit of trouble during the night.

Someone dynamited the tree where we were going to hang Pedro Mapimi. You wouldn't know anything about that, would you?"

"How would I know about it?"

"Sam Easton was using the dynamite to clear his field of boulders. He says you helped him lock it away in the shed last night. Later someone broke into the shed and stole some of it."

"I can't help you there, Sheriff. I guess I must have slept through the explosion."

"Fat chance of that!" the sheriff bellowed. "We don't like strangers meddling in town business, Snow! We don't like them dynamiting our only tree just to save a murderer from the gallows! When we hang Pedro in a couple of hours, we just might be able to find an extra rope for you!"

The jail came into view and Ben could see that work was well under way on the temporary gallows. They weren't bothering with steps and a platform— only a tall upright piece of timber and a crosspiece from which the noose would hang. Pedro would be brought to the gallows on horseback in the traditional Western manner. "I can prove he didn't do it," Ben told the sheriff. "You have to listen to me."

"I'm always willing to listen. Start talking."

"Kaiser's neighbor, Mrs. Fernandez, heard a single shot around nine-fifteen. There were no hunters out that night except for Sam Easton, and he told me he didn't fire his gun. That shot had to be Kaiser firing his six-gun at the killer. But Pedro couldn't have been at his house at nine-fifteen because he was with Molly Tyne from before nine to nine-thirty."

Sheriff Scott listened in silence, then motioned Ben to follow him into the jail. He opened the drawer of his wooden filing cabinet and took out a shiny long-barreled revolver. "This is Bert Kaiser's pistol. I found it myself, next to his body. Go ahead—look at it."

Ben opened the cylinder and saw that the weapon was fully loaded. He sighted down the inside of the barrel. "It hasn't been fired since it was last cleaned," he said.

"That's right. That's how I found it. Mrs. Fernandez didn't hear any shot."

"Why would she lie?"

"Because she's a Mexican, like Pedro. She was trying to save him."

"Pretty funny way to do it. She couldn't have known about this gun, or about Pedro's alibi, for that matter."

"A couple of hours from now it won't matter," the sheriff said, looking out the open door at the scaffold.

"It'll matter to Pedro and it'll matter to me. Look here, you get Earl Kaiser to call that court into session again and I'll prove Pedro didn't do it."

"How you goin' to do that? I just showed you Kaiser's unfired pistol. Pedro's alibi isn't worth a damn!"

"I think it is. That unfired pistol not only tells me Pedro is innocent, it tells me who's guilty."

By ten o'clock that morning, Earl Kaiser had reluctantly agreed to reconvene the trial of Pedro Mapimi on the basis of new evidence. "It's highly irregular," he told Ben at first. "The man's already been tried and convicted."

"It's also highly irregular for you to serve as judge," Ben pointed out. "If you deny a rehearing now and go ahead with the execution, it will appear that you did so only because the victim was your father."

"I'll give you an hour," Kaiser said finally, overruling Sheriff Scott's objections. "We can still hang Pedro before noon."

Even as the six-member jury was reassembling and Pedro was being brought from his jail cell to the barroom that served as a courtroom, he was still complaining. "What about dynamiting the tree? Are we going to try the fellow who did that?"

"If you have any evidence, Sheriff," Kaiser said.

"Sam Easton will testify that Snow knew about the dynamite."

"That's not enough," Kaiser told him. "Forget the damn tree and let's get started." He turned to Ben. "You claim to have new evidence in the case of the People versus Pedro Mapimi?"

Ben got to his feet. "I have, Your Honor." He glanced around and saw that Molly was seated among the spectators, not far from where Pedro sat. Mrs. Fernandez was there, too, and Sam Easton with his wife Julie.

"Proceed with it." Outside, the hammering on the scaffold in front of the jail had ceased. It was ready for the hanging.

Ben cleared his throat and started talking. "When I arrived in Tasco yesterday, the trial of Pedro Mapimi was already over. He'd been convicted of murdering Bert Kaiser, president of your bank. So far as I know, there was nobody to speak in his defense, and the evidence was flimsy at best. He'd been denied a loan by Mr. Kaiser, he'd made some sort of threat against him in this barroom, and Kaiser had been viciously murdered by a knife such as Pedro always carried. No one else in town appears to carry such a weapon regularly. That was the extent of the so-called evidence. Placed against it is Molly Tyne's testimony that Pedro was with her at the time of the killing."

Earl Kaiser spoke. "It has been shown that my father could have been killed before or after the alibi period."

"True enough," Ben agreed. "But then we're confronted with Mrs. Fernandez and her story of hearing a single shot around nine-fifteen. My first thought was that this had to have been fired by Bert Kaiser in defense of his life, but Sheriff Scott showed me the pistol, which hadn't been fired since its last cleaning. I refuse to believe Mrs. Fernandez invented the shot to help Pedro, because it did no such thing. If she'd wanted a false story that would help him, she'd have claimed to have seen a mysterious stranger near the Kaiser house. We must accept her story of the shot as true, and that raises an interesting question. What gun was fired, and where did the bullet go?"

"Hunters," Sheriff Scott muttered.

"Not hunters, according to Sam Easton's story," Ben said. "If Mrs. Fernandez thought the shot came from the direction of the Kaiser house, I'm willing to accept the fact that it did. Bert Kaiser's weapon was unfired, and we can rule out the presence of a third person in the house at the time. If a shot was fired, it was fired by Kaiser's killer."

There was a stir among the spectators and Earl Kaiser pounded his gavel for order. "Proceed, Mr. Snow."

"Assuming that any obvious bullethole would have been spotted by the sheriff, we must ask where the bullet went. I think the answer is obvious. It went into the body of Bert Kaiser. He was killed by a bullet, not a knife."

"That's crazy!" Sheriff Scott protested. "If a bullet killed him, why was his chest cut open like that?"

"To recover the bullet that killed him, Sheriff. The victim was cut open after death so the killer could retrieve the bullet. It's the only explanation for that awful gouging you've described."

"But why?"

"Because the bullet would have identified the killer without question. Who among you could be identified by a bullet from your gun? Who among you has the largest-caliber rifle in the county, by his own admission? Who was hunting with that rifle not far from Kaiser's home on the night of the murder?"

No one had to answer. Sam Easton sprang from his seat and ran for the door, where he collided with the same two deputies Ben had observed standing duty outside the jail the night before.

Molly brought Pedro to speak with Ben later. "How can I thank you?" Pedro said. "I would be dead by now if it wasn't for you."

"We were lucky the right information came my way," Ben said. "From the beginning it seemed to me the sheriff was overlooking a lot. He seemed to assume only you carried a knife, but anyone out hunting would be carrying a knife. Easton was unlucky in one way. Ordinarily a bullet that powerful, fired at close range, would have gone right through the victim's body and come out the other side. In this case it must have hit a bone or been otherwise slowed down. When Easton realized it was still in the body, he knew he had to use his knife to retrieve it. He mentioned having some disagreements with Kaiser over money and I suppose that led to the killing."

"The sheriff says he's admitted everything. Kaiser wanted to foreclose on a loan. Easton stopped by the house after hunting and they argued about it. The banker picked up a pistol and ordered him out of the house, and Easton shot him in the chest with his rifle."

Ben thought about the waiting scaffold. "Will they hang him now?"

"There's no chance of that," Molly replied, a trace of bitterness in her voice. "He's not a Mexican, and he's a landowner. He'll be held in jail and then taken to the county seat for trial. I imagine he'll hire an attorney and plead self-defense."

"I guess I'll be on my way," Ben said. "I'm glad I was able to help you, Pedro."

On the way out of town he passed the splintered stump—all that remained of what had been the only tree in Tasco.

A LONG WAY FROM HOME:
THE TRAVELS OF BEN SNOW

by Marvin Lachman

In "The Headless Horseman of Buffalo Creek," a woman notes that Ben is a long way from home. Ben says, "I've always been a long way from home." This is the man his creator describes as having "the smile of a wanderer . . . Trouble seemed to follow him like a restless hawk waiting to pounce, and he knew he should be moving . . ." The accompanying list covers the locations of the Snow adventures; internal evidence in the stories indicates he has been in many other states as well. In his travels Ben is involved in important historical events.

In 1889 he is in the Indian Territory only days after the famous land rush that eventually led to its statehood as Oklahoma. In the very first Ben Snow story published we learn that he was with the Army in 1890 at Wounded Knee, the battle generally credited with ending the Indian Wars in the U.S. (We never learn whether Ben was in the Army or was a civilian employee.) Ben went up to the Yukon in 1898, shortly after the gold rush, and he was present at the 1901 assassination of President McKinley, tracking his killer. He was present at the Wright Brothers' flight at Kitty Hawk in 1903. At Teddy Roosevelt's inauguration in 1905, Ben's assignment was to protect the great Indian warrior Geronimo, with whom he became friendly.

Ben's path even crossed that of the famous circus elephant Jumbo in 1885 and Lizzie Borden in 1894, the year after her acquittal.

Ben Snow's occupations have been many, though he was most often a cowboy or ranch hand. Though he consistently denies being a gunfighter, because of his prowess with a gun he is often hired as a bodyguard. Eventually he opens a security agency when he moves East, retiring his faithful horse Oats, who has been with him for fifteen years, to stud at age nineteen.

In many adventures, Ben is traveling from one location to another, usually on his way to a new job. In the best tradition of the amateur sleuth, he is always ready to stop and solve a crime to prevent injustice. Indeed, in "The Man in the Alley" he says, "My occupation might be listed as a justicer," using an archaic word for a judge or magistrate.

In my favorite Snow story, "The Problem of the Haunted Tepee," at age 76 Ben consults Hoch's other great historical detective, Dr. Sam Hawthorne, about a mystery that took place on the Sioux encampment in 1890. We learn in this story that Ben had a security business in Richmond, Virginia and that he married in 1905, though the *name* of his wife is not given. The most recent Snow story, "Suddenly, with Fangs," reveals that he married Tamia Ponter, whom he met when she accompanied the Indian chief Geronimo to Washington that year in "The Geronimo Option."

A recurrent theme throughout the Snow canon is his alleged resemblance to Billy the Kid. Ben has acquired a reputation for being as quick on the draw as that famous outlaw. He protests when people claim he is Billy, but the possibility often gets him into fistfights, or even gun battles. The Billy the Kid confusion has even led to doubts about Ben's birth and upbringing. Ben once claimed to have been born in the Midwest, but usually says he's from New Mexico, where he spent his first eighteen years.

Almost half of the stories are consistent with a birthdate of 1859, a year Ben cites himself in some stories. However, in "Ghost Town" he claims to have been born in 1861! Attempting to clear up the matter in "An Early Morning Madness," Hoch has Ben respond to a question regarding his age as follows: "My folks always said I was born in sixty-one, but if I'm Bill I was born in fifty-nine. Sometimes I get mixed up myself. Anyway, I'm either twenty-eight or thirty." Perhaps Hoch is keeping alive the possibility that Ben *is* Billy the Kid, and someone else was buried in Fort Sumner, New Mexico. After all, Hoch did describe Ben as having "the smile of a gun fighter."

BEN SNOW:
A CHRONOLOGY BY ORDER OF PUBLICATION

[Note: *SMM = The Saint Mystery Magazine. EQMM = Ellery Queen's Mystery Magazine.*]

"The Valley of Arrows," *SMM* (British), March 1961; *SMM* (US), September 1961
"Frontier Street," *SMM* (British), May 1961; *SMM* (US), February 1962
"Ghost Town," *SMM* (British), September 1961; *SMM* (US), January 1963
"The Flying Man," *SMM* (British), December 1961; *SMM* (US), July 1962
"The Man in the Alley," *SMM* (British), April 1962; *SMM* (US), June 1963
"The Ripper of Storyville," *SMM* (British), September 1962; *SMM* (US), December 1963
"Snow in Yucatan," *SMM* (US), January 1965

"The Vanished Steamboat," *EQMM*, May 1984
"Brothers on the Beach," *EQMM*, August 1984
"The 500 Hours of Dr. Wisdom," *EQMM*, December 1984
"The Trail of the Bells," *EQMM*, April 1985
"The Phantom Stallion," *EQMM*, October 1985
"The Sacramento Waxworks," *EQMM*, March 1986
"The Only Tree in Tasco," *EQMM*, October 1986
"Poker Game at the Golden Nugget," *EQMM*, March 1987
"The Hearse with a Heart of Gold," *EQMM*, October 1987
"The Nude Over the Bar," *EQMM*, February 1988
"The Victorian Hangman," *EQMM*, August 1988
"Sacajawea's Gold," *EQMM*, January 1989
"The Circus Murders," *EQMM*, August 1989
"The Trial of Ben Snow," *EQMM*, January 1990
"The Pirate of Death Valley," *EQMM*, July 1990
"The Problem of the Haunted Tepee" (with Dr. Sam Hawthorne), *EQMM*,
    December 1990
"The Edge of the Year 1900," *EQMM*, February 1991
"The Headless Horseman of Buffalo Creek," *EQMM*, June 1991
"Five Days in a Texas Town," *EQMM*, January 1992
"The Trail of the Golden Cross, *EQMM*, September 1992
"The Geronimo Option," *EQMM*, January 1993
"The Passion of Lizzie B.," *EQMM*, September 1993
"An Early Morning Madness," *EQMM*, April 1994
"Horse Thief Haven," *EQMM*, December 1994
"The Granite God," *EQMM*, June 1995
"Banner in Blood," *EQMM*, February 1996
"Dagger Money," *EQMM*, January 1997
"Suddenly, with Fangs," *EQMM*, August 1997

BEN SNOW:
WHEN AND WHERE THE STORIES TAKE PLACE

"The Trail of the Golden Cross," 1882, New Mexico
"The 500 Hours of Dr. Wisdom," November 1883, probably Oklahoma
"The Sacramento Waxworks," 1885, Sacramento, California
"The Circus Murders," September 1885, Windsor, Ontario, Canada
"The Only Tree in Tasco," 1886, New Mexico
"The Trail of the Bells," 1887, New Mexico
"The Trial of Ben Snow," 1887, New Mexico

"The Pirate of Death Valley," 1888, California
"An Early Morning Madness," April 1889, Indian Territory (later, Oklahoma)
"The Problem of the Haunted Tepee" (early events), Summer 1890, Sioux
    encampment, South Dakota
"The Victorian Hangman," August 1890, south of Los Angeles, California
"Sacajawea's Gold," early 1891, Yellowstone Park, Wyoming
"Frontier Street," late winter-early spring 1891, Arizona
"The Valley of Arrows," 1891, Arizona
"The Phantom Stallion," about 1892, Texas
"Horse Thief Haven," December 1892, Utah and Arizona
"The Hearse with a Heart of Gold," 1893, Tombstone, Arizona
"The Passion of Lizzie B.," July 1894, Omaha, Nebraska
"Ghost Town," 1895, probably California
"The Headless Horseman of Buffalo Creek," October 1895, Montana
"The Nude Over the Bar," July 1896, Oklahoma
"The Flying Man," September 1896, Arizona or Texas
"The Granite God," Spring 1897, near Las Cruces, New Mexico
"Poker Game at the Golden Nugget," Summer 1898, Yukon Territory
"Dagger Money," Spring 1899, Arizona
"The Edge of the Year 1900," December 31, 1899, Arizona
"Banner in Blood," June 1900, El Paso, Texas and Mexico
"Snow in Yucatan," about 1900, Texas and Mexico
"Five Days in a Texas Town," November 1900, Texas (near Louisiana border)
"The Man in the Alley," 1901, Kansas City, Missouri; Buffalo, New York;
    New York City
"The Ripper of Storyville," 1901, Texas and New Orleans, Louisiana
"The Vanished Steamboat," 1902, Vicksburg, Mississippi
"Brothers on the Beach," December 1903, Kitty Hawk, North Carolina
"The Geronimo Option," February-March 1905, Virginia and Washington D.C.
"Suddenly, with Fangs," August 1908, Utah
"The Problem of the Haunted Tepee" (later events), September 1935,
    Northmont, a town in New England

THE RIPPER OF STORYVILLE

The Ripper of Storyville and Other Ben Snow Tales by Edward D. Hoch is set in 11-point Times Roman and printed on 50 pound Glatfelter Supple Opaque acid-free paper. The cover painting is by Barbara Mitchell and the design by Deborah Miller. "A Long Way From Home: The Travels of Ben Snow" is by Marvin Lachman. The first edition is comprised of approximately one thousand two hundred copies in trade softcover, notch-bound, and two hundred copies sewn in cloth, signed and numbered by the author. Each of the clothbound copies includes a separate pamphlet, *Five Rings in Reno*, by Edward D. Hoch (originally published under the pseudonym R. L. Stevens). *The Ripper of Storyville* was published in November 1997 by Crippen & Landru, Publishers, Norfolk, Virginia.

CRIPPEN & LANDRU, PUBLISHERS
P. O. Box 9315
Norfolk, VA 23505
USA

Crippen & Landru publishes first editions of important works by detective and mystery writers, specializing in short-story collections. The following books have been published:

Speak of the Devil by John Dickson Carr. Eight-part impossible crime mystery broadcast on BBC radio. Introduction by Tony Medawar; cover design by Deborah Miller.   Out of Print

The McCone Files by Marcia Muller. Fifteen Sharon McCone short stories by the creator of the modern female private eye. Winner of the Anthony Award for Best Short Story collection. Introduction by the author; cover painting by Carol Heyer.

> Signed, limited edition, Out of Print
> Softcover, third printing, $15.00

The Darings of the Red Rose by Margery Allingham. Eight crook stories about a female Robin Hood, written in 1930 by the creator of the classic sleuth, Albert Campion. Introduction by B. A. Pike; cover design by Deborah Miller.

> Softcover, second printing, $15.00

Diagnosis: Impossible, The Problems of Dr. Sam Hawthorne by Edward D. Hoch. Twelve stories about the country doctor who solves "miracle problems," written by the greatest current expert on the challenge-to-the-reader story. Introduction by the author; Sam Hawthorne chronology by Marvin Lachman; cover painting by Carol Heyer.

> Signed, limited edition, $38.00
> Softcover, Out of stock

Spadework: A Collection of "Nameless Detective" Stories by Bill Pronzini. Fifteen stories by a Grandmaster of the Private Eye tale. Introduction by Marcia Muller; afterword by the author; cover painting by Carol Heyer.

> Signed, limited edition, $40.00
> Softcover, $16.00

Who Killed Father Christmas? And Other Unseasonable Demises by Patricia Moyes. Twenty-one stories ranging from holiday homicides to village villainies to Caribbean crimes. Introduction by the author; cover design by Deborah Miller.

Signed, limited edition, $40.00
Softcover, $16.00

My Mother, The Detective: The Complete "Mom" Short Stories, by James Yaffe. Eight stories about the Bronx armchair maven who solves crimes between the chicken soup and the *schnecken*. Introduction by the author; cover painting by Carol Heyer.

Signed, limited edition, $40.00
Softcover, $15.00

In Kensington Gardens Once . . . by H. R. F. Keating. Ten crime and mystery stories taking place in London's famous park, written by the recipient of the Cartier Diamond Dagger for Lifetime Achievement. Illustrations and cover by Gwen Mandley.

Signed, limited edition, $35.00
Softcover, $12.00

Shoveling Smoke: Selected Mystery Stories by Margaret Maron. Twenty-two stories by the Edgar award winning author, including all the short cases of Deborah Knott and Sigrid Harald. Introduction and prefaces to each story by the author; cover painting by Victoria Russell.

Signed, limited edition, $40.00
Softcover, $16.00

The Man Who Hated Banks and Other Mysteries by Michael Gilbert. Eighteen stories by the recipient of the Mystery Writers of America's highest honor, the Grandmaster Award, including mysteries featuring Inspectors Hazlerigg and Petrella, rogue cop Bill Mercer, and solicitor Henry Bohun. Introduction by the author; cover painting by Deborah Miller.

Signed, limited edition, $40.00
Softcover, $16.00

The Ripper of Storyville and Other Ben Snow Tales by Edward D. Hoch. The first fourteen historical detective stories about Ben Snow, the hired gun who is often confused with Billy the Kid. The stories include a vanishing steamboat, a stallion that can be seen only by the victim, a patent medicine man who claims to stop time, and serial killings in old New Orleans. Introduction by the author; Ben Snow chronology by Marvin Lachman; cover painting by Barbara Mitchell.

Signed, limited edition, $40.00
Softcover, $16.00

The following short-story collections are forthcoming:

Do Not Exceed the Stated Dose by Peter Lovesey.
Renowned Be Thy Grave; or, The Murderous Miss Mooney by P. M. Carlson.
Carpenter & Quincannon, Professional Detective Services by Bill Pronzini.
Not Safe After Dark and Other Stories by Peter Robinson.
The Concise Cuddy: The Casebook of John Francis Cuddy, by Jeremiah Healy.
A Harlot's Tears and Other Stories by Ed Gorman.
Fortune's Fortunes by Michael Collins.
Murder—All Kinds by William L. DeAndrea.
All Creatures Great and Mysterious by Doug Allyn.
The Spotted Cat and Other Mysteries: The Casebook of Inspector Cockrill by
   Christiana Brand.
The Tragedy of Errors and Others: The Lost Stories of Ellery Queen.

Crippen & Landru offers discounts to individuals and institutions who place
Standing Order Subscriptions for its publications. Please write for details.

Website: http://www.avalon.net/~scott/cl/

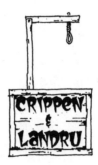